The
SERPENT
of
ERIDOR

Alison Gardiner

Matador
9 Priory Business Park
Kibworth Beauchamp
Leicestershire LE8 0RX, UK
Tel: (+44) 116 279 2299
Fax: (+44) 116 279 2277
Email: books@troubador.co.uk
Web: www.troubador.co.uk/matador

ISBN 978-1784620-783

Artwork used for cover courtesy of Gary Bonn

British Library Cataloguing in Publication Data.
A catalogue record for this book is available from the British Library.

Printed and bound by CPI Group (UK) Ltd, Croydon, CR0 4YY
Typeset in 11pt Aldine by Troubador Publishing Ltd, Leicester, UK

Matador is an imprint of Troubador Publishing Ltd

To Adam, Natasha, Alex, Charlie and Sophie with many thanks for their love and support

CHAPTER 1

Why don't they make mouse-flavoured cat food? Discuss.

Alex Weston smiled. Great essay title: it would do for English and, with a few strategic changes, Food Tech. He reached down to stroke the cream hamster sleeping beside him, without receiving a flicker of response. 'You're awake so little, Skoodle,' he told the fur ball. 'You could be a sleep donor.'

Ignoring his heavy eyes and numb bum Alex started typing, amused at the rubbish he was turning out. He had begun writing about the difficulty of getting food tasters to work in a pet products factory when a soft ping announced the arrival of a message. He flicked a glance down to the time on his screen. Midnight.

Alex clicked on the email which was from his father. The horrifying contents flashed up in front of him. His parents were missing; possibly even dead. Mind numb, he stared at the screen. It had come from his father's email address. Shoulders hunched, head drooping, he punched in a reply.

Dad. Someone has hacked your account. Just had a horrible email from your address. It's got to be rubbish but please let me know you're OK.

He picked up a photo of him and his parents with their surfboards; all blond-haired, soaked in seawater, happy, carefree. He gazed at his parents' laughing faces then clutched the picture to his chest. Nauseated, cold sweat trickling down the back of his neck, he stared at the screen. 'Come on, Dad, answer me. You've got to be there,' he whispered.

1

Body trembling, he waited. *It can't be true*, he kept telling himself, failing to gain control of his fear. Twenty minutes crawled past, hope draining as every second evaporated. Yet no further email arrived. He scanned the message once more, as if rereading would somehow change what it said.

Dear Alex,

If this ever gets to you, something serious will have happened to us. This email has been held on delay and will only go out if we fail to keep moving the send date. Even explorers as careful as we are can come unstuck. If we're still alive, we'll be fighting to get back to you. We're so, so sorry to cause you pain. Aunt Lisa will take care of you. Look to her for love and advice.

'Sorry, Dad,' Alex murmured, shaking his head. 'Can't. If only you knew the truth about her. I care more about Skoodle.'

I know it's a terrible time to ask this, but it's vital that you let our friend Zorrin know that we've disappeared – not returned to England – otherwise disaster will occur, wrecking everything we've fought for. Get a message to him via Ethan Bailey at Frank's Bar on Tikopia. You can't contact Ethan by phone or email as the place is so remote. You'll have to go there. Please do this immediately. Book a flight to the Solomon Islands and then a ticket for Tikopia on a boat called the Coral Grove.

Use the credit card in my top desk drawer and take the envelope of Solomon Island dollars. Take a copy of the map of Tikopia from my netbook, but leave the netbook in England. Do not, under any circumstances, attempt to get on to Eridor. Following us could put your own life at risk.

Always remember that we love you.
Dad.

A deep-seated ache gripped his chest, like a boa constrictor squeezing his heart and lungs. Putting down the photo Alex curled round Skoodle, stroking the soft warm body.

The door crashed open. Aunt Lisa lurched in, vodka glass in hand, dyed blonde hair an unbrushed mess, dirty dressing gown flopping open to reveal a stained nightie. 'Have you had an email from Mark too?'

Alex dropped his eyes back down to Skoodle and nodded.

'Dreadful news.' Lisa came over and sat on his bed, wafting the smell of cigarettes and alcohol towards him.

'You care?'

She drained her glass. 'Of course I do. It's a complete disaster. My allowance will stop if they're dead.'

Alex stared at her. 'That's harsh.'

'Realistic. Also, it takes years to declare somebody dead with no corpse. No bodies, so no inheritance. No cash.'

'You vicious witch. Are you really saying you'd prefer they were definitely… ' Alex swallowed, '… gone forever, instead of there being any chance that they could be alive?'

Lisa gazed at him, face like a disappointed bloodhound. 'See it my way. I've spent a year looking after you with them popping up at intervals like fairy godparents, clutching presents, oozing charm. Each time I've had to suddenly become Mrs Perfect.' She jabbed a grubby nail-bitten finger repeatedly into his chest. 'I've had to put up with filthy sports kit, constant cooking, having a fourteen-year-old eating machine invading my space. And now this. We'll have to live on what you get. I can't even sell their house for seven years. At least they can't interfere any more. From here on I run this place my way.'

'Same as now. It's just what's really important that's changed.'

'Shut it. You'll hand over your allowance or take the consequences. Behave well, then things will only get a bit worse. Remain lazy and lippy… ' She shrugged and staggered to her feet. 'I'm going downstairs for a top-up.'

Alex dropped his gaze. 'Vodka won't give you two dead bodies.'

'Might give me one. Yours, if you drink enough of it.' She laughed. 'Oh, lose the face. They've not been around much for a year. You should have got used to being alone. Well… abandoned, really.'

'It was necessary,' Alex yelled. 'They'd never have left me if it hadn't been vital for their work.'

'Yeah, right. Believe that if you must.'

'I do believe it, because it's true. Get out.'

Curling back over Skoodle, Alex thought about the task his father had given him – the last thing he could ever do for his parents. Whatever it cost him – his home, friends or even his life – he'd go to Tikopia. If it hadn't been seriously important they wouldn't have asked. Then on to Eridor, whatever his dad had said. Maybe they were alive but in serious trouble. He had to find them.

Lisa paused at the door. 'He said he wanted you to take some message somewhere foreign – but even you are not stupid enough to go, are you?'

Raising his head, Alex looked her straight in the eyes. 'No, of course not.'

CHAPTER 2

Alex leaned against a palm tree in the early morning sun on Point Cruz docks, studying a boat. Grey, its paint blistering, with two tattered flags drooping over the bridge, the *Coral Grove* looked more suited to a scrapyard than to a Solomon Island cruise. No choice. There was no other boat. He'd have to risk it.

Dumping his rucksack, Alex pulled a mobile out of his jeans and started texting.

Gone to take message to Tikopia.

He hit *Send*. Seconds later, Lisa's reply whizzed back.

Come home instantly.

Sorry. Can't. Boat goes in two hours.

Alex sat down on an overturned oil drum and leaned back against the wall of a boat shed.

Where are you?

Solomon Islands.

Lisa's reply messages became more threatening as Alex repeatedly refused to return to England. Finally she gave up.

Have it your own way.

Will do.

Sliding the phone back into his jeans Alex gazed at the low forested hills beyond the docks, past distant white sandy beaches framing the turquoise sea, down to the local bustle of the quay as fishermen prepared their boats. Several of the glossy black-haired local children stared at him openly.

Skoodle stuck his head out of Alex's pocket, nose twitching, glancing around.

'Looks strange to me too.' Alex stroked the silky cream head. 'I'm loving the temperature, though.'

A laugh came from nearby. Looking up, Alex saw a boy about his own age with a black ponytail and a round Asian face.

'Are you really talking to that rat in your pocket?'

'He's a hamster, and yes.'

'Are you crazy?'

'Don't think so, but I could be. I'm Alex. The hamster's Skoodle.'

'Hoku.'

Putting down a dive tank, Hoku pulled two cartons of mango juice from his rucksack, handing one to Alex. 'Going somewhere?'

'Tikopia. On her.' Alex jerked his thumb towards the *Coral Grove*. 'If she makes it that far.'

Hoku shrugged. 'Got two lifeboats. No obvious holes in the hull. I'm risking it too.'

Alex shifted along the oil drum. Hoku sat down and wiped a hand down his cargo shorts, leaving a streak of dirt and oil.

'You local?' asked Alex, digging a packet of cookies out of his rucksack.

'Yup. I help my dad teach scuba-diving on the ships. There are 250 passengers on the *Coral*: a lot of them dive, so we're busy.'

Alex offered a biscuit to Hoku, then gave one to Skoodle. Teeth working like a tree grinder, Skoodle crunched his way through it in four seconds then stared at the packet.

'Don't think you could shove any more in, balloon face.' Hoku winced. 'Oh, no. Now I'm talking to that animal.'

'At least you don't expect him to answer,' replied Alex, grinning. 'So you're not too crazy. Yet.'

'Who are you travelling with? Your parents?'

The dull heaviness in Alex's chest returned. Same as every time he thought of them. 'If only. They've disappeared. Don't know what happened or even if they're… ' Alex stopped, trying to swallow the enormous lump blocking his throat. 'Anyway, I found out forty-eight hours ago. Just flown over from London to see if I can find out more.'

'Bummer. Sorry.'

'Stuff happens.'

Hoku gazed over the harbour, silent for a minute, then said, 'So let me get this straight: immediately on landing, you bought a hamster. Not even slightly cool.'

'Wrong on two counts. Hamsters are dead cool, and Skoodle travelled with me. Nobody knew; he slept most of the way.'

Skoodle started to scramble out of Alex's pocket. Alex pulled him into the open and handed the fur ball to Hoku.

'Hold him for a sec.'

'Didn't they pick him up at security? He might have been some sort of mini terrorist.'

Alex shook his head. 'If I'd put him in my hand luggage they probably would've but I kept him on me in an inside pocket.' From the top of his rucksack, Alex brought out a deep plastic box. 'But he's pretty dangerous at the moment.'

'Why?'

'Poop time. Happens almost every time he eats.'

Transferring his grip, Hoku suspended the small cream body over the ground. Alex stuffed a couple of tissues into the plastic box, then took Skoodle from Hoku and put him on top of them.

Hoku crushed his juice carton and tossed it in a bin. 'Well, I guess I'd better look out for you. No parents; best friend is a rodent. You're some loser.'

'Hang on. Take a look at yourself. Living on a tropical island, surrounded by palm trees, diving off cruise ships – yet you're making friends with someone who talks to hamsters. Even bigger loser.'

Hoku grinned. 'Unless being better at being a loser makes me a winner. Want me to show you around the boat?'

'Sounds great.' Alex picked Skoodle up off the yellowed tissues, which were now scattered with tiny black pellets, and dropped the furry body into Hoku's lap. 'Safe now.'

'Sure?'

'Totally.'

Skoodle curled up, closed his eyes and lay still, his breathing deep and rhythmical.

Hoku poked him. 'Surely he can't be asleep already.'

'He is. It's a talent.'

Dropping the poop box into a bin, Alex put Skoodle back into his pocket and slung his rucksack over one shoulder. They strolled along the quay, past holidaymakers who – in their brightly-coloured clothes and constantly chattering – resembled a flock of parrots.

A tall man with long straggling black hair was sitting on a bench nearby, eyes narrowed, frowning, watching the passengers. Dressed in dark trousers and a long-sleeved top, he looked like a raven: watchful, hunched. His sweatshirt lay on the bench and, as Alex watched, a young woman in a faded floral dress dumped a rattan case of chickens on to it. Turning her back to him, she pulled out her phone and started chatting. The sleek brown-feathered chickens peered out through the holes, heads cocked to one side.

Alex nudged Hoku, pointing. 'That man doesn't seem to have noticed the lady dumping her dirty old box on his clothes.'

'You're right. When he grabs his sweatshirt the chickens will go flying. Should be funny.'

As they got to the end of the gangplank, Hoku stopped beside an official in a white shirt and trousers who was holding a clipboard. Hoku leaned over and ran his finger down the passenger sheet. 'New victim for you, Tiki. He's there at the bottom. Cabin eight.'

Tiki glanced down at his list. 'Welcome aboard, Alex Weston.'

There was a clatter behind them, followed by a raucous squawking. They all swung round to see the woman's case upended on the ground, chickens flapping and scrabbling around. She started shouting at the dark-haired stranger as he strode away towards the ticket office.

Laughing, the boys walked up the swaying gangplank on to the grimy metal boat.

'Interesting smell,' said Alex.

'Oil mixed with seawater; not great. You get used to it, though.'

'And the rocking?'

'That too, when you've finished vomiting. This cabin is yours. Comfortable enough, but not exactly luxury.'

The small sparsely furnished room contained two chairs and a narrow bed, which was covered in a bright orange throw. A picture of a volcanic island brightened up one of the grey walls. The tiny shower room was tucked in beside the porthole.

Hoku flung himself into the only comfortable chair while Alex dumped his stuff on the bed, then made a nest for Skoodle out of some tissues and a metal waste-paper bin.

Alex pulled a photo out of his pocket and handed it to Hoku. 'My parents.'

'Your dad looks like you: skinny, blond, tall. That your own surfboard you're holding?'

'Yeah. Why?'

'It's too long. Clumsy.'

'Like you're a surfing expert.'

'Like I really am.'

'OK. Maybe I'll try a shorter one some day.'

From far below them came the noise of the engines starting, then the boat began to vibrate. There was a muffled roar from the crowd on the dock and then Alex could feel the boat moving forward.

Alex opened his father's netbook. 'Anyway, this is what brought me here.'

Hoku leaned forward to have a closer look. 'Why does the top look so odd?'

'Cover or lid?'

'Both.'

'The lid is a solar panel, powering the machine. My parents were explorers, so often went to places without electricity; always had sun, though. The cover is waterproof, for when they ended up being caught in tropical storms.' Alex clicked on his inbox. 'This is the email that brought me here. It's from my dad.' He swung the screen round.

Hoku read the first few lines, then glanced up. 'You're stuffed if you don't find this Bailey person.'

9

'Totally. Eridor's not on any map or internet search. So either my parents got the name wrong – not likely, or spelled it wrong – equally unlikely – or there's something weird about it.'

'I go for weird.' Hoku finished reading it. 'And the bit about leaving the netbook?'

Alex shrugged. 'Ignored it. I wasn't going to leave anything behind that might help me find them. Would you have a look at a file of my dad's? I don't understand much of it but I thought you might, being local. There's a pile of information about Eridor, including a map which mentions the West Pole.'

'Sure, but I'll need to read it later as I'm working in ten minutes. Coming to help?'

'OK. Better than being here with my brain going round in depressing circles.'

'Correct.' Hoku hitched himself out of the chair. 'I need to get some kit. Bring the netbook. We can work on it as I sort my stuff out.'

Leaving Skoodle sleeping in the waste-paper bin, Alex followed Hoku to his cabin. By the time Hoku had explained all about his diving kit and found a rash vest for Alex, it was time to leave.

'We'll come back here after supper and have a go at your dad's file,' said Hoku.

They found a group of tourists waiting for them on the deck and pitched in to sort out their diving kit. Soon the boat had left the port far behind, skimming through tranquil turquoise waters past tiny green islands rimmed with sand.

During the afternoon Alex began to feel almost chilled as he helped Hoku. The guests were in holiday mood, chatty and friendly. Yet Alex couldn't shift the shadow from his mind that these people were having fun together as families. For him, that might never happen again.

Alex learned fast from Hoku, deciding to dive with him at their first stop. By six o'clock it had clouded over.

'Storm coming,' said Hoku, glancing up at the sky.

'Think so? Looks a bit grey, that's all.'

'Trust me. It'll be a biggie. Better pack up and shower.'

★

As Alex rounded the corner on the way to his cabin, a tall man in black stepped out from a doorway, blocking his path. Alex had only a second to register that it was the man from the dock when a hand grabbed his throat, ramming his head against the wall. Stars filled Alex's vision as iron fingers choked off his air supply. His heart thundered in his chest, pulse pounding in his ears. The man slammed Alex's wrist against the wall. Alex's back arched as pain shot through his arm. He clawed at the stranger's hand. The cold blade of a knife pressed hard against his neck. Alex stopped fighting.

Violet eyes glared at him. 'Your parents had some information I want. I believe that your stupid trusting father would somehow have got it to you. I searched your cabin. It's not there. Where is it?'

The man loosened his grip slightly, giving Alex only just enough breath to reply.

'I've got nothing,' Alex choked out. 'Leave me —'

The vice-like fingers tightened around his windpipe, bruising his throat, not even allowing a grunt in reply. Alex couldn't move enough to shake his head. His ribs ached as his diaphragm spasmed, tearing against the blockage, trying to haul in oxygen. Tiny stars appeared in his darkening vision.

'I'll come for it at midnight. If you don't have it by then I'll kill you. A swift slash through the ribs, body dumped overboard. By the time the boat turns around, sharks will have eaten your blood-seeping carcass, whether you'd gone in alive or dead. Clear?'

Sweat trickled down Alex's face as his pupils dilated, his mind filled with a vision of the sharks' feeding frenzy. The hand released him. Alex was aware of running footsteps as the man retreated, but even in his fury he didn't have enough breath to follow him. He dragged in air, coughing, throat aching, head pounding. The stars disappeared as his vision cleared.

Alex reached around to the back of his head, wincing as he found

11

a soft bruised lump. Holding his left arm across his chest, breathing hard and fast, Alex made it to his cabin. He found Skoodle awake, sitting up on his back paws.

'Been assaulted,' he told Skoodle, crouching next to him. 'I'm angry, but I need to think. Why would a mad stranger want to kill me? He really meant it. How do I stay alive?' He closed his eyes, his breathing and pulse slowing as his system righted itself. 'Better go talk to Hoku.' Putting Skoodle in his pocket he ran to Hoku's cabin, mind in overdrive.

Hoku opened the door, rubbing his wet hair with a towel. He stopped as soon as he saw Alex. 'You look upset. What's wrong?'

'Someone attacked me.'

Dumping the contents of Hoku's bin on the floor, Alex placed Skoodle in it. He told all about what had happened as Hoku listened, frowning.

'He meant trouble. My head's splitting. My wrist's really painful.'

'Let me look at it. My cousin's a doctor.' Hoku prodded the swollen wrist and moved it up and down. 'Think it's OK. Still works. It's pretty red and swollen, though. This guy is serious. Just give him the info.'

Alex shook his head. 'No way. Maybe hiding it cost my parents their lives, or at least their freedom. If I give in, it was a wasted sacrifice. Where can I hide on this boat for the next thirty-six hours?'

'Nowhere. Believe me, I know this boat inside out. It would be difficult even to hide Skoodle. You'll need to stay with somebody 24/7.' Hoku filled the handbasin with cold water.

'That won't work. All he needs is two seconds. One thrust of a blade… I'm gone.'

'Stick your arm in this.'

Alex plunged his slammed wrist into the chilly water. Picking up a jug of water and ice, Hoku dumped it in the basin on top of the swollen arm.

'Sorry, but that'll help.' Hoku dropped the empty jug on to a table. 'Anyway, the bottom line is that you're not safe anywhere on this boat.'

'That's exactly it. I'll have to get off the *Coral*. Now.'

'The nearest land is one mile away. Straight down. Or are you intending to swim for ten hours to the nearest island?'

'Nothing as stupid as that. I'm going to take a lifeboat.'

'No way. That won't be safe, either.'

'Why not?'

'You know there's a storm coming. The lifeboat might not survive it.'

Alex frowned. 'But aren't they built for bad weather?'

'Look, they've not been properly maintained.' Hoku began twisting his leather bracelet round his wrist. 'They reassure the tourists, but no one ever checks them.'

'Tough. There's no other option. I'm dead if I stay.'

'Or if you go. They might have holes… rusty equipment… no supplies.' Hoku got up and started pacing the cabin, hands shoved into the back pockets of his jeans.

'There's no choice. I'll have to risk it.'

Hoku stopped and faced Alex. 'You're either very brave or really not thinking straight.'

'Neither. It's just that some chance of living is better than none. I'll go tonight.' Alex pulled his wrist out of the icy water and wrapped a towel round it. 'Tomorrow morning, get the captain to put out a rescue call. Some boat should find me.'

'Why tomorrow? Why not tonight?'

'Because the *Coral* would be the closest boat. Once she turned round she might find me. I'd have dumped myself in a whole heap of danger and gained nothing.'

'I hadn't thought of that.'

'He'll need to see me escape. If I just disappear he might come after you to find out what you know.'

Hoku shrugged. 'Might anyway.'

Alex shook his head. 'No point. Once I've gone he can't get the information, so killing or even hurting you would be an unnecessary risk. He'd do better to keep a low profile and see if he could find out which boat rescues me.'

For a few minutes Hoku sat thinking. 'OK. You're right,' he said finally. 'It's mad, but it's the only answer.'

'This is my plan. I'll hide near my cabin before midnight. When he arrives I'll let him see me, then bolt for the lifeboat.'

'I'll help you get away.'

'That's really kind, but you could be killed. This is my fight. I can manage alone,' Alex said, attempting to sound confident.

'Yeah, right. Like you've managed so well alone this far. You're completely wrong about your surfboard, then you go and get yourself assaulted. You need me, so I'm in.'

'And if I say "No"?'

'Tough. You're stuck with me.'

During the evening the weather howled into a storm, as Hoku had foretold. By late evening, typhoon winds tore at the ship, rattling anchor chains. Salt water crashed over the decks, dragging anything loose into watery depths.

By 11.30 p.m. Alex stood wedged inside a narrow cleaning cupboard at the end of his corridor, netbook in his rucksack, Skoodle in his top pocket. Sweat dripping down the back of his neck, he kept watch through a tiny crack in the panelling.

A few minutes before midnight the stranger strode down the corridor. As soon as the footsteps had passed him, Alex crashed the cupboard door open. As the stranger swung round, Alex bolted, aware of footsteps thundering after him. Eighteen needle-like claws pierced his skin as Skoodle clung on through his shirt.

Heart banging, Alex sprinted up the stairs. As he pulled open the door to the outside deck, wind slammed into his body, shoving him backwards. Alex forced his way into the storm, eyes screwed up against the driving rain which soaked him to the skin in seconds. Glancing back over his shoulder, Alex saw the man following. Head down, shoulders hunched, Alex pushed on.

A crash momentarily swung his attention behind him. The man lay sprawled on the deck. A shadow slid back under a table. Alex instinctively understood. Hoku. Tripwire. A leaving present of a few vital seconds. He felt a wave of gratitude at Hoku's loyalty.

14

Nearby a lifeboat groaned on its metal davits, like a grotesque cradle rocking in the belly of the storm. Alex stumbled towards it through torrents of water and wrenched up the corner of the tarpaulin. He tumbled into the boat and heaved on the launch mechanism. The lifeboat crashed on to angry seething waters, sending Alex sprawling.

Breathing hard and fast, he reached down to check Skoodle. He could feel the tiny heart hammering against the furry chest wall. Scrambling on to his knees, Alex fumbled for the loose edge of the tarpaulin. Finding it, he ripped back the corner and stuck his head through the hole. Rain pounded his skin, assaulting his eyeballs, as he stared straight into the face of the storm. He no longer felt fear, only triumph that he had escaped assassination.

The stranger stood alone on deck, watching, body motionless, apparently unmoved by the downpour. Alex raised a clenched fist above his head then retreated under the tarpaulin, securing the loose corner with stiff cold fingers.

'At least we're not dead yet, Skoodle. Now we must wait for this boat to survive the storm. If it can.'

CHAPTER 3

Lightning ripped through the black underbelly of tempest-laden clouds. The skies unleashed a fresh torrent of rain, whipping the sea into a frenzy. The boat bucked like a deranged bronco. Head-splitting crashes of thunder blasted through the electric air, pounding Alex's brain. Terrified, he hung on to the sides, hands in a vice-like grip welding him to the boat.

With every heave of the waves, Alex's body was wrenched sideways, hauling on his anchored arms. His muscles were stretched to the limit as rods of agony shafted into his wrists and shoulders.

Furious with the fates, he jammed his feet harder between the slats. 'I'm not giving up,' he yelled at the storm-ridden night. 'Whatever the pain, I'm holding on.'

After what felt like a lifetime, the storm began to settle; the thunder less monstrous, the rain subsiding. Alex waited until the wind damped down before loosening his grip.

After checking on Skoodle, Alex crawled forward to find the emergency box, hoping it would have blankets, drinks and food. He found a torch, flashing its beam around the tented interior. No holes in the canvas so far. The boat wasn't big, but would do for two. He pulled a blanket around his aching body and tried to settle on the hard boat base. Reluctantly, he switched off the torch to conserve batteries.

'Nothing more I can do, Skoodle. The wind and tide will decide what happens to us.'

Exhaustion carried him into an uncomfortable, broken sleep at some time during the restless hours that followed.

When Alex woke, the storm had settled. The only noise reaching his storm-shocked ears was the quiet lapping of a gentle sea, now more of a kitten than the raging tiger of last night. The boat lay totally still. Alex's tired brain worked out that he must have been washed up on land somewhere. He felt his shirt pocket and found Skoodle asleep, breathing rhythmically. Muscles aching as if he'd been run over, Alex lifted the edge of the tarpaulin and looked out.

Sunlight cascaded into the boat. Brilliant white stretched ahead for miles, flanked on one side by calm, azure seas, on the other by lush jungle. Emerald leaves framed a mass of jewel-coloured flowers: ruby hibiscus, slender yellow lilies like slivers of sunlight, sapphire orchids with their hearts slashed by deep burnt-orange stamens. It was like looking into an exploding rainbow.

Alex whooped, punching the air. He got out of the boat and wandered a short way beside the sea, loving the sensation of the sand beneath his feet, the sun on his face and the light breeze in his hair.

'We'll have to explore the jungle for more fresh water,' he told the still-sleeping Skoodle as he walked back to the boat. 'Assuming we don't get eaten before we find food.'

Unable to haul the boat away from the water's edge, Alex tied the bow rope to a nearby palm with a couple of knots. Grabbing a hunting knife from the emergency box, he headed down a wide path into the muggy interior of the jungle. The strong perfume of orchids blended with the heavy musty scent of damp earth and trodden leaves. Many animal tracks showed in the dirt – some hoofed, others of large cats. None were human.

After twenty minutes Alex arrived in a clearing about twice the size of a football pitch. Hundreds of brightly-coloured birds flew above his head, swooping across the clearing and landing in the surrounding trees. Feeling tired, hot and thirsty, Alex sat down on a grassy mound. *This is a pretty hostile place*, he thought.

I disagree, a voice replied. *It's very homely, as well as ace-superbly beautiful.*

With a shock, Alex registered that he hadn't spoken out loud. In a double whammy, he realised that the other voice hadn't been aloud, either. It had come from inside his head. Alex looked around the glade, puzzled. *Why doesn't the voice sound like me?* he asked himself.

Why should it? It's not you replying.

I've never used 'ace-superbly'.

Can't have because I've just made it up.

So if this voice is someone else, not me, where are you? In my head?

Yeah, right. That would be a bit crowded. Actually, thinking about it, maybe not. I'm up here. In a tree on the other side of the clearing.

Alex looked up into the thick emerald canopy of trees which was pierced by shafts of bright sunlight. A small brown monkey, fur tipped with red, was perched in a tree some distance away. *It seems to be waving at me,* thought Alex.

What do you means 'seems'? Not impressed? OK, watch this.

The monkey swung itself upside down, suspended by its tail.

But you're a monkey.

Oddly enough, I know that.

How do we understand each other?

Thought transference. Mind broadcasting. Don't you use it in your bit of the jungle?

I don't have one. I've just arrived, in a boat.

Keeko, came a deeper voice, also female. *Who are you talking to?*

Don't know. Who are you?

Alex.

Bizarre what parents call their children, said the new voice. *Cruel, really.*

Where are you, Ikara?

On the way from Tariq's clearing.

A minute later the creature emerged out of the undergrowth.

'You're a snake,' said Alex, stepping back.

'Wow. That's brilliant. And can you name this green stuff I'm lying on or that blue expanse above me?' asked Ikara.

'Sorry. Stupid to state the obvious, but I've never seen a snake so close up before.'

'It's the jungle. Get used to it.'

A vivid picture of the reptile house at Regent's Park Zoo flashed into Alex's mind: rows of clear-fronted cages, trapping an astonishing variety of snakes. Yet none looked like this version: four metres long from nose tip to tail, shimmering green and gold. He hoped that pictures wouldn't transfer.

'Pictures don't transfer,' said Ikara. 'But trapping animals in cages doesn't sound good.'

'No, I guess not.'

Sleepily, Skoodle poked his head above the edge of Alex's pocket. Alex took him out and put him on his palm.

'Lunch,' said Ikara, her green eyes locked on to Skoodle.

Putting a protective hand in front of him, Alex said, 'Pet. Special kind of friend. Not for eating.'

'Hello, small animal,' said Ikara, sliding closer.

Crisis. Play dead, said a new voice in Alex's mind.

Skoodle rolled on to his back, legs sticking stiffly in the air, not breathing.

'No use,' hissed Ikara. 'I know you're alive. You moved.'

'Skoodle. Can you talk?' asked Alex.

Maybe, but not if it proves I'm alive.

'I won't eat you, rat lookalike,' said Ikara. 'I make it a rule never to eat anything that lies about whether or not it's dead.'

'Promise?' asked Skoodle, opening one eye.

Ikara sighed. 'I suppose so.'

'Got to love the rodent,' Keeko called from her perch on a narrow branch above them. She threw a plum stone into a nearby bush. Startled, several crimson and yellow parrots rose into the air shrieking.

'It's so cool that you can speak,' said Alex. 'Why have you never done so before?'

'Never could.' Skoodle rolled back on to his feet. 'Anyway, I probably wouldn't have bothered at home. It might have shocked the adulty ones. Your aunt would have run away shrieking.'

'Possibly,' agreed Alex. 'Great image, though. It's not usual for animals to talk where we come from,' Alex said to the others. 'By the way, where are we?'

'Eridor,' replied Ikara, winding her tail around a large bush. She started to shake it violently. A hail of shiny black beetles fell to the ground. With a swift flick of her tongue, several vanished.

'We were on our way to Eridor. Odd that we've managed to be blown here,' said Alex.

Ikara shook her head. 'Not really. The current from miles around swirls round the island, so everything gets dragged towards us.'

'Kind of a whirlpool effect,' said Keeko. 'I once found an elephant on the beach.'

'Really?' asked Skoodle.

'No, but it makes a good story.' Laughing, Keeko swung herself upside down by her tail.

'That makes me slightly less worried about the boat. It's our home and food supply currently. I couldn't drag it up the sand.'

'Tariq will do that for you. He's a bear. Very strong. He'll be in the river clearing.' Ikara pointed her tail at a path on the far side of the clearing. 'Coming?'

Yeah, right, thought Alex, forgetting his thoughts could be heard. *This bear might have a passion for crunching human skulls. All the bits of him which aren't muscle or claws will be teeth.*

'Leave the boat,' said Skoodle. 'I have a hunch that it'll be fine where it is.'

Alex gave him a hard look. 'Chicken-heartedness overrides logic. Possibly a big mistake.'

'Yeah, but the cowardly road gives me the chance to live '

'Tariq's OK,' said Ikara. 'He's a real softie. Unless you're against him in battle: then he'll rip you to shreds.'

Great, thought Alex. *Truly terrific.*

'Yup. Trust or die,' hissed Ikara, setting off towards the far side of the clearing.

Keeko threw a nectarine at Alex. 'Food.'

'Watch the hamster,' yelled Skoodle, ducking the shot. 'I'm already traumatised by the lifeboaty-storm experience.'

'Stop complaining. You're alive, owing to my brilliant navigating,' said Alex, passing him a bitten-off lump of fruit.

Skoodle snorted. 'We'll follow,' he said, cheeks stuffed, juice running down his chin. 'But if he starts the ripping stuff, I'm off.'

'Thanks. I hope you die of a guilty conscience.'

'Not me. I don't do guilt or conscience. Get going, human. Follow that snake.'

CHAPTER 4

Alex set off across the clearing, wondering why he was taking orders from someone weighing about two hundred times less than he did. Sense of fun? Limited other options?

'Logic,' said Skoodle. 'If I make the decisions we don't mess up.'

'It's a real pain that you can read my thoughts,' said Alex.

Keeko tilted her head to one side, looking at him, frowning. 'Then block them.'

'How?'

Ikara sighed. 'Takes a while. We'll teach you once the boat's safe.'

On the track the trees grew close together, choking out nearly all light. They travelled up the shadowy green tunnel of leaves, plunged into deep gloom.

'Walk louder,' said Skoodle.

'Can't. Moss underfoot. Why?'

'I'm spooked by all the creepy, slithering, snapping sounds from the jungle around us. If you made more noise I wouldn't be able to hear them.'

'The animals would still be there.'

'Not if I pretend they aren't.'

After a steep climb they emerged on to a long strip of sun-drenched grass. Several mango trees stood at the edges of the clearing, their branches heavy with ripe golden fruit. At the far side ran a river. Downstream to the left the waters fell over a waterfall, crashing with a muffled roar to the earth far below.

As Alex gazed around, part of a shadow detached itself from the edge of the trees. It solidified into a huge golden-haired bear, brilliant eyes fixed on the newcomers. It reared eight feet into the air, razor claws unsheathed, teeth a row of ivory daggers.

Alex's heart began pounding as if trying to escape on its own. Yet his legs, jellified, failed to move. *Fool,* he thought. *At any minute I might be shredded. Perhaps they're wrong that he's friendly.*

'I don't do wrong,' said Ikara. 'I respected the petness of your rodent. I didn't eat the rat: Tariq won't eat you.'

'Yes, but look at the size of him.'

Ikara coiled herself into a neat stack. 'He's one of my best friends although, astonishingly – despite the resemblance between us – not family. So I know exactly how big and powerful he is, also how fast he can swim. Any further Tariq facts needed, don't hesitate to ask.'

The bear dropped to all fours and shambled across the grass. Alex started backing away, palms damp, heart drumming a tattoo of fear. *Useless,* he thought. *The bear would outrun or outclimb any human.*

'Put me down,' hissed Skoodle. 'Fear has got to my gut.'

Alex placed him on the ground. Skoodle rushed to hide behind a nearby bush. A small splatting sound followed a second later.

Close enough for Alex to smell bear fur, Tariq halted. In a deep and resonant voice he said, 'Hi.'

'Five,' replied Keeko, offering him her paw.

'One,' said Ikara, holding up her tail. 'This is Alex. From the sea. He needs a boat dragged up the beach. Will you do it?'

Tariq looked Alex full in the face. He was even more terrifying up close. A creature of the jungle, unpredictable, savage, with vicious teeth bared. *Smile or grimace?* Alex wondered. At any second he could find out the hard way.

'You're frightened of me,' Tariq said, sounding amused. 'Don't be. I'll help you.'

'Thanks,' replied Alex, trying hard to envisage Tariq as something less scary, like a monster wave – but surf didn't have claws, enormous muscles or teeth.

'Told you he'd help,' crowed Keeko, doing cartwheels across the glade.

'Actually, it was me who said that,' hissed Ikara.

Keeko did a flick-flack, landing neatly. 'Whatever. Still clever.'

'Do you like hamsters?' Skoodle asked Tariq, poking his head round the bush.

'Absolutely; for lunch,' replied Ikara.

'Any friend of Ikara's or Keeko's is mine too,' said Tariq, sitting down. 'Besides, I don't eat rodents. I'd rather have a banana.'

'I don't know whether to be relieved or insulted,' replied Skoodle, wandering into the open.

'Choose both,' replied Keeko.

Ikara rolled her eyes up. 'Economy of emotion not your forte, furry face?'

'Never.'

'It'll soon be dark. We'd better sort your boat out now. There could be a storm later,' said Tariq.

'Perfect idea,' said Keeko, jumping on to Tariq's back. Ikara curled herself round Tariq's leg then, in a shimmer of green and gold, slithered up to curl round his neck and torso.

'Piggyback?' Tariq asked Alex.

Alex looked at the bear-snake-monkey combo. In an odd way he wanted to join them, feel the thrill of riding a bear. His fear levels were falling, but not low enough to ride. 'Thanks,' he said. 'I'll walk. It's good for me.'

'Taxi,' shouted Skoodle.

Alex reached down and scooped him up.

'Shoulder, not pocket.'

'Like a pirate's parrot,' said Alex. 'A human's hamster.'

'Or a rodent's ride. Let's keep perspective.'

As they reached the lighter, more open track, Keeko launched herself into some low-hanging trees. She threw a large knobbly orange fruit at Alex. It looked like a misshapen grapefruit. Curiously, he held it to his nose. It smelled fabulous – a cross between a pineapple and a mango. 'Is it safe to eat?'

'Of course.'

Alex peeled it, passing two segments to Skoodle, who crammed both into his mouth at once.

'Instant balloon,' said Ikara. 'More of a meal that way.'

Skoodle swallowed quickly, as Alex shoved him back into his pocket.

'Joke,' said Ikara. 'Although not actually very funny for me. I'm starving.'

She slithered off the path, reappearing about a minute later. 'Delicious,' she said, voice muffled as she swallowed. 'But it would've been even more terrific with a fruit garnish in its mouth.'

'You're winding me up,' said Alex.

'Snake kebab,' Skoodle called from his pocket. 'Reptile on toast. Serpent burger. Overgrown-worm nuggets.'

'Insignificant fur ball: hardly even a snake snack,' replied Ikara. 'If I tried to eat you, I'd choke on all the acid in your heart.'

After three of Keeko's fruits, Alex was beginning to feel full for the first time in twenty-four hours. Life didn't seem so awful when he was neither starving nor about to vomit. They hadn't drowned. They'd made friends with talking animals: bizarre, but great. Also, because of the tides, they'd made it to Eridor. *Life could be a lot worse*, he reasoned.

'Optimism. I thought it couldn't get worse,' groaned Skoodle.

'Just did, 'cause you started talking,' said Ikara. 'Silence is considered to be a great attribute in a rat.'

'Hamster, ignorant worm.'

★

Once on the beach Alex untied the bow rope, retying it around the great bear's waist. On all fours, Tariq dragged the dead weight up the beach, Keeko riding on his back, bombarding him with unnecessary advice. Within minutes he had pulled the boat out of the sea's reach.

Alex refastened the rope to a huge palm. 'Nothing but a hurricane or tsunami will shift it now.'

'It shows what real muscle can do.' Skoodle hopped on to the rope to have a better look. 'Knots are okay. At least you got that right.'

A glorious sunset in shades of brilliant orange, burnt umber and blood red lit the sky as they finished. The jungle seemed impenetrably dark in contrast. Alex almost wished that his boat was back on the water's edge, not quite so close to the black expanse filled with ominous noises.

'You go to the river clearing with Ikara,' Keeko told Tariq. 'I'll sleep here. Alex and Skoodle don't know the ways of the jungle.'

'I'd feel a lot safer,' said Alex.

Skoodle snorted. 'What? Being protected by a monkey?'

'She may be small but she's no fluff-ball,' said Ikara. 'If something attacks, you'll see a whole new side of her.'

'The word attacks is not reassuring,' said Skoodle. 'If anything happens we'll yell for Tariq.'

'Thought transference travels further than speech, even hamster yell, so use that,' said Tariq. 'See you in the morning.' He set off into the inky depths with Ikara wound casually round his neck like a scarf.

Over the next hour Keeko taught the others how to block their thoughts. 'You think the words *Non sprugguli* while envisaging a huge breaking wave. But no sun, no clouds, no fish. Only sky, surf, water.'

Since Keeko had said "No sun", Alex found it difficult not to keep seeing it in his mind. Finally he got the picture fixed, with only a bit of sunlight.

Non sprugguli. How's that?

Not great.

Alex rearranged his vision mentally, blocked the sun with a storm cloud, and then recalled that no clouds were allowed.

Any better?

Needs work.

After about twenty minutes of practice, Keeko's face finally remained blank in answer to Alex's mental questions. Unblocking proved easier. *Sprugguli*, with the same mental image, took only four attempts. Skoodle cracked both with two attempts.

'Easier for you,' said Alex, watching Keeko and Skoodle sitting on the sand opposite each other, toe to toe. 'Less imagination.'

'More skill, intelligence, genetic ability, willingness to listen – shall I go on?' asked Skoodle.

'You can, but I'm going to bed. Do carry on talking to yourself if you want,' replied Alex.

'Nope. I'm shattered too,' said Skoodle, trotting across to the boat.

'Sand will be better. I'll sleep out here,' said Keeko. She scrabbled around making a comfortable hollow then lay down, curling her tail round her body. 'Sleep well,' she called.

'No chance,' said Skoodle. 'Bet I'll be awake all night.'

Alex lifted Skoodle over the side of the boat then pulled the tarpaulin over their heads. Almost instantly both fell into a deep sleep, such that only the dead could rival.

CHAPTER 5

A loud bang rocketed Alex back to consciousness, ripping him out of his dreams. His mental processes were still foggy from sleep, made worse by dehydration.

His eyes jerked open. Completely useless. His brain cells showed nothing on the vision front. He lay entombed in complete darkness, apparently buried alive.

Confused, aching, his mouth tasting as if his tongue had been dragged through a pigsty, he desperately tried to work out where he could be. It could be anywhere horrendously uncomfortable and stiflingly hot. The crash came again, this time closer to his feet. An attack. By whom? Why?

'You awake?' asked Keeko, from above him.

With the sound of her voice, yesterday's experiences flooded back: Eridor, his new friends, the lifeboat. Suddenly, the hardness underneath him and the pitch black made sense.

'Yes,' Alex mumbled, through dry lips.

'It's been ages since the sun rose,' continued Keeko. 'I've been gathering your breakfast.'

Alex shoved back a corner of the tarpaulin to reveal a clear sunny day, already hot despite being relatively early. The deep blue sky hung cloudless above the stunning vista of the jungle.

Grape-sized red fruit had been thrown on to the tarpaulin, splattering juice and seeds in a sticky explosion. The fantastic smell brought a sharp pang of hunger, made worse by the food being a squashed inedible mulch.

Keeko sat balanced at the top end of the bow rope, laughing. 'Fentice fruit. It was breakfast, then it broke, fast. Hungry?'

'What do you think?' replied Alex, not bothering to keep the fatigue out of his voice. 'Starving. Thirsty. Looking forward to a chunk of barbecued monkey.'

'OK. Tiny hint taken, but avoid going into the jungle while I'm gone. If you must, stick to the paths.'

Flinging herself into the trees Keeko swung rapidly up the jungle path, her brown and red furry body soon swallowed by the dense green foliage.

'I hope she hurries back,' Alex said to Skoodle, sitting down on the sand. He ripped the top off an emergency water bottle and glugged most of it down in one go.

'She'll probably forget. I expect we won't see her till lunchtime,' said Skoodle, long brown whiskers trembling in irritation. 'Although she could be quite quick if she wanted. Monkeys can travel up to thirty-five mph.'

'How do you know?'

'I've walked across a lot of your books.'

'Have you always understood English?' asked Alex, wiping his mouth on the back of his hand.

'Of course.'

Holding the bottle for Skoodle, Alex clumsily tipped it down his tiny chest, soaking his cream fur. 'Fascinating. Hamsters can raise their eyebrows.'

'Dull. So can humans.' Sitting up on his back legs Skoodle began to brush the front of his chest, frowning.

'Do other animals in England understand speech?' asked Alex.

'The clever ones do. Naturally, animals such as chickens can't. Cats understand pretty much everything. In fact, I once knew a cat who could read Greek.'

'Oh, come on.'

Skoodle rubbed a wet paw on Alex's jeans. 'Actually, it's true. Minty could also read Latin.'

'I believe you about that. What's ridiculous is that you knew this Minty creature. Cats and hamsters don't get on.'

'You are,' replied Skoodle coldly, 'confusing me with a mouse.'

'You come from the same family, don't you?'

'There is no mouse that I'd call cousin. We're about as closely related as you and the average smelly gorilla.'

'Don't you be rude about my Uncle Gus,' replied Alex, grinning. 'He may be hairy, odour-challenged and eat bananas, but he's a fine guy to be with if you can understand his grunts.'

Skoodle made an L sign on his forehead, turned his back and started picking sand out of his tail. Oozing sweat from every pore, Alex lay down in the shade to wait.

Before long Keeko returned with food, arms laden as she ran. The three sat on the warm white sand, listening to the chorus of parrots in the jungle behind them, munching fentice fruit.

Once they were stuffed, they made their way up the hill to Tariq's place. As they entered the clearing, a feeling of being in the presence of evil passed over Alex, rapidly evaporating. Ikara lay sunbathing on the grass.

'Busy?' asked Alex.

Green eyes flecked with gold swivelled round to fix on him. 'Don't knock it. Power snoozing. We cold-blooders need a sun blast at times.'

Skoodle's body had gone rigid. Alex stuffed a finger under Skoodle's nose, blocking his nostrils. As the hamster opened his mouth to breathe, Alex removed his finger and crammed more fentice into the tiny mouth.

'Eat. Chill out. It's OK to be friends with a snake.'

'Eating's okay,' mumbled Skoodle. 'It's the thought of being eaten that I find less relaxing.'

'Then stand away from the snake. Go buddy up with the bear.'

Tariq was lying stretched out on his back on a patch of thick grass, huge arm across his eyes. He looked perfectly content in the caress of the sun's warmth. Thoughts unblocked, Alex wondered if he was asleep.

'Asleep?' asked Keeko. 'We'll soon fix that.'

Shinning up a nearby tree, she picked a handful of nuts. Taking aim, she pelted the bear with them.

'Stop, Keeko,' Tariq said, not moving a millimetre.

Ignoring him, Keeko continued the barrage. Tariq picked up a nut and threw it hard. It pinged off the monkey's chest.

'That hurt. I'll get you.' Swinging through the branches above their heads, Keeko flung herself on to Tariq, kicking and punching.

Tariq play-wrestled back, pushing her fists away, groaning in overacted agony.

'Great. A fight,' shouted Skoodle, mimicking Keeko's every move, ducking the phantom blows from Tariq. 'Right hook. Unlucky. Slug with the left.'

Lying still, Tariq said, 'Getting tedious, Keeko.'

Keeko bared her long teeth and bit him.

'Not funny.' Tariq stood up, grabbed Keeko by her feet and dangled her upside down – the other paw holding her upper spine to stop her twisting to bite him.

Still acting as if he were Keeko, Skoodle was forced into a handstand. 'Crisis,' he said. 'Bad vibes.'

Keeko punched and kicked at Tariq, hitting only air, screeching and wriggling.

'No more biting or fighting. Pax?' asked Tariq.

'Fat chance.'

Boxing the breeze Keeko fought on, not one paw finding bear flesh. Skoodle gave up, righted himself and changed sides, imitating Tariq waiting.

Finally Keeko hung limply. 'Pax,' came a small voice.

'Good.'

Tariq tossed her up into the air, catching her in a hug.

'Not happy, though. Don't think you can get round me by being nice,' she said, baring her teeth.

Tariq growled loudly.

'But that'll work,' she replied with a smile.

Wearing Keeko on his chest like a small furry bib Tariq asked, 'What news from the beach?'

Before anyone had time to answer, a blast of wind ripped through the clearing. Jungle birds were flung out of the trees in a shrieking, multicoloured blizzard. Black clouds scudded across the sun as the temperature plummeted.

The wind dropped, leaving an unnatural stillness in the polar air.

'The news is...' thundered a voice, filling the clearing. It seemed to come from everywhere but nowhere. It paused ominously. For several seconds everyone froze, petrified. The suspense was agonising. Skoodle disappeared into Alex's pocket.

Into the terrified silence the voice spoke again. 'Alex will die.'

Time seemed to stop. The glade was silent. Alex's heart was pumping hard as he struggled to work out if this could really be happening.

Tariq stood up, handing Keeko to Alex. 'Virida, O Powerful One. For what reason do you make such a dreadful statement?'

A deafening clap of thunder answered him. In the same instant a column of swirling blue smoke rose from the centre of the clearing. Within seconds it towered as high as the treetops, spitting red, green and orange sparks. Alex sat transfixed, terrified by a force powerful enough to control nature.

'Because, O Stupid One, the Weston boy must bear the sins of his parents. They wronged me deeply. For that he shall pay.'

'Such is not justice,' replied Tariq, facing the column without flinching. 'The parents commit the crime, yet the son is to be punished?'

The column of smoke rose higher, swelling thicker. 'You question my judgement? Be careful, or those who defend him may also die.'

'The deeper laws of Eridor do not permit such injustice,' said Tariq, taking a step closer to the swirling smoke, apparently unmoved by the fear that paralysed the rest of them.

'A death for a death is permitted,' spat out the voice. 'Blood has been shed by the Westons. The evil in them is embedded in the kinfolk also. The boy must be eliminated. I have spoken.'

The wind whipped up again, bending trees, snapping vines, tearing branches off bushes. Flattened by the force Alex grabbed on to a tree, arms scraped by branches hurtling past, Keeko clinging to him. He caught Ikara as she blew towards him in a bruised tangle. Holding the tree with one arm, he clung to Ikara until she wriggled up his chest, wrapped herself around the tree, thus anchoring all three of them.

Only Tariq stood unmoved, his great weight and courage fixing him to the spot. The column started to fall as the cascade of smoke turned in on itself. Within moments, the pillar stood at barely half its peak height.

'Wait, Virida,' growled Tariq. 'Is there anything you would accept other than the life of such a miserable creature?'

The wind dropped. The column halted, hanging swirling in the air, internal lights sparking. The centre glowed red, a poker of heat straight through the smoke's heart. The whole column pulsated as if a life force beat within it.

Seconds passed. Sparks spitting and hissing were the only sounds in the terrifying silence. Then the voice came again. 'There is a price I would accept.'

'Name it.'

'The Sapphire of Akan. Bring it to me and Alex goes free. Fail and you all die with him. Unless you speak now, you have all agreed.' With not even half a second's pause to allow an answer, Virida swept on. 'The pact is made. You are bound by its terms.'

The column started to fall once more.

'Stop, Virida.'

The column halted, centre glowing darker, pulsating heat. Red sparks, like long nails, rained on to the ground, scorching moss, setting tufts of grass alight.

I hope he knows what he's doing, thought Alex, mind blocked. *The column looks as reasonable and as safe as the core of a nuclear reactor.*

Tariq's face remained expressionless. 'Where can we find the sapphire?'

'Ask Zorrin.'

'No one knows where to find him, except the Elemental Wizards,' replied Tariq.

'Tough.' The column began to shrink again.

'If you help us we have more chance of getting the gem for you. If we die finding him we're only a pile of corpses, no use to you.'

The column quietened, apparently thinking. 'Try the Single Redwood. Zorrin sometimes goes there.'

A wild gust of wind swept the smoke straight up into the sky where it hung for a moment, then vanished in an explosion of purple and red sparks. The black clouds slid away from the face of the sun, yet the atmosphere remained icy.

Alex frowned at the space where the column had been, stunned. Could this be possible? Had he really been condemned to death? Who would have this much power, even controlling the weather? In a cold sweat he let go of Ikara's tail as she unwound herself from the tree. He pulled himself to sitting.

Keeko's sobs broke the horrendous silence. 'We're all to die. Nothing can save us.'

CHAPTER 6

'We'll find the crystal and hand it over. Then everything will be all right,' said Alex, trying to sound calm.

The temperature had risen, the birdsong returning, but the glade still felt sinister.

'The sapphire may not even exist,' said Ikara. 'It's probably only a legend.'

'She's being cruel,' cried Keeko, rocking back and forth, arms round her knees. 'We'll run around trying to find a mythical gem then, when she's bored of the game, she'll kill us.'

Tariq shambled over to join them. 'Yet we have to assume it exists and search for it if we want to stay alive.'

'Alive is good,' said Skoodle. 'I go with that.'

'Surely she cannot kill the rest of us. Our death sentences must be an empty threat,' said Ikara, looking up at Tariq.

Tariq shook his head, deep sadness in his eyes. 'Unfortunately not. She'll execute us unless we get the sapphire. Evil witches are not known for compassion. The pact, although unfairly made, will be binding.'

Shuddering, Keeko buried her face in her hands. Alex lifted her on to his lap. Skoodle started biting his toenails.

'But what if Zorrin's not at the Redwood? How are we going to find his hideout?' asked Ikara.

'I'm not sure,' Tariq said.

'I know where Zorrin lives,' said Alex.

Ikara stared at him. 'How?' she asked. 'That would be impossible if you'd really only just arrived.' Her head rose, the sides of her neck winging out like a cobra. 'We were wrong to trust you. We were safe before you turned up. You're the cause of our death sentence.'

A sense of injustice boiled up inside Alex. 'It's not my fault,' he shouted. 'You can't blame me for something my parents may or may not have done. Furthermore, it's in your country where all this magic and death-binding stuff occurs. It doesn't happen in mine.' Spitting out each word, he continued. 'This has nothing to do with me.'

'Go, Alex,' yelled Skoodle.

Ikara glared at Alex. 'Thinking about it, you must be one of Virida's spies.'

'I'm not,' Alex replied, furious. 'You heard her. I'm under the death penalty too.'

'And me,' shouted Skoodle.

'It could be a cover,' said Ikara, sounding increasingly hostile. 'Virida threatens you, but only intends to kill us. If we travel together she'll know exactly where we are going and what we are doing, with you acting as her informant. Perhaps the plan is for us to lead her to Zorrin, then the sapphire. Doubtless she'll destroy us once we hand over the stone, sparing you of course.'

'And me,' yelled a squeaky voice.

'Not helping,' Alex muttered.

'That can't happen,' Tariq cut in. 'She couldn't kill us if we give her the sapphire. Even the witch cannot override the deeper magic that governs the pact she has thrust upon us.'

'It seems weird to me,' continued Ikara, as if she hadn't heard Tariq. 'This human claims he has just arrived on the beach. From where? Then he says he knows how to find Zorrin when he has been here for only one rising of the sun – whereas I, who have lived here all my life, don't know. How? He appears, then bang – the witch comes and curses all of us. Too much of a coincidence. I say he works for her.'

'I don't work for her,' said Skoodle.

'Thanks,' said Alex.

'Nor does he,' added Skoodle.

36

Keeko wriggled off Alex's lap and slipped across to Tariq. The bear's face remained unreadable, but his honey-brown eyes looked troubled.

Getting up, Alex stood eye to eye with the uncoiled snake. 'There's a map showing Zorrin's hideout in something I brought with me.'

'Virida could have planted that on him,' hissed Ikara, unmoved.

Anger exploded in Alex's head again. 'All I've done is follow my parents, nearly getting myself drowned in the process. It wasn't my fault that Virida landed us with a death sentence. So why am I suddenly the bad guy?'

'The time has come for you to tell us how you got here and why,' said Tariq calmly.

Alex turned his back on Ikara.

'Tell them,' said Skoodle.

'Why should I?'

'If it comes to a fight we're dead meat.'

'So we leave.'

'We need their help to get the stupid sapphire, break the curse, then get on with finding out what your parents were doing here.'

Alex walked away a few paces and stood looking at the jungle, trying to regain calm. Whichever way he looked at it, Skoodle was right. He turned back to the others and motioned for them to sit down.

Tariq and Keeko sank on to the grass nearby. Ikara remained upright, towering above him.

'My parents were explorers, often away for months at a time so I live with my aunt Lisa in England,' said Alex, tone surly. 'A few days ago I received an email. An electronic letter.'

He dug in his rucksack. Pulling out the netbook, he found his father's email and handed the computer to Tariq. 'Read it.'

Alex paused as they read the email. 'Yes, you can read it calmly. I couldn't. That day I booked a ticket to Tikopia.'

On Tariq's and Keeko's faces Alex could see interest: on Ikara's, frank disbelief and impatience. Skoodle caught his eye and shrugged.

Settling himself more comfortably on the ground, Alex went on. 'However, on the boat, a man in black threatened to kill me.'

'Can you describe him?' asked Tariq.

Alex described the man in detail, ending with, 'Oddly enough, he had violet eyes.'

Tariq nodded as if he had been half expecting this last piece of information. 'What happened next?'

Alex told them about casting himself adrift in the lifeboat, ending up on the beach. Silence fell on the group as he finished. Keeko sat twisting her tail, frowning.

'Lies,' Ikara said, rising higher, tension in every muscle of her body. Skoodle ran and hid behind Alex.

'I think not.' The bear motioned for Ikara to coil up again. 'Don't you recognise the man?'

Ikara shook her head remaining rigidly upright.

'It was Karlan.'

Ikara sank back on to the ground, resting her head on a wide coil as Keeko started tying and untying knots in her tail. Skoodle stuck his nose out from behind Alex's jeans.

'Who?' asked Alex.

Tariq looked worried as he sat with his huge golden-brown arms resting on his knees. 'A powerful, evil wizard. Yet he would have had little magic away from the circumferential forces of the island, which is why he had to resort to threatening you with a knife.'

'Before we get too carried away with this belief business,' said Ikara, 'we should have a little proof. Where is this map of Eridor?'

Anger ignited within Alex again. He turned a hostile pair of eyes towards Ikara. 'I've nearly been killed hiding my netbook. The information's mine. I no longer trust that you're on my side.'

'Our side,' said Skoodle.

'He's right. There are two of us.' It sounded good to be a team, but Alex couldn't help thinking that an added couple of ounces of hamster didn't make him the strongest fighting unit on Eridor.

'Yet,' replied Tariq placidly, 'if you try to escape the death sentence alone, you won't live long in the jungle. The rest of us will also be as good as dead. If you show it to us, we can work together and may find the sapphire. We have to trust each other for survival.'

'Like that's going to be easy. She's just attacked me, said Alex.'

'It was only words,' said Skoodle.

'Provoked by anger, which you felt too,' said Tariq. 'Since when has something become impossible just because it's difficult? An animal survives or dies on instinct. What was your impression, Ikara, when you first met Alex and Skoodle?'

Ikara dropped her eyes. 'I liked Alex. The rodent took longer to accept.'

'You, Keeko?'

Keeko was absent-mindedly pulling a leaf to pieces. 'I took to them. They seemed fun, if a little strange.'

'For me the connection was also good,' said Tariq. 'You're an animal too, Alex. What were your feelings?'

Alex's wrath was draining away as he recognised Ikara's honesty, doubtless at considerable cost to her pride. He owed them the truth, however wound up he felt. 'You all seemed OK. Well… great, really.'

'Skoodle?'

'Fine, once I got over my fear of the legless one.'

'Then there must be a pact between us,' said Tariq, 'Ensuring openness, trust and honesty. When we fight, as we surely shall, we'll be victorious together or die defending each other. Salute.'

Tariq held his paw out, back uppermost, so that his flesh-shredding claws pointed downwards. Without hesitation, Keeko reached out and placed her small red and brown paw on top of the heavy golden one. Ikara paused, looking at Alex long and hard. Finally she uncoiled her heavy tail and placed the tip on top of the paws.

Decision time. Alex knew that if he failed to reach for the others, he would be alone in a hostile jungle. But did he truly trust Ikara? Just now she had turned against him, so how could he believe that she could become totally loyal to him? It needed to be a two-way confidence. Still uncertain, Alex hesitated.

Skoodle scrambled on to Keeko's arm and placed his small paw on Ikara's tail.

Decision made. The final hand reached out and joined the heap.

'Until the sun implodes,' said the Eridor three.

'Until the sun implodes,' echoed Alex and Skoodle.

'Right,' said Ikara, pulling her tail away. 'That binds us. Tariq, what do we do next?'

Before Tariq could answer, Alex made a decision. They were now bound together, like blood brothers. 'I'll show you my map, but not here. I'm worried about this clearing. It feels evil to me.'

'That's interesting,' Tariq said. 'This could be useful. You may have the power of predor.'

'Of what?'

'Predor. The ability to detect evil when there is no visible sign. You're right about the atmosphere here. This clearing has been used for evil ceremonies. Let's get back to the beach,' said Tariq.

No one spoke as they strolled back down the jungle path. On arrival, Alex pulled out his parents' netbook and found the map. 'Over here up in the north east is Zorrin's place, Ravenscraig, with an eagle sign above it.'

'We are directly south,' said Tariq. 'There's the Single Redwood, immediately north of us on the way there. We'll carry on to Ravenscraig if Zorrin is not at the tree.'

'Who is Zorrin, anyway?' asked Alex.

'The most powerful of the elemental wizards – the good guys,' said Tariq. 'He looks like a pirate: long, curly, black hair down to his waist; brilliant blue eyes. I met him at the Battle of Gelforth.'

'We can't set off now; too late in the day,' said Ikara.

'Meet at my clearing at day break,' replied Tariq. 'Then we'll cross the river to the path going directly to the Single Redwood. Questions?'

'None. I'm too tired to think,' replied Skoodle, as Alex hoisted him into his top pocket.

'Not like you. You'll be OK tomorrow,' replied Alex.

'If we're really unlucky,' muttered Ikara, slithering up Tariq as he rose upright on his back legs.

Snake aboard, Tariq shambled back into the dense undergrowth.

CHAPTER 7

As Alex watched them walk away, a buzz of excitement shoved out his fear. Odd, but the adrenaline whizzing round him felt great.

'Stress makes me hungry,' said Skoodle. 'There are some nuts in the emergency box.'

'I'll get them.' Alex scrambled over the side of the boat, but lost his handhold on the wet edge.

'You nearly squashed me,' said Skoodle.

'Sorry.'

'Not much point in being sorry once I'm dead and with Uncle Toomba.'

Alex put the grumpy rodent on the boat edge and climbed aboard. 'Who?'

'Toomba. Long-dead uncle. Invaluable, though. Gives me all sorts of advice.'

'Isn't that tricky if he's not exactly alive?' Finding the nuts, Alex passed a couple to Skoodle.

'No. I ask questions and his voice replies inside my head.'

'Mad people hear voices. Probably mad rodents too. How do you know it's him?'

'It sounds like him; his advice is the kind that Uncle Toomba gave. Why do you ask all this? Don't you get advice from life-challenged relatives?'

'Only in my worst nightmares.'

Alex had a sudden wave of longing. Advice from his parents would be great. To talk to them again would be amazing, even if he couldn't see them. For a moment sadness overwhelmed him. He sat down and gazed out to sea.

'You OK?' asked Skoodle.

'Yeah, just missing my parents.'

'Then there's only one thing to do.'

'What's that?'

'Dance.'

Standing up on to his back legs – small front paws in the air – Skoodle started flinging himself about energetically, singing loudly and tunelessly. 'Join in,' he called.

After watching for a few more minutes Alex got up and started to dance, copying Skoodle's moves. After twenty minutes he collapsed in a heap, laughing, while Skoodle jived on.

'That's awesome. I feel a zillion times better.'

'I have to practise at night,' panted Skoodle. 'It would look a bit odd if a human saw a hamster dancing.'

'Lisa would have run away screaming. Brilliant thought.'

Finally, Skoodle lowered himself down on to all fours again. 'I'm shattered. Why don't you look for food? I'll sleep.' Without waiting for an answer, Skoodle curled up in the shadow of the boat.

'Sleep tight, Skoodle Van Winkle.'

'Always.'

Alex walked the length of the track to the clearing, but no fruit hung within reach. The jungle on either side of the path was dense and forbidding, the forest floor alive with multicoloured insects. Beetles the size and colour of lemons tramped silently through the undergrowth. Lines of giant flying ants marched in winding trails, their wings folded on to their backs as they stamped across the ground or snaked up tree trunks.

Almost on the point of giving up, Alex saw some juicy-looking dark purple fruit hanging a short distance off the path. One of the purple fruits had fallen, bursting as it smashed to earth, releasing intense fragrance like an overripe nectarine. For a moment he stood looking at the fruit longingly, unable to decide whether to try and reach them.

'Uncle Toomba, should I try and get that fruit?'

I'm losing the plot, he told himself. *Asking for advice from a dead rodent.*

Too hungry to resist, even if Uncle Toomba refused to help, he forced his body through the undergrowth towards the food. Thorns scored deeply into his arms as the jungle enclosed him in a painful embrace.

A sudden puff of wind wafted a scent of fruit through the humid air. Acute hunger felt like a drill boring into the pit of his stomach. Resolutely, Alex shoved on another step.

Without warning the ground gave way, pitching him into a mudpit hidden beneath the heavy carpet of leaves, roots and fallen branches. Thick black glue-like mulch enveloped his lower legs. Alex grabbed the solid edge beside the mudbath, wrestling to get his legs free. Struggling drove him deeper into the cold, foul-smelling muck. Gripping like a python, the lake sucked him down into its black depths. Within minutes, both legs were compressed up to the thigh by the deadly embrace of the mulch.

A graphic picture filled Alex's mind of drowning in this filth – slowly, horribly, his mouth filling up with black tarry mud as he suffocated. Breathing fast and ragged, he fought the slime, muscles screaming. Virida's death sentence had seemed horrendous, but now he would be grateful to live long enough to be killed by her.

From the distance came the pad of heavy paws. The horror of being ripped apart while lying trapped immobilised him. The footsteps paused. Totally still, hardly breathing, Alex waited silently, powerless to stop himself sinking. The footfalls set off again, becoming fainter.

As he started to struggle another sound reached him: the unmistakeable slithering of a snake. Desperate, Alex grabbed a thick stick, even though he knew how little use it would be against some of the deadly serpents that lurked in the jungle. The leaves in front of him parted. A snake's head shot out, poised for attack, neck winged, green eyes glittering.

'Ikara.' Relief surged through Alex.

'In trouble, I see,' said Ikara, lowering her head.

'Get Tariq quickly. This stuff is like a vice.'

'Too late by the time he arrived. You'd be gone by then. I'll do it.'

'You're not big enough,' yelled Alex. 'Throw me a vine.'

'It would snap. Don't keep struggling. Things will get worse.

43

You're already in deeper than when you started fighting, aren't you?' Ikara dropped her head and stared at the ground, immobile.

Alex held still. Frustration filled him, made more intense by the flash of hope being ripped away. *Why doesn't she do something?* he wondered. *Anything. Cry, get help from someone else, bite me so I die of poison… anything other than this unbearable frozen inaction.*

As he glared at Ikara he noticed that the tail lying on the jungle floor had begun to slide away. Then he realised that she was not uncoiling but enlarging. Fast. In one minute Ikara had doubled in width and length.

'That's impressive, but scary,' said Alex.

'Would you prefer me puny?'

'No, but I'm not exactly used to snakes yet. Particularly giant ones.'

'Frankly, I'm not entirely comfortable with humans. Even moderate-sized ones.'

Alex leaned forward on to his arms, concentrating on breathing slowly, trying to calm the crashing waves of fear in his head.

Within another minute a massive snake lay before Alex, its body as wide as a football. Two vast discs of green flecked with gold gazed unblinking at him.

'Stay still while I slide around you,' said Ikara, her voice deeper and stronger.

Slithering forward, Ikara coiled her upper body round Alex's torso, the great head swaying past inches from his face. Her skin didn't feel slimy, as he had expected – more like the roughness of chain mail. Her tail encircled the closest tree.

'Brace yourself.' Ikara contracted, snapping tight like whipcord, forcing the air out of Alex's lungs in a whoosh. Her body hauled against the mud.

Pressure built up in Alex's chest as his airless lungs compressed agonisingly. Oxygen starvation gripped his brain, making stars dance in front of his eyes. In a reflex attempt at survival, his hands tore at Ikara's body, but uselessly. He had no breath to shout for release, despite the pain. The sounds of the jungle floated away as Alex started to slide towards death.

With a huge squelch, she wrenched him free. As Alex flew out, the tenacious goo fell away from his lower body like the unclasping of a straitjacket. He still couldn't breathe, but even on the verge of unconsciousness he was ecstatic at being released from the slime.

A second later, total-body agony ripped away the joy of escape as he crashed on to solid ground. Ikara relaxed, releasing his chest. Heavy breaths filled Alex's tortured lungs – air burning his throat, the taste of blood in his mouth. For a moment his body hurt too much for him to care that he was still alive.

'Exciting,' said Ikara.

Despite being numb from shock, his brain registered that her voice seemed normal. Dazed, Alex raised his head. Facing him lay not the vast monster who had rescued him, but the usual four-metre version.

'How did you do that?' he asked, voice hoarse.

'Genetic ability from my mother's side. It's a rare power.'

Slowly Alex rolled on to his back then sat up, wincing. 'How big can you get?'

'About five times that size. Tell me, what were you doing in the depths of the jungle?'

'Food. I was starving.'

Green flecked eyes surveyed the trees beyond. 'Were you aiming for that purple fruit over there?'

'Yes. It smells amazing.'

'Extremely poisonous.'

Even through his pain, the irony got to Alex. 'Fantastic. So having been squeezed to within an inch of suffocation and catapulted on to rock-hard ground, I'm now supposed to be grateful that I fell into a deadly man-eating mud pit?'

'As it happens, yes.' Ikara coiled as she spoke.

Wearily, Alex picked himself up from the ground. From his hips down, both legs were covered in what appeared to be tar. His muscles ached as if he had run a marathon. Pain shot through his lungs each time he took a deep breath. 'By the way, thanks. Body-crushing is a real winner compared to a one hundred per cent, full-on death experience.'

'No problem,' replied Ikara. 'There will probably be worse on the way to the sapphire. I'd give you a lecture on the dangers of the jungle, but I'm too shattered.'

'I can empathise with shattered. Also ripped, broken, bruised, mauled and terminally spooked. I'll never trust mud again.'

'We'd better go back to Tariq's clearing. I'll meet you there with some food.' In a murmur she added, 'Novice.'

Shoving his aching body through dense undergrowth, Alex eventually made it to the path. Legs weighed down by thickly-caked jeans, he plodded to the river.

Not bothering to undress, Alex walked straight into the shallows, swinging round to lie with his head on the bank. Cold water swirled past him, healing, strengthening. He pulled up his shirt to see the snake damage. An angry red band encircled his chest, swollen and grazed. *A small price to pay for life*, he thought.

He was lying on the bank drying in the sun when Ikara reappeared, a bunch of red bristly fruits suspended from her mouth by the stalk. 'Orton. Try one. It's a pain getting rid of the husk, but the fruit inside is worth the aggro.'

Starving, Alex ripped several open. Munching contentedly, savouring the exquisite taste, he chose two of the biggest and shoved them in a pocket for Skoodle. As he demolished the rest of the pile, Ikara slid away, reappearing a few minutes later with her tail wrapped round a large green fruit.

'More food. Great.'

'Wrong. It's a giffrod. To drink. The juice is fantastic.'

Using a jagged flint, Alex cut into the emerald shell to find a sea of pale green fluid. He handed it over to Ikara. 'Want some?'

'Thanks.'

Alex watched as mouthfuls of fluid passed down the snake's neck like a row of ping-pong balls. Once Ikara had finished Alex reached forward to drink. A sudden thought struck him. He halted with the giffrod almost to his lips. 'You're not a venomous snake, are you?'

'Not my style to rescue you from the mud and then poison you.'

Alex lifted the giffrod back up, and then paused. 'By the way, I'm not venomous either.'

'I've realised that, although you were poisonous after Virida blew through.'

'History, and it was both of us.' Alex finished the juice in one hit.

'Agreed. You'd better get back to the beach before it gets dark. I'll leave some fruit by your boat later.'

On arriving at the beach, Alex found Skoodle shredding the lifeboat instruction manual to make a nest. Over a shared tin of cold macaroni he told Skoodle about nearly dying in the mud swamp. After Skoodle had finished laughing, they settled down to watch the deep orange and red tropical sunset.

Eventually Alex turned his attention to the emergency box, pulling the large hunting knife and a waterproof torch from its interior and putting both in the rucksack with the netbook. 'That's it; packing done. Better turn in. No sun equals no light, as I don't want to use up the torch batteries.'

Skoodle finished the last orton and wiped the juice off his face on to Alex's jeans. 'You could have packed a few extra. You're a failure at this survival stuff, aren't you?'

'Oddly enough, I didn't expect to be cast adrift. You?'

'Nope. Not a usual hamster experience, so Uncle Toomba tells me.'

Alex picked up Skoodle and climbed over the edge of the boat. 'At least I got us to shore.'

'Yeah, right. Like it was you, not the tide. Anyway… good going, Weston. Positive score: three new friends. Negative: five death sentences. Looks like the opposition wins.'

'Not yet, they don't. It takes more than a talking smoke column to muscle me out of the picture.'

'Even if it's really an angry witch bristling with evil spells?'

'I'm still fighting,' replied Alex, settling himself on the hard floor. 'Step one: find sapphire. Step two: break curse. Step three: have hamster's jaws wired together.'

That wouldn't work. Remember thought transference?

'Blast all weird perceptions. Why did my parents come to this bizarre place? What was wrong with Brighton?'

'Limited opportunities for explorers. Sleep tight, death-curse brother.'

CHAPTER 8

When Alex woke the next day, every particle of his body ached after yesterday's mud wrestle. He tried to roll over and snooze a bit more but the boards at the bottom of the boat were too hard to let him recapture his dream. Irritatingly, Skoodle lay snoring beside him. Eventually Alex gave up trying to sleep. He crawled forward, pushed up the edge of the tarpaulin and clambered out.

Dawn was breaking, the likes of which he had never seen. The sky hung in a citrus palette, sweeping from palest lemon to the scarlet heart of a rose grapefruit. Gradually soft blue crept in, deepening until the sky became rich turquoise.

Alex mulled over life as he watched the colours change, sipping from a giffrod. So this was the world his parents had been exploring: one of magic, danger and intrigue. They might have been proud of him for finding his way to the island. He doubted that they would have been quite so pleased about him landing a death sentence within twenty-four hours of arrival. Thinking of his parents gave him a familiar ache in his chest – unpleasant, but oddly welcome.

Deciding to try for another nap, Alex pulled the tarpaulin over his head and fell asleep. A gentle knocking woke him later. 'Come in,' he mumbled.

'Come out,' said Ikara.

Alex pulled back the corner of the tarpaulin and found himself inches away from Ikara's nose. In her mouth she held a large bunch of fentice.

'You look half asleep,' she said, dropping the fruit. 'It's been daybreak for hours. Either you're very lazy or you were badly hurt yesterday.'

'Bit of both,' replied Alex, rubbing his eyes. 'Even so, not many humans would naturally get up with the sun.'

'Odd,' said Ikara, helping herself to a fentice. 'Must add that to my list of facts about humans. Number one: smart alecs, or Alexs, shouldn't be let loose alone in the jungle, especially when hungry. Fact two: humans believe that if some fruit is edible, all must be. Fact three: humans are not logical. Seems there's a link there.'

'Cut the lecture. Hand over a fentice,' replied Alex, draped over the wooden side.

'Make it two,' said a small voice as Skoodle scrambled over the side of the boat and dropped on to the sand.

'Done, rodent.' Ikara flicked a fentice at Skoodle. It hurtled straight into his stomach, bowling him on to his back. Skoodle scrambled to his feet and threw it back at her. Ikara took the hit on her head, dramatically flinging herself backwards on to the sand where she lay groaning.

'Hardly seems possible,' said Skoodle. 'Fewer legs but acres more sarcasm.'

'You two could form a mutual dislike society. After a while you might get to like each other.'

'Yeah, like a vampire loves a neck,' muttered Skoodle.

'No, more than that,' replied Ikara, shuddering the sand off. 'Like my stomach acid adores fresh protein.'

'Don't wind me up. I may be small but I'm fierce.'

'Terrified,' squealed Ikara. 'Keep him away, Alex. Don't let him hurt me.'

'Peace and harmony,' said Alex. 'Or I'll thump you both. So… anyone for fentice?'

An hour later they joined the others in Tariq's clearing. Keeko was hopping from one leg to the other as if standing in a bed of nettles.

'Go get yourself mango,' Alex told Keeko. 'It'll take your mind off things.'

'It won't,' said Keeko. She set off for the nearest tree, pulled off a huge mango and dropped back to the ground, chewing on it unpeeled.

'We need to walk upstream for a few hundred metres,' said Tariq, gazing over the river. 'The waters are narrower there.'

Ikara shook her head. 'Danger freak. There are crocodiles in the upper parts of this river. Crossing here makes more sense, unless we'd rather be eaten by carnivorous flesh-eating reptiles than nuked by the witch.'

'Here suddenly seems ideal,' replied Skoodle.

'All agreed?' asked Tariq. 'OK. Decision made. But beware the waterfall downstream. It drops a hundred metres on to rocks. Get swept over, you die. Clear?'

'Unpleasantly so,' muttered Skoodle.

Estimating the distance, Alex asked, 'How do we get out? The far bank's a solid wall of plants.'

'There are a few tunnels, made by large animals, through those mangrove roots,' said Tariq. He pointed to a black area in the barrier of vegetation, slightly upstream. 'Beyond that one lies the path to the Single Redwood.'

Ikara smoothly slid into the water, her body held up by surface tension, and whipped rapidly towards the opposite bank.

'You next, Alex, with Skoodle,' said Tariq. 'If you're doing OK I'll bring Keeko.'

'What a morning. Waterfall, crocodiles, imminent death,' said Skoodle. 'Wonder what he's got planned for this afternoon.'

'Rhino wrestling?' asked Alex.

Skoodle scrambled on to his scalp. The pain of his needle-like claws was cushioned only slightly by Alex's blond hair being longer than school allowed. Walking forward into the cold river, Alex sank up to his waist within six steps. Two more and the bottom of the river fell sharply away, plunging him in chest deep. Alex struck out in crawl, aiming upstream to compensate for the current.

Head up, transferred Skoodle. *Every time you roll to breathe I get dunked.*

Not refreshing?

More like repetitive drowning.

Are many people's lives ruled by a rodent? Alex wondered as he lifted his head and swam water-polo crawl, in time to hear a splash behind them as Tariq powered into the river.

Doubt it, but they should be. More chance of world peace. Better food.

This is tough.

So is holding on.

At least you're not in wet jeans and waterlogged shoes, swimming across a strong current.

Pretend you're on a surfboard.

Surfing doesn't include a waterfall and you in my head space.

Me being in there stops it being empty.

Up ahead Ikara lay coiled round a branch, surveying the scene below. 'Come on, sloths. I've been here for ages. Very dull, waiting.'

Tell someone else. We're as interested as that log over there, transferred Skoodle.

'It's a crocodile,' Ikara screamed.

Whipping his head around, Alex saw the log upstream open its mouth to snap up a water rat. The reptile's fearsome head swung around, its malicious eyes on Alex.

'Head down, Alex. Swim for it,' yelled Skoodle.

Totally focused on forcing his body forward, Alex carved his way through the water.

He's gaining. Faster.

This is fastest.

'Want a snack, snub face? Over here,' called Ikara. 'Or are you frightened of a little snakey-wakey?'

Mid-stroke, Alex lifted his head to see Ikara hanging suspended by her tail at the water's edge. The monster hesitated, glancing from Alex to Ikara. The snake was closer but smaller. The two reptiles locked eyes. Ikara held her ground, swaying, a millisecond from death. The crocodile surged forward. Ikara swerved, but remained in range. The enraged croc lunged again as the snake's head swung out of reach.

Two more strokes, transferred Skoodle. *Come on, Alex.*

An instant later Alex's fingers touched roots, each the thickness of a footballer's thigh.

51

'Climb. Get us out,' shrieked Skoodle.

'Can't. No grip. Too slippery.'

The roots stretched along in a dense row, too solid to penetrate. The only hole through that Alex could see lay upstream, beyond the croc. Heart pounding, Alex grabbed his knife, scraping it against the nearest mangrove.

'Kill the croc, not the root.'

'Getting the slime off.'

'Won't work. Get the croc.'

'Against him my knife would be as much use as a toothbrush.'

'Come on, old lumpy skin,' Ikara yelled, dipping closer. 'Give it your best shot.'

As the croc threw himself at Ikara, missing by millimetres, a bear and monkey arrived at the bank in an explosion of water.

'Jump, Keeko,' shouted Tariq.

Keeko threw herself off, landing high on the nearest mangrove root. All four limbs clamped round its green slipperiness. Her tail looped round the dry branch above, swinging her out of danger.

Tariq changed course, thrashing through the water, heading directly for the crocodile. His furry fist swung out of the water and punched the croc. As the stunned reptile recoiled, Tariq leapt on to the animal's back, arms clamped round the ripping jaws. Infuriated, the croc submerged itself. The terrified watchers could see dark shadows wrestling in the murky depths. Bloodied water swirled above the fighters.

Keeko shinned down the mangrove and grabbed a large rock from the shallows.

'Don't throw,' called Alex, treading water, still scraping at the root. 'You might hit Tariq.'

'But he'll drown. He'll run out of oxygen first,' shouted Keeko.

The animals resurfaced, Tariq's powerful arms flung around the croc's scaly head in a hideous embrace. Keeko hurled the rock, slamming it accurately on to the reptile's skull.

The crocodile lashed his tail into the bear's side. Roaring his rage and pain, Tariq raked his claws down the reptile's underbelly. Scarlet ribbons spurted from the open flesh, staining the water crimson as they were swept downstream.

Look out, Tariq. The waterfall, transferred Keeko.

Tariq must have heard but didn't look up, his body remaining locked against the crocodile's.

Let go, Tariq, screamed Alex inside his mind. *Swim for it.*

Can't. He'll get back upstream quicker than me.

A moment later the two figures were swept from view. It was over.

'Tariq,' screamed Ikara, her voice ragged with pain.

Horrified, Alex stared at the head of the falls. He couldn't believe that seconds ago his friend had been fighting for all their lives. Now he was gone. Immobile, Alex hung on to the slippery roots, his body drifting in the water.

Splashing nearby made Alex drag his eyes away. Two more crocodiles were swimming towards them with lashing sweeps of their scaly green-grey bodies. Ikara slithered towards Alex like greeny-gold lightening. Powered by adrenaline blasting through his system, Alex shoved his knife in his belt and began grappling with the slippery mangrove roots.

Ikara's tail reached down. A clamp of snake wound round Alex's chest, squeezing the air out of him as he scraped painfully up the side of a mangrove. Sore, unable to breathe, Alex grabbed for the higher, dry roots. His grip held. The pressure round his chest was released.

The closest croc jumped at Alex, using his tail to propel himself out of the water. Alex jerked his feet up just before they were crunched off. Keeko sat within easy reach, face in hands, sobbing.

'Get away, Keeko,' yelled Alex. 'More crocodiles.'

Her head swung towards him, tear-filled eyes blank.

'Tariq died saving us,' screeched Skoodle. 'Don't waste his sacrifice.'

Her trance of pain shattered, Keeko scrambled upwards. 'You won't get me,' she yelled at the crocodiles. 'I'd murder you if I could.'

The reptiles circled below Keeko, malicious eyes fixed on her body. Then they headed upstream.

'They're aiming for the tunnel through the roots,' called Ikara. 'Get to that path before they do.'

Alex clambered through the mangroves until he reached a branch that hung over the track. Taking a deep breath he launched himself into space, hitting the ground running. From behind him came the sound of lumbering crocodile feet. Alex pounded down the path, but his wet jeans and shoes weighed him down. Tangled roots threatened to trip him at any moment: thick vegetation overhung the path, tearing at him. Slow meant dead. Injured meant dead.

Not rocket science, transferred Skoodle, reading his thoughts.

Nope, it's logic. Inescapable.

Like the crocodiles?

Wrenching branches out of his face, Alex ran after the retreating body of Ikara. The crocodiles moved steadily, getting closer.

They're supposed to be slow on land, transferred Alex to Ikara.

Not on Eridor, she returned. *They don't tire easily, either. Keep running.*

Exhausted, losing ground, Alex ran on. Wet jeans chafed his legs; his trainers felt like concrete.

Tired? asked Skoodle.

Shattered.

How long can you keep going?

Easy answer: *Not long.* His lungs ached as if hot steel wires had been rammed through his rib cage; his heart was banging, muscles leaden. *Ask me in five.*

Minutes?

Seconds.

He forced himself through the lower branches of another prickly bush then stopped, horrified. An enormous lake of mud stretched in front of him, the path round it only a very low tunnel through dense vegetation. There was no other escape route. As he hesitated, the crocodiles closed in further.

Alex grabbed the branch of an overhanging tree and hoisted himself upwards, trying not to look down at the mudbath. The gaping black expanse would suck him in like quicksand if he fell. Once had been enough.

He gripped the branches, ignoring the stings of red fire ants crawling along the bark. Scrambling from tree to tree, he aimed for the other side of the lake. The branches acted like crazy wooden scaffolding, gradually taking him higher. Finally reaching the far side, Alex stood on a twisted eucalyptus branch. The jump to the last mahogany tree looked impossible. Six metres below, the edge of the mudbath met solid ground. If he missed, pitiless jaws would shred his broken body as he tried to crawl away.

Alex hesitated. Momentum had kept him running, then climbing. Now he faced a suicidal-looking jump.

Retreat, transferred Skoodle.

Can't. Crocodiles will follow.

Stay.

Can't. No food. No water. Tariq dead. Another two about to follow.

'We aren't ready to die yet,' yelled Skoodle. 'You'd better make that jump.' He sank his teeth into Alex's chest. 'If you think that hurts, times it by a hundred for crocodile teeth. Go for it.'

Decision made, Alex launched himself into space. Sheared off by the force of his push-off, the bough crashed to earth. His grasping hands found hard wood, clutching the branch. Alex's shoulders took his full weight as his body jerked out of free fall. It felt as if his arms had been wrenched out of their sockets.

Looking down made his head dizzy, his hands sweaty. The ground seemed miles down. The closest foothold lay a couple of metres away. To get to it he would have to let go with one hand. Cold sweat poured from his body, making his hands slippery.

'Move. This branch could crack too,' yelled Skoodle.

Licking his dry lips, Alex let go with his right hand to grab the branch closer to the trunk. Calling on his reserves of strength he crept, hand over hand, to the trunk.

'Doing fine,' said Skoodle. 'Uncle Gus would have been proud.'

One more shuffle of his hand, then a soaking trainer found a solid perch. Transferring his footing to a wide branch, Alex grabbed the trunk.

'By Vertog, flying is foul,' said Skoodle.

'Flying's OK, but landing may kill you.'

Alex climbed down to a branch above the path then dropped to the ground, touching down hard, joints robbed of all spring by fatigue.

Pushing onwards, legs working on automatic pilot, Alex raced down the trail, breath rasping in his throat. Relentlessly, the murderous feet thundered closer. *This'll soon be over. They're quicker.*

Too much honesty.

As the crocs bring me down, I'll throw you into the jungle.

Great. So I'll die alone.

Stay with?

No chance. Alone's good.

Ikara's voice tore through his thoughts. *Keep running. I see an escape route.*

CHAPTER 9

Alex rocketed round a hibiscus bush, wrenching its dense, flower-laden branches aside. Ahead stood a massive redwood tree, its base as wide as a house. Carved into its dark bark face stood an arched entrance. Beyond the open door Ikara's tail was disappearing up the first few treads of a staircase. Keeko dropped from a mahogany tree and ran for the entrance, Alex sprinting in behind her.

Flickering candles suspended high on the dark wooden walls lit the cool, cathedral-like interior, from which low, wide stairs spiralled up out of sight. Keeko and Ikara had already vanished round the first curl upwards.

Alex wrenched at the front door, but it wouldn't budge.

'Leave it,' yelled Skoodle. 'Run. Crocodiles can't climb stairs.'

I hope you're right, returned Alex, too breathless to speak. He belted towards the ancient treads, footfalls echoing across the hall. From behind came the sinister scraping of sharp claws on the stone floor of the entrance.

As Alex climbed, the clatter came closer. Disbelief paralysed his mind, yet there could be no doubt. The crocodiles were starting up the stairs behind him.

Although it felt as if his legs were about to drop off, terror forced him to keep running. If he found no hiding place, he was trapped. The image of saw-edged white teeth in gaping jaws hung vividly in his mind. The stench of rotting flesh mingled with stinking river mud floated up to him.

Drenched in sweat, Alex ran round the central column of the spiral staircase. From ahead came the faint rhythmical scratch of claws as Keeko swung from lamp to lamp. Pointlessly, painfully, his legs pumped up and down like a machine, slower with every step, muscle power blown away by lack of oxygen.

'Alex, door ahead,' yelled Ikara from above him. 'Keep going, Keeko. You're safe on the brackets.'

Around another turn he found Ikara coiling her powerful body around the brass handle, twisting. Alex lunged at the door, battering it open. As he catapulted into the room, a coil of dizzy snake landed at his feet. Recovering his balance, Alex twisted back to slam the door. He heard a loud thud as flesh hit wood.

Alex shot the heavy brass bolt home then stood panting, eyes fixed on the door. Heavy blows hammered on to the wood as the huge reptiles blasted at the barrier. The door shuddered as the metal hinges strained to resist the assault. Alex backed away, expecting that at any second he would be nose-to-snout with one of the river monsters.

'*Somnato,*' cried a commanding voice.

The blows stopped instantly. Astonished, Alex turned round to face the room. A tall figure rose from the high-backed armchair which had shielded him from sight. The man appeared to be about thirty, curly black hair tumbling down to his waist. A wide streak of white hair scorched backwards from his forehead. The face was strong, with high cheekbones. Silver writing writhed over his loose black shirt, letters forming lazily as they snaked their way across his chest. Swiftly Alex blocked his thoughts, unwilling to let a stranger into his head

'Sleep spell. There's no danger now,' the man said.

'Zorrin?' asked Ikara.

'Of course he is,' said Skoodle. 'He exactly matches the description Tariq gave us.'

'Welcome. Rest yourselves,' said the wizard.

Alex collapsed into a nearby chair, legs in spasm, muscles screaming. He closed his eyes for a moment, sweat trickling down his face as relief washed over him. Every deep, painful breath reminded him that he was alive. Desperation fell away like a heavy cloak, loosening the tight band round his chest.

After a few minutes he opened his eyes and surveyed his refuge.

High-ceilinged, it was lit by groups of slender candles each the height of a man. Heavy crimson rugs covered the flagstone floor. On one wall hung an immense tapestry depicting a snarling panther battling strange winged creatures, while goblins and trolls lay dying nearby. A fire of silver and blue flames crackled in the great stone fireplace.

'Seems like heaven,' said Alex, stretching his stiff legs out in front of him.

'Haven, anyway,' replied Skoodle. 'Well decorated for a prison. How do we get back out? Jump over the playful old crocs?'

'The crocodiles will remain unconscious. Forget them,' said the wizard. 'Tell me, why have you journeyed here?'

'To bring you a message from my parents, Mark and Virginia Weston. They've disappeared. They said it was really important that you knew,' said Alex, relieved to have this off his chest.

'Also, we're seeking the Sapphire of Akan,' said Ikara. 'Can you help us?'

'Doubtless. But before we talk, eat and drink. As you see, food is ready for you.'

Fragrant warm bread, bowls of steaming rice, hot chicken, a hand of bananas and an enormous bowl of golden-yellow ice cream appeared on a table near the fire. A huge pitcher of red juice sprang up in the middle.

'Great,' said Alex, struggling to his feet, but before he could get to the table there was a loud banging on the door.

'Let me in,' yelled Keeko.

Alex ran to the door, opening it a crack, allowing Keeko to swing in. He slammed it and rammed the bolt home.

Trembling, Keeko pointed at the man. 'He's an impostor. He's not Zorrin.'

'What would you know, ignorant ape?'

Lifting his arm, the wizard pointed straight at Keeko. A bolt of purple light shot from the tip of his finger, hitting Keeko in the chest, slamming her backwards. She screamed as she hit the wall.

Alex flung himself on his knees beside her, not daring to touch her body in case any bones were broken. 'You OK?'

'No. I hurt.'

Alex glared at the wizard. 'Why did you do that?'

The wizard raised an eyebrow. 'The monkey is delirious. Perhaps it's the air in the corridor, or maybe she has eaten something unwise. She needed to be tranquillised so that I can help her.'

'Believe me,' whispered Keeko through her pain. 'It's not Zorrin.'

The man raised his arm again. 'I'll just—'

'No,' exploded Ikara, as Alex swung his body between Keeko and the wizard. 'Keeko doesn't lie. You're a fake.' Ikara coiled to strike, the hood on the sides of her head flaring out as she swelled and lengthened. As she lunged forward to attack, the killing finger swung towards her.

Alex grabbed a pewter vase from the table next to him and flung it at the wizard's hand. Metal met bone with a sharp crack. The wizard's deadly bolt of light missed Ikara, exploding in a shower of red sparks on the wall beyond, carving a jagged black fissure deep into the wood.

Ikara struck, whipping round the wizard's body – tightening, wrestling, trying to drag him to the floor. He grabbed her round the throat and started to squeeze. *She'll only have seconds to live*, thought Alex. Grabbing a heavy brass candlestick he lunged forward, brandishing it above his head. The deadly finger swung to aim at his heart. Instinctively, Alex swung the candlestick across his chest.

The narrow beam blasted the weapon out of Alex's hands, slamming him backwards. His head hit the stone floor. Sick, unsteady, he tried to stand, but could not make it up past kneeling. Clinging to the back of a heavy chair he hauled his body up, legs sagging – forcing himself to move despite the pain in his pounding head, desperate to get to Ikara.

The wizard screamed. Alex looked up to see the furry body of Skoodle, front teeth buried deep in the wizard's wrist, blood oozing from his mouth. In agony the wizard let go of Ikara's neck, raising his fist to pulverise the hamster.

Alex tried to launch himself forwards but his legs failed. He crumpled to the floor, yelling, 'Jump.'

With terrified eyes fixed on the approaching fist, Skoodle dug his teeth in deeper, body stiff, braced for the blow.

Her body still wound around the wizard, Ikara swung her head above Skoodle. The fist hammered on to her skull. Eyes rolling, she sagged as her body loosened.

'Let go, Skoodle,' Alex yelled as the wizard's hand rose again.

Skoodle dropped to the floor, then bolted under a chair. The wizard's furious eyes focused on him for a second then swept unpityingly past Keeko, who was clutching a chair leg, trying to scramble upright.

Alex's fingers found the candlestick. He grabbed it, clawing his way up the wall to a standing position. He lurched towards the man like a seasick fencer with the candlestick as a foil.

'Die, snake.' The wizard aimed his deadly digit straight at Ikara's head.

With an unsteady swipe, Alex crashed the wizard's arm away. The killer shaft of purple light missed Ikara's head by a centimetre, blasting a smoking hole in the ceiling.

The wizard kicked Alex hard in the stomach, doubling him up. A red beam shot out of the tip of the wizard's finger, transforming a coffee table into a snarling Rottweiler. The huge beast leapt at Keeko, who flung herself on to a wall bracket. The dog stood below her, snarling.

Swiftly, the finger moved on. Another shaft of light hit a walking stick, transforming it into an enormous serpent twice as large as Ikara. It towered upright over Alex who froze, powerless to do anything.

Before the wizard could morph anything else, Ikara sank her teeth into his forefinger. Sparks flew from the tip beyond her mouth, sending balls of red and blue light flying round the room like small meteors.

The wizard grabbed Ikara's neck. 'Here is the deal, boy. You have information I want. Give it to me and command your snake to let go. In return I'll keep my serpent at bay.'

'But if Ikara lets go you'll kill us anyway.'

'Of course, but I'll make it quick and fairly painless. It will be better than watching the monkey and the snake get torn apart as you die screaming in agony from the venom of my serpent.'

Alex could feel the hard blade of his hunting knife against his belly, frustratingly useless. In the time that it would take to reach it, the serpent would attack him. Anger surged through him. *Death either way, but I'd rather die fighting than give in.* Balancing himself mentally, he prepared to grab the knife for one final desperate effort.

The last fighter bolted from under a chair. Skoodle halted directly under the nose of the serpent. The vast lidless orange eyes swung to fix on the tiny animal. The terrifying jaws started to open as the serpent arched for the strike. Yet he hesitated. His master had not yet given the command to kill.

It was the two seconds that Alex needed. He wrenched out his knife. The serpent's glittering eyes flicked back to him.

'Kill,' screamed the wizard.

The serpent's huge head plummeted down, venom-filled fangs aiming straight at Alex's heart. With a scything uppercut, Alex struck at the snake. The knife's arc slashed through the serpent's throat with a rasp, releasing a jet of bright green blood.

The amputated body of the serpent fell to the floor like a cut-off rope, as the monster's venom-filled head rocketed towards Alex's heart. Alex flung himself out of the path of the severed head, crashing to the floor. The knife spun out of his hand, slippery with snake blood.

With a heavy thud, the huge scaly head landed inches away in a sticky emerald pool, vast dead eyes open. A moment later, the snake had transformed back to a walking stick, top broken off, lying in a patch of sawdust.

'The dog,' squealed Skoodle.

Alex's head jerked up. The dog was crouching only feet away, ready to spring, teeth bared. Glancing over at his knife, Alex realised it was too far away. He'd never get to it before the beast sprang.

Keeko launched herself on to the Rottweiler, landing legs astride his back, grabbing his ears. The dog snapped at her legs, teeth ripping through the flesh of her foot. She squealed but hung on like a rodeo rider, clamping her legs round the dog even harder, claws digging into his ears.

Alex snatched the hunting knife. Lunging forward, he rammed the blade deep into the dog's chest. The animal sagged to the floor, howling. As his life evaporated, the Rottweiler transformed back into wood.

'What happened?' cried Keeko, legs now astride a table.

'Two dead. Progress,' Alex said, wrenching hard at the deeply embedded knife. It didn't budge.

Keeko sprang at the wizard, landing flat across his face. Digging her claws into his scalp, she fixed herself to him like a living balaclava. Fur blocked the wizard's nose and mouth, suffocating him. The wizard pulled his hand away from Ikara's throat to try and claw Keeko off his face: the more he fought the tighter she clung. Ikara coiled her body around the wizard's chest and began to squeeze, forcing air out.

Giving up on the knife, Alex grabbed a book to pummel the wizard – then realised how pointless it would be. The two animal faces in front of him were determined, victory in their eyes.

'Squeeze him, squeeze him, ape and snake. Take his air, that evil fake,' sang Skoodle.

The man's writhing became more frantic as the agony in his air-starved lungs built up. He swayed, knees sagging, then slid to the floor. As he went limp Keeko jumped off, landing heavily on the dog-table next to Alex.

'That was close,' said Ikara, hoarse from the wizard's stranglehold. 'Keeko, how did you know?'

Breathing hard, Keeko peered down at her bleeding leg. 'I found the true Zorrin. He's trapped upstairs.'

'How are you so sure that the other one is the real wizard?' asked Ikara, loosening her hold around the wizard's chest. 'We were convinced by this one at first.'

Keeko stopped licking the blood off her dark fur. 'Zorrin bears the mark of an eagle on his right forearm.'

'Like a tattoo?' asked Alex, lying flat on his back, arms outstretched, waiting for his heart to stop banging.

'A bit, but much more complex. It's made of streaks of gold and silver, which shine with the brightness of sunlight. Really pretty. It's ancient elemental magic which no one else could copy. Only Zorrin's got one.'

'We'd better go and release him,' said Alex, attempting to rise. A bolt of pain shot through his left shoulder. Wincing, he stood up. 'How did he get captured?'

'How should I know?' Keeko leapt on to Alex's uninjured shoulder, landing on her good leg. 'I didn't stop to ask. I shot straight back down to rescue you.'

'Thank the stars you did. Ikara, can you stay on guard while we go for Zorrin?'

'No problem. My head still aches from his fist. If he starts to come round I'll give him another blast of agony.'

Alex grinned at her. She'd burned pity for breakfast, ripped up compassion. He got the point, though. Sympathy wasn't on the list of combat necessities. Impatiently he shoved his fringe out of the way, finding his blond hair thick with clots. He wiped the blood from his hand on to his jeans then headed for the door, pausing to scoop up a shaking Skoodle.

'You're amazing,' said Alex. 'That was so brave.'

The little hamster squared his shoulders, chin rising upwards. 'Correct. Leonine courage. If I had nine lives like cats, I'd be one down from heart failure.'

'We didn't fail. Still got nine. Maybe.'

Trying to avoid getting more blood on Skoodle, Alex placed him in his pocket. 'Were the crocodiles still asleep when you came in?' he asked Keeko.

'Flat out. Still, be careful.'

'Or the terrible jaws will snap,' said Skoodle. 'Flesh will rip: yours, a scream of agony… yours again, then death by being torn limb from limb in a bloodbath.'

'And where will you be during the body-rippage?'

'With Keeko, on a wall light. But upset, of course.'

'It's great to know that you'll be safe.'

'I'll shout advice.'

'Helpful.'

Alex opened the door a crack as Skoodle put his paws over his eyes. Outside on the steps lay an unconscious crocodile, head lolling. The body of a second curled round the central pillar, tail out of sight. The rhythm of drawing in clear air and pumping out foul breath remained unbroken.

Hesitating only long enough to be sure that they weren't moving, Alex slid past the snout of the closest crocodile, pulling the door closed behind him. He ran upstairs, Keeko swinging between wall brackets ahead of him. Four spirals round the central marble pillar gave them sight of another dark wooden door, slightly ajar.

'In there,' murmured Keeko.

She landed on Alex's shoulder. Wincing, Alex pushed the door fully open and walked in.

CHAPTER 10

The dark, damp room was like a dungeon. The sombre walls were bare: neither pictures nor tapestries relieved the gloomy expanse. No rugs covered the hard floor. The stone fireplace was empty of both heat and light. A black panther lay crumpled on the far side, unconscious.

On a low stool sat a man almost identical to the wizard downstairs, both in face and clothes. Yet this one was paler, with dark shadows under his eyes.

He smiled wearily as they entered. 'Welcome, Alex and Skoodle. Keeko said you would come. You must have defeated Karlan to make it here.'

'Are you really Zorrin?' asked Skoodle.

The tired lines round his eyes deepened in amusement. 'I am.' He indicated a large rip on his sleeve. 'Your friend tore a hole in my shirt with her teeth to check if my brand was real. Luckily she missed my skin, despite her haste.'

The wizard pulled aside the torn folds. Emblazoned across his forearm was a golden eagle, the light radiating from it powerful enough to illuminate the room.

'Told you,' said Keeko, triumphantly.

'But if you're Zorrin, and such a powerful wizard, how did you get caught?' asked Skoodle. 'Not impressive, really.'

Zorrin frowned. 'I was tricked into believing that my sister was in mortal danger. Karlan, an evil master was here, waiting for me. He couldn't kill me, but was able to trap me.'

'Are the other evil wizards still here?' Skoodle asked, sliding back into Alex's pocket.

'No. They left Karlan to guard me.' Zorrin grinned. 'I don't think Karlan expected to be defeated, especially by so tiny a gang.'

'Small but fierce,' said Skoodle.

Alex sat on the cold, hard floor. 'That was Karlan? When he attacked me on the boat he looked totally different, not identical to you.'

'Transmorphing is child's play to him. It stopped you being suspicious, didn't it?'

'Yes,' said Alex, feeling slightly better that he hadn't been so very stupid. 'It was almost fatal for us.'

'It's very weird here,' said Skoodle. 'At home people always look pretty much the same week after week.'

The stool creaked slightly as Zorrin shifted. 'I can explain more about Karlan later, but perhaps for now you would be kind enough to release me and Myth.' He pointed at the sleeping panther.

'Of course. How?' Alex asked.

'There's a brown leather pouch in Karlan's right-hand trouser pocket containing powder which can break the hex that binds us.'

Alex closed his eyes, head drooping. Back past the crocodiles. When would this nightmare end?

'OK, Wiz,' said Skoodle. 'Crocodile hopping is our speciality. Consider us gone.' He gazed at Alex. 'My ride looks a bit tired, though. Perhaps a small bite would pump up the adrenaline.' He bared his teeth.

'Bite me and die,' said Alex, pulling his hand out of reach. 'Or maybe I'll pull your ears off and feed them to the crocs.'

'Finally, fighting talk. Crocodile row, here we come. Although, thinking about it, I'll wait up here. No need for us both to go.' Skoodle started to climb out of Alex's pocket.

'I'm not doing this alone,' said Alex, pushing him back in. 'Anyway, another couple of meetings and you may get to like the scaly ones.'

'Not fantastically likely, but I'll consider it on the way down to my next near-death experience.'

'I'll stay here. Guard Zorrin,' said Keeko, loping closer to Zorrin's stool and sitting cross-legged on the floor.

'Fine by us.' Alex set off with his hand loosely over his pocket, trapping Skoodle.

'That translates into shotgun the cushy job,' muttered Skoodle under his breath as they reached the first step.

'It's uncool to be harsh.'

'Not for a rodent.'

Footsteps echoing against the stone walls in an eerie drumbeat Alex retraced his steps downstairs, hoping that the crocodiles would still be asleep.

'From saviour to errand boy,' said Skoodle, resting his chin on Alex's pocket edge. 'Next Zorrin'll want tea: one sugar; white; two biscuits.'

'Don't even go there,' replied Alex. 'He might have had a tougher time than us.' For a second he reflected. So far today they'd endured the death of Tariq, nearly been eaten alive and almost died fighting a powerful wizard. He added, 'Probably.'

The room downstairs was as they had left it. Ikara remained loosely coiled around the unconscious wizard's chest. As Alex rummaged in Karlan's clothes, Skoodle explained what had happened upstairs – giving a graphic description of how heroic he had been in spurring Alex into action, risking death or body-maiming.

Alex snorted. 'Zip the lip or I'll throw you to Ikara for lunch.'

'Wouldn't eat him now that I've got used to him. I'm a carnivore, not a friendivore.'

As Alex grabbed the powder bag Karlan stirred, his eyelids fluttering half open. Ikara tightened her body. With a grunt, as air was forced out of him, the man lapsed back into unconsciousness.

'Practical demonstration of how to tame a wizard. Hurry up,' said Ikara. 'Being down here with him is seriously unpleasant.'

'So is killing snakes, playing dodge with crocodiles and belting around rescuing people,' said Skoodle.

Ikara sighed. 'Accepted. Just go.'

They arrived upstairs to find Zorrin squealing and grunting at Keeko, the only recognisable sound being 'Gelforth'. Alex raised his eyebrows questioningly at Keeko. Zorrin didn't look mad, but you could never really be sure. Not with wizards.

'Simian tongue,' Zorrin said. Then, as Alex looked blank, he added, 'Monkey language.'

'Fairly sane explanation. I had assumed you were one toad's gizzard short of a potion,' said Skoodle. 'How many languages do you speak?'

'About thirty.'

'How about Hamster?'

'Unfortunately not, but willing to learn. Got the powder?'

Alex held the pouch up.

'Fantastic. The pattern you need to trace with it is extremely precise. If the lines are not perfect the spell won't break.'

Following instructions, Alex began to sprinkle dust on the floor, starting at the door. As it touched down, the powder changed from sparkling red to bright yellow.

'Get it right,' sighed Skoodle as Alex redid a crescent for the third time. 'Lucky there's bags of it. Or bag of it, I mean.'

Alex scraped some bright yellow powder into a line. 'I don't see you doing any of the crawling around.'

'Not hero material, me. You do the rescuing. I'll advise, map read, eat, organise – that sort of thing.'

'The easy bits?'

'No, the intellectual stuff,' replied Skoodle. 'I'm not built for the physical business. You're the athletic one. I'm the brains. Life fact.'

Too tired to argue, Alex finished tracing a thin line circling Zorrin's chair then extended it around the panther.

'Now a few grains on to my feet,' instructed Zorrin.

As the first few atoms of powder touched Zorrin, the whole line roared into flame. Gigantic red tongues of fire exploded up to the ceiling. Wizard and panther were engulfed in an inferno.

'Beat it out,' yelled Skoodle. 'Use your shirt.'

Alex dumped Skoodle on the floor and started tugging his shirt off.

Zorrin called out, 'Ignore the fire. Get back.'

Halting, Alex stepped away. The wizard sat calmly in the centre of the intense blaze. Myth slept on. Neither made any attempt to save themselves.

After a few seconds the flames extinguished, leaving the room filled with dense red smoke. The black panther yawned and rose, trotting over to sit at Zorrin's feet.

Zorrin scratched the cat behind his ears. 'Good to see you awake, Myth.'

'And you,' came a deep and resonant voice. Myth stretched his front legs out and settled down to lie at Zorrin's feet.

'What happened?' asked Skoodle.

'The Chi Llang spell combusted. Spectacular, but – as you see – the victims remain unharmed. Quick, stand back.'

There was a loud crack. Gale-force wind whipped up from the floor below Zorrin, slamming Alex, Keeko and Skoodle against the wall. Alex forced his eyes to stay open despite the stinging wind, determined to see what was happening. Zorrin's hair was blowing wildly above his head as if he were in a tornado. Myth's fur, tail and ears were standing straight up.

The roof yawned open. Through the chasm Alex could see swirling blue and gold mist. The thick red smoke whirled up through the gap. With a crash, the fissure in the ceiling closed.

As the wind died, Skoodle slid towards the floor. Keeko caught him inches above the hard tiles.

'That was a blast,' said Skoodle.

'Totally,' replied a field mouse from nearby. It staggered across the room to hide near the fireplace. A whole family of cockroaches had been peppered against the walls: dead on contact, now like black ink blots.

Brushing the last traces of smoking yellow powder from his robes, Zorrin stretched. 'Tell me, why have you come?'

Alex told him about his parents' email, then Keeko related the story of Virida and the sapphire. Meanwhile Skoodle was muttering to himself at speed. Alex caught the words 'Uncle Toomba', 'disaster' and 'hurricane'.

Zorrin shook his head as he stood up. 'There'll be bad times up ahead: possibly wholesale death and destruction. Heroes will emerge: undoubtedly we'll need them. But for the moment we must deal with Karlan. Let's go down to Ikara.'

Alex handed the brown pouch to Zorrin. 'What are you going to do with him?'

Zorrin's face became serious. 'He must be permanently imprisoned. He'd have killed me if he had been able to.'

In silence they followed Zorrin and Myth down the stairs. Wizard and panther stepped over a sleeping crocodile as if it were a low scaly wall. Zorrin opened the oak door and froze. Before them Ikara lay motionless, loosely coiled on the rug. The wizard had gone.

'See to Ikara,' Zorrin shouted. Sprinting across the room, he wrenched aside the heavy curtains and flung the sofa aside. 'No one's here. It's not a trap.'

Alex dropped to his knees beside Ikara. Her eyes were staring lifelessly at the ceiling. Keeko covered her face with her hands and began to sob.

'Is she dead?' Alex asked as Zorrin knelt beside him. Skoodle scrambled down to sit hunched next to the still head.

Zorrin ran his hand over the green and gold scales. 'No. She's deeply unconscious, but alive.' He jerked the brown leather pouch out of his pocket and sprinkled a line of Chi Llang powder down Ikara's back.

Flames ignited, travelling down her full length, vanishing in an instant. As the smoke cleared, a faint rhythmical movement started in her upper body.

'She's breathing,' Alex shouted.

Keeko stopped sobbing and flung her arms around the glistening green neck.

A befuddled voice floated up from the floor. 'I'm very, very sorry.'

'What happened?' Keeko asked, stroking her scales.

'I ate something from the table. After you left. So hungry. Must have been enchanted. Probably why he wanted us to eat. Such a stupid snake.'

Pearly white tears fell from her eyes. Sobs sent waves down her body, like ripples down a whip.

'Not really. You couldn't have known,' said Zorrin. 'Not all food offered by wizards is enchanted.' He rose. 'Karlan will be far away by now but we'd better leave for my home, Ravenscraig, immediately. He or one of the others may return.'

He turned towards the door and snapped his fingers, the sound reverberating unnaturally loudly like a small thunderclap in the still air. The crocodiles woke and started lumbering forward.

'Slam the door,' Keeko screamed at Alex.

'Please don't,' said Zorrin. 'I need them.'

As he spoke three crocodiles trundled in, all aggression gone. Zorrin held up his hand. They halted, heavy heads swaying from side to side, teeth sheathed.

Zorrin looked at them as if he were a conjuror with a newly de-hatted rabbit. 'The crocodiles will get us home.'

'Blast,' said Skoodle. 'How about a horse or two instead?'

'These will be quicker.'

Zorrin held his hand over the head of the closest crocodile and murmured, *'Argentaro volam.'*

The tip of the crocodile's nose turned metallic grey. The wave of colour travelled down his body until an entirely silver reptile shimmered at Zorrin's feet.

'Like it?' he asked Ikara, who was wiping snake snot on to the corner of the tablecloth.

'Impressive.' She dropped the glistening cloth. 'But is it useful?'

Zorrin nodded, then repeated the spell with the other two crocodiles. 'Next… something to ride in.' Holding his hand over the middle of a crocodile he said, *'Galeni contrapsione.'*

A mist rose from the centre of each of the three beasts' backs, gradually forming into padded armchairs balanced on small wooden platforms, covered by glass domes.

Zorrin looked at Alex. 'Want your chair a little bigger?'

'No, thanks. It's great as it is,' said Alex, so stunned at the transformation that he would have absent-mindedly refused anything, even chocolate.

'Ever travelled by crocodile before?' Zorrin asked.

'Never,' Alex replied. 'Should be pretty cool.'

'It's a little bumpy when we're on the land, but fabulous in the air.'

'Sorry. I must have misheard,' said Skoodle. 'I could've sworn you said "The air."'

'I did.'

'Wouldn't a crocodile fly like a rock?' Alex asked.

'Good theory. Wickedly inaccurate.'

'This must be a Cinderella-pumpkin sort of spell,' said Skoodle. 'Although enchanted coaches generally don't have teeth, if I remember the story correctly.'

Alex threw a glance of regret at his wedged hunting knife. 'Any chance you could release that for me, Zorrin?'

'Of course.'

A small circle of the table melted back into bloodstained fur. Alex ran and pulled his knife out. In seconds the circle became wood once more, the blood on the knife floating to the floor as sawdust.

'Please unblock your minds. We'll use thought transference on the journey.'

A door opened in the glass cubicle nearest Zorrin. He climbed into the navy velvet chair and settled down as Myth padded in to lie at his feet.

As Alex moved towards the next cabin the door opened automatically. He got in, reaching down to stroke Skoodle's shaking head. Keeko climbed in the last one, perching herself on the edge of her seat like a constipated parrot, Ikara sliding in after her.

'Portus ferme,' called out Zorrin.

With not a whisper of sound, the doors shut.

'Levator reptilia superioris,' Zorrin shouted, his voice clear despite the barrier of glass.

Clutching the edge of his chair, Alex waited for something amazing to happen. Unspectacularly the crocodiles lumbered across the room, away from the door.

They've gone the wrong way, transferred Alex.

No, they haven't, came back Zorrin's voice. *Trust me. I'm a wizard. And lizard pilot.*

73

So they'll circle back?

Not exactly.

Alex realised with horror that the crocodiles were picking up speed, still aiming for the solid wall. Helpless to do anything, Alex clutched his seat, waiting for the impact.

'Worse than I thought,' wailed Skoodle. 'Uncle Toomba, I'll be with you any second.'

Alex could see Zorrin's crocodile passing through the wall ahead of him. The snout of Alex's own crocodile entered wood. He himself must follow shortly. He braced himself for the unknown, unnerving experience of passing through something solid.

Silence and misty blackness closed in. Freezing wind ruffled his hair, as if he was flying through a freezer. He felt weightless. After a few seconds the darkness evaporated. The front of his reptile had emerged from the tree, the back still passing through wood.

A pair of long scaly wings swung smoothly out of each side of his crocodile. Glittering in the sunlight they rose and fell gracefully even before they finished unfolding, propelling them upwards.

He could hear Keeko transferring to Ikara, *Help, we're going to crash. Why has it gone dark? I feel really odd. Cool, look at that.*

Alex turned to watch their crocodile emerge from the tree. He waved at Keeko, grinning as he saw Ikara wound tightly round the chair leg – the tip of her tail across her eyes. Keeko scrambled on to the back of the seat, peering down at the jungle below.

Gathering speed, the trio of reptiles rose into the sky, heading for the wispy clouds above. As the jungle fell away from them the massive redwood soon became the size of a tallish ant. The crocodiles levelled out, glittering silver wings rhythmically beating.

Are you all OK? transferred Zorrin.

Fine. I was right. This is cool, Alex replied.

Magic is. We'll be at Ravenscraig in a couple of hours. There you'll meet my sister, Flick. Relax. Enjoy the scenery. Soon we'll fly over the living Mountain of Makusha.

Skoodle frowned. *Sounds scary.*

Not really. He's a friend.

This is fantastic, returned Keeko. *I'm hungry, but otherwise... Wow. Doughnuts. Thanks, Zorrin.*

Are they enchanted? asked Ikara.

Not even slightly. Enjoy.

The slight swing of the crocodile and the soft rush of the wind whistling past made Alex feel sleepy. He curled up, laid his head on the cushions and drifted into a dreamless vacuum.

CHAPTER 11

A few hours later Alex was woken by Zorrin's voice. *We're nearly there. Down to your right is Ravenscraig.*

Through the glass dome Alex could see a few ruins: blocks of white marble breaking through the tangled emerald jungle, as if randomly tossed around by a giant.

Where? I can't see anything, Alex transferred back.

I know. It's a great piece of magic, replied Zorrin. *I'm really pleased with it. We'll go in round the side by the stables.*

The crocodiles circled down towards a lake. Banking sharply, they flew straight at the water. Their silver noses broke the surface as they plunged into the turquoise lagoon.

Wings working like gigantic flippers, the crocodiles spiralled downwards past shoals of tiny blue fish, electric eels, orange-striped starfish and golden seahorses. Lobsters scuttled for cover under coral banks as the crocodiles ploughed past. The surroundings lightened and they popped through the water into clear air. Looking back, Alex could see the bottom of the lake.

It's like a floating slice of water. A liquid door, transferred Alex.

Sooo pretty, said Keeko.

Below them lay a huge old-fashioned farmhouse made from blocks of pale stone, covered with a black grey slate roof. The crocodiles touched down in a courtyard which was surrounded on three sides by the house. The fourth side was made up of a row of stables.

As soon as the dome doors opened Alex climbed out, grinning at Keeko and Ikara as they got down from their crocodiles. 'So this is where we were aiming for. The place on my map.'

Zorrin nodded. 'Yes, but you would never have got past the magical defences. Come on in.'

He strode through a doorway into a vast kitchen, which was warmed by a crackling fire. In the centre stood a long oak table, beyond which sat a cluster of navy sofas and squashy chairs.

A beautiful young woman was hanging upside down from the ceiling by her toes like a bat, eyes closed. Bunches of long candy-pink hair cascaded upwards over her black cotton trousers and shirt. Everything hung neatly, as if she were the right way up. As they entered she somersaulted down, landing lightly on her feet, running across to hug Zorrin.

'Welcome to Ravenscraig. I'm Flick. His sister,' she said, her voice bubbling with laughter. 'Zorrin, it's good to get you home. The crystal picked you up once the spell began to shatter.'

She swept a hand over her hair. It changed into a mass of red smoke and silver sparks, as if the Chi Llang spell was combusting round her head.

'No concern, tears, pleas not to get captured again or wild hysteria?' replied Zorrin.

'Not my style. Although I was worried when you vanished from the crystal. At least the Live Wizards List confirmed that you weren't dead.'

Flick waved her hand over her head again. Her hair became a short dark green bob. 'Why don't you ever change the resting colour of your mood streak? Blue could be nice.'

The streak on Zorrin's hair changed to brilliant blue then white, followed by blue with white stripes, as the wizards fought for supremacy. Myth pricked up his ears as he watched, growling softly.

'Don't worry, Myth. She's only teasing,' said Zorrin as he held Flick's gaze, while turning his locks back into pure white.

For a moment the hair streak became pale blue, then sparkling white with blue blotches. A few blue sparks spat from Zorrin's hair, then the strip changed back to pure white and stayed that way.

'You win,' said Flick, bowing to Zorrin. 'Park your posteriors,' she said to the visitors. 'I'll dig out something to tide you over till supper.'

Alex gazed around the kitchen, fascinated. High up, on the wall to the left of the fireplace, was a shelf filled with rows of weird containers. A bright blue glass one contained gnarled black mushrooms; a yellow one held snail shells; the one next to it held dried lizards. Assorted plants suspended on invisible shelves grew in rows along the walls, tangled roots free in the air. Though revolted, Alex couldn't take his eyes off the bottles. Flick intercepted the look.

'Don't worry,' she said, placing a plate of biscuits and a large sticky chocolate cake on the table. 'Those ingredients are for my medicines – they don't go into the food.'

'She's a very talented healer,' said Zorrin, picking up a bright yellow biscuit. 'Can fix almost anything. Only death is beyond her. You'll be safe while she's around, other than if her cooking poisons you.'

Flick aimed a blow at Zorrin's head, which he ducked. 'I've saved him from the verge of death several times. Now I wonder why I bothered. I'll take you round the ingredient garden sometime. But touch nothing or… ' Flick grasped her neck, rolling her eyes up to the ceiling.

'You're on,' said Skoodle.

'Interested by something that's not food? That's odd,' hissed Ikara.

Keeko grabbed a bunch of grapes and started tossing them in the air, catching them in her mouth.

'Come on, the rest of you. Eat. I'll be offended if you don't clear the table,' said Flick.

'Love a challenge,' said Alex, reaching for a blueberry muffin.

'Tell Flick your story. Also, I want to know how you found me,' said Zorrin, pouring juice for everyone.

Interrupting each other often the four related their tale, starting from Alex's email and his decision to find out what had happened to his parents. Keeko's eyes filled with tears as they got to the river battle.

'Then Tariq disappeared over the waterfall, still wrestling with the crocodile,' said Ikara in a brittle voice.

Alex's chest felt heavy and strange. 'Tariq warned us that the fall would be fatal.'

'Maybe he was wrong. I'll check if he's OK on the crystal.' Flick vanished, leaving behind a faint waft of perfume.

'Where did she go?' asked Skoodle.

'Disparticulated. Dematerialised to become solid somewhere else. Sort of instant transport.'

'Amazing,' said Keeko. 'What crystal?'

'An entire wall in Flick's bedroom, which shows where anyone is. Only the more powerful of the evil ones don't show up, nor does anyone who's in their power. So, alive or— ' Zorrin stopped and coughed, '… otherwise, she'll find him.'

They heard Flick's voice even before she reparticulated. 'I've found Tariq. He's alive.' A hazy shadow appeared and began to turn into the solid body of Flick.

'Fantastic,' shouted Keeko, cartwheeling across the kitchen.

'Alive's good, but is he OK?' asked Ikara.

'Seems so. He's making his way through the jungle towards us.'

'This news is ice,' said Alex, punching the air.

Zorrin frowned slightly. 'Pardon? I thought you said "Ice".'

'I did. It means fantastic. You know: if cool is very good, then ice is the best it can get.'

There was a strangled sound behind them as Flick choked on her coffee then started laughing.

'Ordinary words don't need new meanings,' said Zorrin. 'Ice is frozen water. That's all. There are many other words for the best – like superb, overwhelming, fantastic.'

'Or make up your own,' said Flick, grinning. 'Like squasjig, galumphen or rapti.'

Zorrin looked at his sister sternly. 'Don't you start. This conversation is getting beyond ridiculous.' He rose swiftly to his feet, brushing yellow biscuit crumbs off his trousers. 'Would you send Viskar on a carpet to get Tariq? While we wait for him I'll show the others round Ravenscraig, starting in the gloomy bits.'

'Of course.' Flick took a sheet of thick cream paper from beside a copper cauldron and wrote in lavender ink: *Please collect Tariq. Large golden bear. For whereabouts see crystal.* She picked up a small silver bell, shook it and put it down on the note.

'No sound?' asked Alex.

'No need. You go on. I've got to pop out to the garden for a minute.'

They arrived back up from the cellar to find a massive golden snail – as tall as a man from its slimy foot to the top of its shell – in the kitchen. Its huge, pale green eyes stuck out like periscopes on glistening stalks. Myth lay by the back door purring loudly as Flick, now sporting spiky purple hair with silver streaks, stroked him.

'Your hair,' gasped Alex, without thinking.

'You don't like it?' asked Flick. 'OK, I'll change it back.' She swept her hand over her hair. It returned to the sleek dark green bob of a few minutes ago. 'Thanks for the drink, by the way,' she added to Zorrin. 'It was yummy.'

'Sorry. Not me, I'm afraid. Must have been Viskar.'

'Are you going to introduce me to your friend?' Ikara asked, indicating the snail with her tail.

'This is Yub,' said Flick. 'He mows the lawn for me.'

'Very slowly, I guess,' said Alex. 'It must take weeks.'

Flick shook her head. 'As it happens, it doesn't. I have jet-propelled him. *Velocita.*'

The snail shot across the kitchen, skidding to a halt inches from the far wall.

'I tie him to a stake in the middle of the garden and set him off whizzing round and round. The rope then winds round the stake, so he eats his way through a spiral of grass.' Flick reached into a cupboard and pulled out a leaf the size of a bath towel. She patted Yub on his slimy brown head, her hand coming away covered in rainbow-coloured snail slime. 'I always give him a little treat once he's finished.'

Flick placed the leaf in front of Yub. With a single crunch and a slurp, the banana leaf vanished.

'How he could be hungry after a lawn full of grass?' asked Skoodle.

'Beats me,' said Flick. 'But he is.'

'Hadn't you better get him outside, my favourite mollusc tamer, before all that grass reappears at the other end in a different form?' asked Zorrin.

'Good point.' Flick climbed on to Yub's neck and grabbed the bottom of each eyestalk.

'Yuk,' Ikara murmured.

'It doesn't hurt him.'

'It's me that I'd worry about, not the snail,' said Ikara. 'Think of all that slime.'

'*Velocita.*'

The pair whizzed towards the open back door.

'We'd better continue our tour,' said Zorrin, watching the golden shell rocket across the stable yard.

'I'll stay here. Have a little sleep,' said Myth, jumping on to a sofa.

They left the kitchen by a wide, stone-floored, high-vaulted corridor lined with ancient battle instruments: spears, balls with spikes and clubs. This led into an immense hall lit by orbs of fire suspended in mid-air, hissing and spitting softly.

Pictures of beasts of a mythical level of weirdness hung on the dark wooden walls. There were ferocious dragons with snakes' heads, a winged lion, an eel with the head of a shark devouring an armoured rabbit four times its size. Alex hoped that they were imaginary, yet the whole set-up was so extraordinary, he wouldn't be surprised to learn that they were Zorrin's pets. They moved on to a long balcony with arches on one side giving a view over the garden and the jungle beyond.

Keeko leapt up on to the low wall which ran beneath the arches. As she leaned forward to peer out there was a crack as she banged her forehead. 'That hurt. The air is solid.'

'A powerful spell, not glass, fills those arches,' said Zorrin. 'I have my enemies. From outside this appears to be tangled jungle. Let's go upstairs to Flick's room. It's amazing.'

CHAPTER 12

On a first floor corridor Zorrin approached an ordinary-looking dark oak door and placed his hand flat where the handle should have been. Silently, it slid sideways into the frame. Dazzling light streamed out of the room, as if they had flung the door open to reveal a sunny July morning. They could hear the low roar of running water from inside. Following Zorrin, they stepped forward into the brilliant yellow glow.

The sound filling the room came from a waterfall that fell from the ceiling and ran away through the floor. In front of them a precipice yawned, with nothing between where they stood and the lush green jungle.

'Another magical glass wall?' asked Ikara, pointing her tail at it.

'Absolutely,' said Zorrin, stroking an orange and green hummingbird that had landed on his shoulder.

'Makes this place look like home. Masses of leaves and flowers.' Ikara pushed off on the stone tiles. As she reached the glass floor there was little friction. She slid towards the jungle, scrambling to slow down but failing.

'Watch out, Ikara. You'll crash,' called Alex, waiting for the bang, the cry of pain. They didn't come.

Ikara had slid off the edge of the visible floor to hang in space ten metres above the ground. 'What happened?' she called, body rigid, peering directly down.

'It's totally safe,' said Zorrin, laughing. 'The magical glass-like floor extends out by about five metres. You'll hear a gentle hiss before you hit the far wall.'

Ikara slid on in mid-air. After a few meanders, they heard a soft whooshing noise. She stopped and reached out with the tip of her tail towards the air in front of her. 'It's solid,' she said, tapping at it.

'Correct. Like it?'

'Amazing,' said Ikara, curling up, surrounded by jungle.

'This floor is pretty,' said Keeko.

A whirl of stars embellished the entire surface of the visible floor. Multicoloured planets, their orbits marked with ribbons of gold, hung suspended in a deep blue sky: names were written in copperplate silver lettering beside each.

'It's not decorative,' Zorrin said. 'It's a dynamic encyclopaedia – a mine of knowledge. It moves in harmony with the stars around us and is useful for various spells, as well as being invaluable for predicting weather conditions such as typhoons and cyclones.'

'It's broken. It's not moving,' said Keeko.

Ikara yawned and positioned her head more comfortably on her tail. 'I suppose you expect planets to be whizzing about all over the place, asteroids zooming under your feet, a hail of shooting stars zipping from wall to wall. Wrong. Owing to the relative proportions of the cosmos and the floor, the movements in this pattern are too tiny to be seen over a short period, like an hour or even a day. Maybe a week would be long enough for you to notice them.'

Zorrin raised his eyebrows. 'Impressive. You understand both astronomy and scale.'

Ikara pointed the tip of her tail at her skin. 'I think you'll find that scale is my forte. I also have an in-depth understanding of relative sizes,' she continued, looking at Alex.

Alex nodded. 'I can vouch for that.' He grinned at Ikara and then – with a look of disgust on his face – mimed shaking sticky mud off his legs then clutching his ribs while gasping for air.

'Interesting dance,' said Zorrin, smiling.

'It's a long story,' said Alex, now apparently forcing his way through bushes, crouching low. 'I'll tell it to you one day.'

'Can't wait.'

'You're right: it could be a dance,' said Skoodle, from Alex's shoulder. He shook his legs in turn, gasping, waving his arms, as he hummed to himself. 'What do you think, Uncle Toomba? No? Perhaps you're right.'

Zorrin raised his eyebrows at Alex.

'He talks to his dead uncle. Apparently he used to do it in Hamster-speak in England. He reckons he gets all his best advice from Uncle Toomba.'

'Interesting concept,' said Zorrin. 'My Aunt Florianne was amazing, if mentally always on another planet. I wouldn't mind chatting to her. How do you dial them up?'

'It's a rare gift,' said Skoodle, stopping his dance and sitting down. 'They have to talk to you first. You can't just barge into their spirit lives.'

'Or deaths?' asked Alex.

Skoodle looked at him without smiling. 'Funny.'

'What's that?' asked Alex. He pointed at a floor-to-ceiling ice-like sheet, whose silver-grey face reflected the sparkle and dance of the waterfall opposite.

Zorrin wandered over to place his hand on its rough surface. 'This crystal wall shows where anyone is. A fantastic piece of kit. I invented it. Ask, and it shows where anyone is, as Flick did to find Tariq.'

'Flick said it didn't work when the evil forces had you,' said Ikara.

'That's true. Yet she knew I was alive by this.' Zorrin pointed to a large board next to it, on which were lists of names written in gold. Some were bright and glittering as if freshly written, others dull from age.

'It's a record of living wizards. Anyone who's still alive appears on the board. There I am.' He pointed to the name Zorrin Horsfeld. 'On a wizard's death the name disappears. When a baby wizard is born a new name appears.'

As he spoke, a commotion started on the board, letters jostling each other as they moved.

'Out of my way. Move down, oaf,' said a tiny voice from the golden list.

'Keep going or that K will get me right in the bottom.'

'Don't shove me. The Zs are still asleep. Someone get the last Y to poke them.'

The letters shuffled and reformed, then stopped moving as the little voices died down. A new name had appeared high up between Angelissa de Pomadori and Degrote de Pomadori, in bright gold letters.

'Baby de Pomadori. An Italian wizard, I presume,' said Zorrin. 'There'll be another fuss when he's given a first name and they have to shuffle again. I don't know why they always grumble about moving. You'd think they would be grateful for a little exercise.'

'Look,' exclaimed Keeko, gazing over a low brick wall. 'Teeny-weeny creatures.'

Alex joined Keeko, who was peering over the boundary of a miniature world. On a flat plain tiny lions lazily swished their tails, watching mini antelope grazing. Close by, in a desert, sphinxes and pyramids trotted around on four legs. Miniature walruses lay on an ice cap, basking in a snowfall. Several penguins played near polar bears who were flicking blue and pink fish out of the sea, catching them in their mouths. In the middle sparkled an ocean, from which minuscule dolphins leapt. Above it hung the sun, brilliant in a clear blue sky, the source of the light that had dazzled them at the door.

'Is it a toy?' asked Alex.

'Far from it,' said Zorrin. 'Those animals are real and, when removed from the compound, normal size.'

'Boring to have the sun all the time,' said Ikara, looking over the edge.

'Flick switches it for the moon at night. She keeps it here.' He pointed to a gold bowl on the shelf. 'But the weather is a bit random. Flick tosses in whatever she feels like.'

He reached towards a shelf on which sat rows of jars. The labels ranged from Hail and Lightning to Spring Breeze. Zorrin chose a jar marked Rain Clouds and sprinkled a few over the mountains. A cry of protest rose from the goats and bears.

'Sorry, but you need rain sometimes,' said Zorrin to the upturned faces.

With a small harrumph the bears trooped off to their caves. A fleet of ducks flew in, giggling, droplets of rain rolling off their heads.

'How do they become big again?' asked Alex.

'These capsules.' Zorrin indicated a bowl of fragile-looking bubbles on a pedestal near the compound. 'They hold a weightlessness spell. If you drop one on an animal you can pick it up. When you burst it the animal becomes normal-sized.'

'Do you have to put the clouds back?' asked Keeko, reaching over to poke one.

'No,' said Zorrin. 'They rain themselves out. Shall we see the rest of the fortress?'

'Sure,' agreed Alex, even though he wanted to stay. 'This is so cool. Even ice. I'll ask Flick to show me the rest of the stuff in here some time.'

As they turned to leave, bickering started again on the Live Wizards List.

'Excellent,' laughed Zorrin. 'Not only have they given the baby a first name, they've double-barrelled his second. Almost the whole lot will need to shift. Riot brewing.'

The noise levels of tens of tiny voices rose as Frederik Zimbalt-Pomadori started his descent through the list of names.

Zorrin addressed the board. 'There must be no torn-off bits of letters when I get back. I'm tired of mending you.'

The last call was Zorrin's study, a cross between a high-tech room and a male comfort cave. A transparent domed ceiling rose above them, slender silver beams visible through the glass. The circular walls were hung with maps, several of Eridor: some astronomical, most of the others incomprehensible. A painting of a sailing boat, with the name *Phaedea* inscribed on the hull, hung behind his desk. At the far side of the room was a doorway filled with a thick mist, like a cloud door.

A large tabby cat sat at Zorrin's immense wooden desk, reading a newspaper. He glanced up at them, nodded hello, then carried on reading. Near him, a tall contraption of glass cylinders, half-filled with liquids of various colours, hung in the air.

'Pretty,' said Ikara, eyeing it. 'But is it useful?'

'Very,' replied Zorrin. 'It's an astromometer, sent to me by a friend of my father's about fifty years ago. Old, but it works perfectly.'

Keeko wandered over. 'Love the colours. What's it do?'

'Predicts the interfacing of time zones, the occurrence of meteor showers and of shooting stars. You're lucky to see it. Quite often it fades out and disappears, sometimes for days, which is extremely inconvenient.'

'And these?' asked Ikara, indicating a small gold bowl in which lay several red beans.

'Orgreeb. If you put one in your ear I can talk to you, even if you're miles away.'

'Why not use thought transference?' asked Alex.

'It's got nothing like the range of these. Also, with transference, everyone can hear your thoughts. Orgreeb are private, transmitting only to whoever is wearing one, so ensure secrecy.'

Keeko opened a red enamel box. 'And this?'

Bounding across, the cat grabbed it and slammed the lid shut.

'Thanks, Clawds. Those are highly dangerous time tears. When two time zones collide, either in the course of nature or by wizardry, an unstable edge forms. The shearing forces rip small droplets of reverse time from the edge.'

'Why are they dangerous?' asked Keeko.

'Touching one without the protection of a glove of Mazal will transport you to the other time zone. The only way to return is by contact with the opposing tears remaining on the other side, but they're amazingly difficult to find. Clawds, would you get Figstaff to bring some drinks, please?'

'Of course. No problem.' Clawds ran from the room, tail held high.

'Does this box also contain time tears?' Alex pointed at an ancient-looking wooden box, a gold mesh glove on top.

'No. Go on, look in the box, but don't touch the contents.'

Inside were four green slimy globules, like massive blobs of snot, quivering in individual black metal compartments.

'Why the glove? Do these things bite?' asked Alex.

'No. They're cabivitrim: a powerful magical adhesive. The only things they won't stick to are the box they're kept in and that glove. Drink?'

'Great,' said Alex, suddenly realising how thirsty he was after the long trek around Ravenscraig.

An emerald-green frog in a flowered waistcoat walked in on his hind legs, rearing up to the height of a man. He held a tray of glasses. Each one was scrolled with gold writing, the stems blood-red. Figstaff put the tray on a table near the fireplace then placed his front leg on it. Pale green fluid bubbled up through the glass stems.

'Thanks, Figstaff,' said Zorrin. 'Is this your mango, orton and passion fruit mix?'

'Absolutely,' said Figstaff. 'Enjoy.'

As Figstaff handed a glass to Alex, a short bald-headed man dressed in a dinner jacket entered the study, his gaunt face unsmiling. Over one arm lay what appeared to be a furry white towel. As the man paused at the door the soft drape moved slightly and a head appeared. Alex realised with a shock that the fluffy something was a rabbit.

'You requested a bear, I believe,' said the bunny.

CHAPTER 13

The man stepped back to let Tariq pass. With a shriek Keeko flung herself at Tariq, landing with her arms wrapped round his neck and her tail curled around his torso.

'You're alive,' she yelled. 'You frightened us.' Crying, she beat on his chest with her fists.

'Had a good swim?' asked Ikara from her perch on the desk. 'I suppose you got bored with your crocodile friends and thought you'd pop over and see us instead.'

Tariq grinned. 'Something like that.' Mud matted his golden fur and a livid red scar ran the full length of his right forelimb.

'Welcome back,' said Alex, so pleased to see Tariq that it felt as if his chest would pop. 'We thought you were dead meat.'

'So did I.' Tariq sat down with Keeko still wrapped round him.

'How did you survive?' asked Skoodle.

Tariq accepted a glass from Figstaff and drank deeply. 'Luck.'

'More detail, croc wrestler supreme,' said Skoodle, as Figstaff handed him a tiny glass. The frog wandered from the room.

'There was a thick branch reaching across the waterfall from a tree on the bank. As we fell I kicked at the croc, using him as a springboard. I managed to grab the branch then climbed it to the side of the gorge. Old leather-face wasn't so lucky. He's fish food now.'

'I expect the croc aerobics were quite tiring,' said Ikara. 'On the positive side, though, the river will have washed the blood away.' Her tone became anxious. 'Unless you're still bleeding?'

'No, I'm not.' Tariq ran his hand over the smooth scales of her head. 'I had a couple of slashes when I first arrived, but Flick made me drink some disgusting green muck. I healed immediately.'

As Tariq withdrew his paw to take his cup, Ikara sank softly to the floor, a soft whisper of air escaping her mouth.

'By the way, thanks for saving our lives,' said Alex.

'No biggy,' replied Tariq with a shrug. 'Don't be too grateful. You may yet need to return the favour.' He turned to Zorrin. 'Does that guy who guided me here never talk? Only the rabbit spoke at all.'

'Yidgit is complex. The pair share a body. The rabbit does all the thinking and talking, but he's almost boneless and has no vital organs of his own. No heart, no lungs, no gut. Without the man the rabbit would die, and vice versa.'

'Amazing,' said Tariq, reaching for a banana. 'So what happened to you guys?'

Keeko launched into the story. She acted out the fight with Karlan, overplaying it. The enemies became larger, the battle bloodier. She passed swiftly over Ikara's defeat by Karlan, moving on to a graphic description of travelling by aerocroc.

'Great acting,' said Zorrin as Keeko bowed. 'We need to work out why Virida sucked you into this task and if it's related to Karlan's attempt to kill me. We must also get more information on the disappearance of Alex's parents.'

'That would be great,' said Alex.

Zorrin took a small white ball from the edge of his desk and flung it into the air. As it rose in a lazy arc it expanded, becoming hazier. It floated down to the floor behind them, becoming a large undulating crescent-shaped cloud, wisps of vapour rising from its surface.

Zorrin sat on it. 'Join me.'

'Looks fun,' said Keeko, jumping on.

'Loving this.' Ikara leaned her head back on to the moving white cushion.

'Thanks. Alex, may I see you your parents' stuff?'

Alex pulled out the netbook, put it on the desk and found his father's Eridor file.

Skoodle scrambled out of Alex's pocket and jumped on to the desk. 'Pull it a bit closer, please. Should be less boring with Zorrin to explain it.'

Zorrin opened the file. 'It's written in Tor. Sensible of them. Almost no one understands that ancient language.'

They waited as Zorrin read – the silence only broken by Skoodle scratching his head, drumming his claws on the desk or sighing.

Finally Zorrin spoke. 'They've collected an amazing amount of info. Astonishing, as they've got no personal magic. The map is highly detailed: it even has the mooring place of my boat *Phaedea* in Petrock Bay on it. Very few know where she lies.' He read on. 'I've found the reason why Virida trapped Alex with the hex. Listen to this prophecy. 'One shall come from afar. Of few years and of human frame, he'll rediscover the Sapphire of Akan, thereby launching a new era.''

'So Virida chose me as her puppet,' said Alex. 'Landed us with a curse.'

'We must stop looking for the sapphire,' said Keeko, grabbing Zorrin's arm and shaking it. 'We can't play into her hands.'

Zorrin shook his head. 'We can't stop. If the stone does exist we have to get to it first. It has awesome power. We'll have to get more information from the Mountain of Makusha.'

He rummaged in the cloud sofa and then pulled out a coloured three-dimensional map. Zorrin hung it in thin air above his desk.

He whistled a note. A thin silver stick appeared in his hand. Zorrin pointed it at the map. 'Makusha is part of the mountain range that we flew over to get here. The journey to him will be appalling: arctic, exhausting, dangerous. But there is no choice, as Makusha knows things that no one alive would be able to remember.'

'I'm confused,' said Alex. 'Is Makusha a mountain or a living creature?'

'Both,' replied Zorrin, putting down his pointer. Immediately it rolled into a ball and attached itself to the sleeve of his shirt as if it were a magnetic button. 'Makusha has an astonishing brain trapped in a granite exterior. He is guarded by the Xo force, which prevents unwanted visitors reaching his heart. Unfortunately it also prevents us from getting there by disparticulation.'

Skoodle trotted over to Zorrin's sleeve and pulled the silver button off. 'Will this Xo stop us getting in?'

'No. If your motives are good the Xo will allow you to pass. If not, it throws you back out into the snow as if you'd been blasted by a cyclone. Bone-shattering stuff. Tomorrow we shall find out what Makusha knows about the sapphire.' Zorrin gestured dismissively at the map.

'Great. So you've finished with me,' said the map. 'No "Thank you" or "Good work". Well, I know when I'm not wanted.'

The map rolled itself up into a long thin tube and shot back towards the cloud sofa, heading straight at Alex. As Alex flung himself forward on to the desk, the map whistled past his left ear, missing by only millimetres. It dived into the sofa, shouting, 'May your brains turn to bogies.'

'A map with attitude. Rare, thankfully, but better than the other kind of troublemaking one which explodes into a shower of beetles when it's angry. It takes ages to piece it back together, as the bits keep running off.'

As Skoodle pulled at the button and shook it, a snarl cut across the air. Clawds stood braced: back arched, fur on end, tail vertical, his gaze focused beyond Ikara.

'Clawds, what's the matter?' asked Zorrin. 'It's only a mouse.'

Clawds gave a savage yowl. 'No. Evil wizard.'

'Blazing asteroids, you're right,' shouted Zorrin, leaping off the sofa.

The rodent pelted across the floor, aiming for the cloud door. Clawds leapt after him, hissing and spitting.

'Don't lose him, Clawds,' yelled Zorrin as the tip of the mouse's tail disappeared through the cloud door, the cat in pursuit.

Zorrin grabbed Alex's arm, holding him back. He took an orgreeb and shoved it at Alex. 'Cram this in your ear. I'll relay instructions. I'm going to the ice wall so I can track him better. Follow Clawds.' Angry black eyes met Alex's. 'Show no mercy. Kill the intruder.'

Scooping up Skoodle, Alex raced after the other three. They threw themselves through the hazy door into a corridor lit up with a soft orange glow. Clawds's tail was disappearing down some stairs at the far end of the corridor. As Alex approached he found the long narrow flight of stone stairs in deep shadow as it plunged downwards; the bottom treads in total darkness. Ikara raced down them, ahead of the others. Near the bottom she stopped suddenly, rearing up on her tail.

'What's wrong?' Alex asked, drawing level with her.

One glance answered his question. A cavernous black hole lay beyond the bottom tread, filling the whole passageway: no other way forward. Clawds had already disappeared down it.

'Jump,' said Zorrin's voice through the orgreeb.

Alex peered into the darkness. 'Are you sure?'

'Positive. The crystal shows Clawds ahead of you, with the mouse not far beyond. Go for it.'

Alex relayed the message to the others.

'Not me,' said Skoodle, clinging on to the edge of Alex's pocket. 'Yes. Us.'

Taking a deep breath Alex closed his eyes and launched himself into the hole, hoping that he wouldn't break both legs on landing.

'Parachute,' yelled Skoodle.

'That's me.'

Alex and Skoodle fell through darkness until a blast of air slowed them to a halt. They touched down in a brightly-lit vast cellar – Ikara, Keeko and Tariq landing a second later. The mouse was still ahead of Clawds, the gap closing as they raced onwards.

'Spread out to herd him towards Clawds,' Alex called to the others. 'We'll trap him.'

The mouse reached some turquoise mosaic tiles close to the far wall. As he ran on to one it flew upwards, whooshing him towards the ceiling.

Body flattened, the mouse clung on to the speeding slab as it rocketed up.

Skoodle's eyes were fixed on the tiny figure. 'Is this Zorrin's magic? Death by splattage?'

They waited for the nauseating crunch. Yet, with a whisker to spare, the roof opened above the mouse. He shot on upwards, unharmed.

'As it turns out, no,' said Skoodle.

Clawds jumped on to the next turquoise tile. As he landed, it began to soar towards the ceiling.

'If the roof doesn't vanish sooner he'll be pulverised,' wailed Skoodle. 'Close your eyes.'

Alex couldn't look away. As Clawds's head reached the ceiling a black hole appeared. He disappeared into it.

'Get on to one,' Alex called to Keeko and Ikara. 'Quickly.'

'What if the roof doesn't open for us?' yelled Skoodle.

'We get crushed,' said Alex, face set in hard lines, hazel eyes serious.

CHAPTER 14

Alex leapt on to a coloured stone. With a jerk it began to rise, faster than the others had done.

'Know where we're going?' asked Skoodle.

'Up.'

Keeko jumped from the floor into his arms as Ikara lassoed his leg with a coil of her tail to haul herself on board. Tariq jumped on to the slab next door, his face showing no emotion.

Alex crouched down, hoping that the roof would open earlier than for the other animals. His eyes were fixed on what seemed to be a very solid ceiling. A second before they crashed into it, it evaporated, leaving a dark hole. The slab below them began to glow. They zoomed upwards in a turquoise column of light. The paving stone halted in a laboratory stuffed with benches of scientific instruments, gas burners, glass beakers and jars of chemicals.

The mouse was streaking down the centre, pursued by the sleek tabby body of Clawds. Both bolted through an open door at the far end.

Zorrin's voice came again in Alex's ear. 'Clawds is closing in. The storeroom has only one door. Guard it. I'll transparticulate there and deal with the mouse.'

'Understood.'

As Alex arrived in the next room he heard Clawds's deep growl coming from the other side of a pile of boxes. He ran round to find Clawds with the mouse clamped in his jaws. Black blood oozed out of the cat's mouth. Then, opening his mouth wide, he engulfed the rodent. Zorrin and Myth reparticulated beside them as the tip of the mouse's tail disappeared into the cat.

Clawds's eyes glazed. His body stiffened. In seconds the cat had frozen into a solid block of wood, perfect in every detail, even in his startled expression. Shocked, Alex stared at the lifeless form.

'He's dead,' cried Keeko.

'No. Only lignified,' said Zorrin. 'I've changed him into wood. If I hadn't transmorphed him, the evil concentrated in that small rodent body would have killed Clawds.'

'But doesn't being turned into wood count as being dead?' asked Skoodle. 'Seems a bit on the terminal side.'

'No,' said Zorrin. 'This spell is reversible. The evil trapped inside Clawds is lignified with him and can't escape. He's safe, at least for the moment.'

He picked up the small wooden figure, turning it in his hands, studying the warm sculpture. 'We'll take him to Flick and see if she can reverse this without killing him. The tree will be the quickest way down.'

A window stretched from ceiling to floor at the far side of the room. Beyond it, a huge oak spread its branches towards the glass. Zorrin opened the leaded casement and climbed on to the low sill. With a quick 'Follow me,' he scrambled on to the nearest branch. Myth jumped on behind him. Placing his feet on the bark in front of him, Zorrin yanked downwards on a small leafy twig.

A hole appeared in the trunk, light blazing from it. The branch tilted slowly, sliding Zorrin and Myth into the gap. As they whisked out of sight, the hole closed and the branch levelled out.

'Me first,' said Keeko, swinging herself on to the branch and yanking on the twig. She disappeared out of sight, shrieking and laughing.

Alex climbed on to the branch, then pulled on the twig. The branch tilted him forward as the yawning hole appeared. As they slid forward into the centre of the tree, candles fixed to the walls burst into flame, lighting up the inside of a polished tube. They flew down as if on a water slide, whizzed through a hatch at the end and slid to a halt on the flagstone kitchen floor next to Keeko. An undignified heap of snake followed a few seconds later.

'Move,' yelled Alex, wrenching Ikara off the landing strip,

knowing that in a millisecond three hundred kilos of flying bear would crush her.

'Clawds took a huge risk and swallowed the intruder,' Zorrin was telling Flick as Tariq crashed into the kitchen. 'He would have died in seconds if I hadn't transmorphed him.'

Flick took the statue into her hands. 'What an amazingly brave thing to do.'

'Can you save him if I change him back now?'

'No. It would kill him.'

'Makusha might know a way to reduce or divert the negative power flow. Then waking him up might not kill him. We'll go first thing tomorrow. Flick, will you stay and guard Ravenscraig? I'll leave Myth with you.'

'Why can't Flick come?' asked Skoodle. 'More wizard power.'

'There could be a rescue attempt,' said Flick. 'Then we'd lose Clawds. That mouse interloper must be an immensely powerful magic force.'

'How do you know?' asked Tariq.

'He broke through our defences. The fortress boundaries are impenetrable unless you are specifically invited or are an elemental wizard,' said Zorrin.

'If he's so powerful, why didn't the mouse kill Clawds as soon as he gave chase?' asked Alex.

'Because Clawds acted so quickly. He never gave the wizard a moment to stop and gather enough energy to transmorph. With even a couple of seconds' pause Clawds would have caught him.'

'He was on the lift to the attic for several seconds,' said Skoodle. 'Could've changed then.'

'I'm guessing that it would have taken all of a mouse's physical strength and mental concentration to hang on to a stone travelling at that speed with the wind streaming past,' said Zorrin. 'It's lucky for us that Clawds recognised the mouse for what he was. Yet I can't think how an enemy, powerful wizard or not, foiled our defences.'

Tariq scratched his head. 'Perhaps he came in on the back of one of the crocodiles.'

'No. Still wouldn't count as being invited,' said Flick.

'What if it became one of the crocodiles?' asked Ikara. 'This evil is able to transmorph so maybe it could change into a croc. As our transport, you invited them in.'

'Clever thought. I'll check the stables.' Zorrin pulled back his sleeve. On his wrist a crystal sparkled with masses of different colours. He looked deeply into it.

'There are only two crocodiles in the stables now. Flick, that's a loophole we must close. Could you work on it as soon as possible?'

'Of course. I'll do it tomorrow while you're away, but now we all need to get to bed. You'll have a very long day tomorrow.'

Alex's bedroom was on the third floor, its windows overlooking an amazing array of huge fuchsias among heavy jungle vines. Dark emerald velvet curtains hung at the windows and cloaked the corners of the four-poster bed. Alex gently pulled a snoring Skoodle out of his pocket and placed him on a clean towel.

'Don't pee on it,' he told the sleeping hamster. 'Manners.'

Pyjamas had been laid out on Alex's bed. He climbed into them and found that they fitted him exactly. With a sleepy smile in the direction of where he thought Flick's room might be, he got into bed and fell into in a dreamless sleep.

The next morning Alex and Skoodle found Myth sitting outside their room. As they emerged, Myth started padding along the corridor towards a broad oak stairway.

'Panthernav,' said Skoodle. 'This place has everything.'

From the kitchen drifted a fantastic blanket of aroma woven from croissants, hot chocolate and freshly-baked bread. As they walked in Flick was placing an immense platter of fruit on the kitchen table.

'Ice,' said Keeko, trotting over and taking a banana.

'That word,' groaned Zorrin, looking up from his book. 'Soon you'll all be using it.'

A wicked grin crossed Flick's face. 'Possibly. If we all did, it would be ice.'

She ducked, avoiding the melon slice hurled by Zorrin.

Alex grinned at Flick. 'Agreed.' He picked up a glass of orange juice. 'Gosh, this is warm. Pass the—'

'Frozen water,' yelled Skoodle. 'Careful. Say it and he may turn you into a skunk.'

'Or something more useful, like a cauldron brush,' muttered Zorrin.

As they ate, he filled them in on the details of the upcoming trek. It didn't sound pleasant.

'It sounds awful. How are we going to get to the mountain?' asked Skoodle.

'Come with me. I'll show you.' Zorrin rose, black hair cascading down his back, high cheekbones emphasised by the morning sunlight. The white mood streak at the front of his hair had pale green edges. He led them to his study.

'This is the Modo: our transporter,' said Zorrin, as they walked in.

'Where?' asked Skoodle climbing on to Alex's shoulder.

'This room,' said Zorrin. 'The controls are in my desk. When I launch us, those silver plates will open up.' He pointed to the clear ceiling, beyond which were thin metal triangles, meeting at their tips. 'The whole room will then take off, like an enormous glass ball.'

'Awesome,' said Alex, trying to imagine the room in flight.

'But what about all the stuff in here? Surely some is too valuable to leave the fortress,' said Tariq.

'You're right. Those things are magically anchored to Ravenscraig so, as we leave, they'll stay.'

'Such as?' asked Keeko.

'The Sword of Alwyn on the wall behind you. It has ended many lives in the past. The goblins have woven strong magic into its shaft. It can even cut through metal: human bones are like twigs to it.'

'Great piece of gory history,' said Alex. 'How did you get hold of it?'

Zorrin shrugged. 'It's a very long story. I'll tell you some day. Now, help me think. We need to take a gift to Makusha, but what do you give a mountain?'

'Something magical?' suggested Alex.

'Something valuable? A gem, for example,' said Tariq. 'Stone for a stone?'

Keeko shook her head. 'Too dull. Must be something quirky.'

'I'm decisioned out,' said Zorrin. 'We'll take all three. That rod leaning on the parrot's cage will do for the magical. Tapped once, it produces fire.' He reached through the solid top of the desk, withdrawing a glass bottle in which was suspended a huge milky pearl. 'Queen Rak-hi-eda's wedding gift from her father. No magic but, being huge and perfect, it's extremely valuable. Let's see. Quirky.'

'Time tears?' suggested Ikara, surveying the desk.

'Too dangerous. Cabivitrim glue and the gold mesh glove – that will do. Please shove them in a pocket, Alex.' Zorrin put the other things into his trousers, collapsing the black and gold rod into a short stick.

He sat down at the desk. With a light touch to one corner and a few muttered words, a control panel sprang up in front of him. 'Keeko, if you would push that blue lever beside you, the doors will seal. I'll then launch us. Once in the air we'll be able to see the earth below through glass panels. From the ground we'll look like a solid silver ball, owing to a one-way mirror effect.'

Keeko leaned hard on the lever. 'So we can see out and they can't see in?'

'Correct. Launching now,' said Zorrin.

With a whoosh, they shot upwards.

'I'm loving this.' Keeko trotted across to one of the windows to gaze down at the receding jungle. 'Flying's brilliant.'

'Bit further to the west,' Zorrin told a map laid out on his desk. 'Yes, about there. Show me a detailed section of the area.' As he spoke a small silver arrow travelled across the map towards Makusha. A small red dot moved in response to his words. 'The crimson light is our Point of Intended Touchdown or PIT,' he told Alex, who had moved across to see what was happening. 'The silver arrow represents the Modo in Flight or MIF.'

'I suppose that,' said Alex, indicating the castle, 'is the Point of Launching at Ravenscraig. POLAR.'

'And this,' said Ikara, pointing with her tail at the Single Redwood, 'Is Many Unpleasant Deeds Done Yesterday. MUDDY.'

'How about,' said Tariq, indicating the river, 'This being the Crocodile Assault; The Friends Attack Together. CAT FAT.'

'And what about,' said Keeko, pointing at Makusha, 'This being the—'

'I don't think you're taking this seriously,' interrupted Zorrin.

'No, but then we don't have to,' said Ikara, curling herself back on the floor. 'We're not flying the joint.'

'Do we get in-flight refreshments, Captain?' asked Alex.

'Of course,' said Zorrin, waving a hand towards a cabinet on the far side of the room. 'Over there.'

'Ice,' said Ikara.

'Now it's you with that word,' said Zorrin.

'It seems to be catching,' said Alex, grinning.

'Not by me it isn't,' muttered Zorrin, as he bent over the map once more.

CHAPTER 15

Deep in the tangled forest, the swarthy goblin leader Tevo threw a broken-legged squirrel on to the fire. Ignoring its dying screams he sat on a rock, eating the animal's barbecued brother. The band of animals around him didn't flinch. They knew how little Tevo valued life; his total disregard for pain. His long brown beard soon filled with bits of flesh as he ate, yellow dog-like teeth tearing at the meat.

Malicious goblin eyes watched the Modo rise, its shape etched out in the steely grey sky. Then a heavy black cloud swept across the heavens, hiding it entirely.

'Good riddance,' spat out Tevo. 'That will be the do-gooder wizard out of the way.' Tevo's voice rose into an imitation of a woman's voice, totally out of keeping with his stocky build and strong face. 'Let's go and rescue the weak ones, Zorrin. Or shall we grow herbs together?'

The pack of animals surrounding him laughed loudly.

'Why does he hate that wizard pair so badly?' Grut, a small badger, asked his cousin Smuddy Binks.

'They captured the Sword of Alwyn. I believe that Tevo's real reason for breaking into Ravenscraig isn't the jewels: it's the sword.'

Tevo's wife Rectoria watched him from the other side of the camp, frowning. She sniffed hard – collecting as much snot into her throat as she could – swished it around her mouth and, with a hard contraction of her abs, spat. A glob of spit-covered nasal gunk sailed through the air, glistening dark green in the sunlight. The foul-smelling quivering mass landed three metres away.

Rycant, the black Rottweiler, trotted over to look at the repulsive snot-ball more closely. He looked back at Rectoria, estimating the distance of the gob's flight by eye.

'It's a winner,' he stated loudly, adding in an undertone to his brother, Hebor, 'She must be about to snap.'

Rectoria strode across to Rycant. 'I heard that. I am. I'd divorce him if I could,' she muttered back.

'Then do it.'

'Can't. Goblin law. He's a life sentence.'

Tevo glanced across at the snot-glob, then pulled a map from his pocket and unfolded it on to the ground. He gazed upwards to the cloud formations scudding across the sky.

'Blasted ferret gizzards,' Rectoria hissed. 'Greatest gob for months, far better than many of his, and he doesn't say a word. He doesn't give a stoat's left ear for any of us, including me. The only two emotions he's got are anger and hate. Even loyalty doesn't feature, useful though it might be to him.'

'I know,' replied Rycant in a low growl. 'In battle I've seen him pass within a pace of his injured comrades, not lifting a sword arm to help. Once you're too badly wounded to fight he has no more use for you. Is there anything at all he cares about?'

'Money. Power. The Sword of Alwyn. But mainly desire to reclaim the goblin rights, taken from the great goblin master. That will keep him fighting until the last breath is slashed out of his body.'

Tevo rooted in the soil with a stick, examining conditions underfoot. He arose, a cruel gleam in his black bulgy eyes. 'It is right. Tonight we enter Ravenscraig.'

'That's good,' muttered Hebor. 'I'm fed up with waiting.'

'The defences at the hideout will be weak,' continued Tevo.

'Will no one be guarding Ravenscraig?' asked Rectoria, her voice harsh and strident.

'Don't be such a complete fool, female,' answered Tevo, looking at her with a sour expression. 'The servants and animals will remain. They wouldn't leave the castle entirely undefended.'

The urge to snap back was strong, but the memory of the

beating Tevo had given her the last time she had angered him kept Rectoria silent.

Smuddy Binks, a large badger with a battle-scarred snout, was standing away from the group. He called over, 'How many servants?'

'The number is unimportant,' Tevo replied.

Rectoria raised her eyebrows. Turning her back on him she mouthed at Rycant, 'He doesn't know.'

'How are we to get into Ravenscraig?' asked Arnak, a fox whose battle skills and courage had made him a subsection leader, feared and respected in equal measure. 'Are we to storm the front door?'

Tevo snorted. 'No one can get in by force. It's guarded by deep magic. The only way in is either to be an elemental wizard, or be invited in by one.'

'As we are neither this has been a lousy waste of time,' muttered Smuddy Binks to Grut.

'Stupid badger,' said Hebor, trotting over to kick Smuddy Binks. 'I've worked it out. Tevo's captured an elemental wizard. He's going to torture him and make him lead us into the castle.'

Tevo produced a hideous grin. 'That wouldn't work. Deeper magic would recognise that there was no free will on the part of the wizard. You've also forgotten the stupid loyalty that all elemental wizards have for Zorrin. Any would rather die than betray him.'

Arnak shook his heavy russet head, bemused. 'There must be something you're not telling us, as we're not elemental wizards and I seriously doubt they've invited us in.'

'I have a visorb,' Tevo said. 'The defence magic will recognise it as being that of an elemental wizard.'

'But that's not possible,' barked out Arnak.

'For me anything is possible.'

'But how?' asked Grut. 'You cannot take a visorb from a living wizard, nor from a dead one: it dies with him or her.'

'So how is this apparently possible?' asked Smuddy Binks.

Tevo leaned back against a tree, arms folded, surveying them with a half smile.

After a minute Rectoria realised that Tevo wanted her to describe his cleverness and the brilliance of his plan. *Fool*, she thought. Deeply irritated, she asked him, 'Shall I tell the story?'

'If you really want to,' he replied. 'You can have centre stage and your bit of reflected glory.'

Forcing her voice to sound full of admiration, she began. 'Some of you may have heard of Olip, an evil wizard who betrayed the elemental wizard Jago. As a consequence, Jago's wife Hera lost her life. Jago swore that she would be avenged: Olip would die.

'Jago told everyone what he planned to do. He wanted Olip to lie awake at night tortured by fear and spend every waking moment in mental agony. As soon as the news of Jago's sworn intent reached Olip, the coward went into hiding.'

Choosing her words carefully and trying to sound more enthusiastic than she felt, Rectoria continued, 'The first part of Tevo's brilliant plan was to become Jago's bodyguard. As Jago's servant he could spy for Olip. The plan worked perfectly. Tevo became a trusted part of Jago's household. Then Olip came back out of hiding and threatened to kill Jago's son, Luke.'

'Why?' asked Arnak. 'A wizard boy of fifteen is no threat. He doesn't even have his own visorb until he's sixteen, so his magic would have been puny – nothing compared to Olip's.'

Tevo took a couple of paces towards Arnak, who backed away. 'That wasn't the real plan. Olip knew that Jago would hide Luke. While they were travelling to a hideout they'd be vulnerable. The concept was working exactly as we'd anticipated.'

'We' my big hairy toes, thought Rectoria. *It was my idea.* Tevo looked across to her. Suppressing a sigh, Rectoria continued. 'Tevo told Olip the route along which they would escape. At a remote spot, high above the falls of Spirox, Olip waited on a stormy night for the two travellers. The horses had to slow down to walk on part of the slippery narrow path. At the sound of their approaching hooves Olip sprang out and hit Jago with a maxalgia curse.'

'Agonising death,' whispered Grut, paw across his mouth.

Smuddy Binks lay rigid, thinking of Jago lying in agony knowing

105

that he'd failed to save his son's life. Mentally he could see the horrified white-faced boy staring down at his father in despair, Olip and Tevo watching and gloating.

'So Olip escaped his death sentence,' said Arnak.

'Not exactly,' said Tevo, frowning. 'Jago killed him.'

'But how?' asked Smuddy Binks. 'It's not possible that a wizard in the grip of maxalgia, limbs broken, could work any form of magic that would kill a powerful wizard like Olip.'

'The boy,' spat out Tevo. 'Jago whispered a few words to him. The boy lifted his dying father's broken arm, ignoring his scream as he did so. Through gritted teeth Jago spat out *"Mortus"* as Luke pointed his spell finger at Olip's heart. Jago gave Olip a better death than he himself suffered a few minutes later.'

CHAPTER 16

Tevo looked back at Rectoria, head tilted, eyebrows raised. Mentally curling her lip at having to glorify the smug toad, Rectoria took up the thread again. 'With his last breath Jago instructed Luke to seek safety with Zorrin, telling him the incantation and where the key vine was. He also told him to hang his own visorb round his neck to gain entry. Tevo heard it all. With the boy at swordpoint, he snatched Jago's visorb and placed its chain around his own neck.'

'Surely the visorb would die. It needs oxygen and blood nearby to live. It's a parasite. It cannot live away from flesh for more than seconds,' said Smuddy Binks.

'Correct, badger,' said Tevo, a strange high note in his voice. He loosened the cord that held his rough shirt closed, to expose his thick neck and hairy chest. Halfway down his breastbone on a thick metal chain nestled a visorb, the flat silver disc covered in weird writing.

'It lives on me.' Tevo lifted the visorb, showing the dark red mark where it had sucked energy from him. He replaced it quickly.

Awestruck, Hebor stared at it. 'Do you have its power?'

'No, I don't. But it will get us past the barriers of Ravenscraig.'

'Is that innocent boy also dead?' asked Smuddy Binks.

'No,' said Tevo, shoving his shirt back into place. 'I chose to capture rather than kill Luke. He could be useful in the future as a hostage. A couple of lower-order goblins guard him in a cave to the north. He's alive. Just.'

'Jago told his friends that they were going away for a long time, so no one seeks the boy. The plan is perfect,' said Rectoria.

Not waiting for a response, Tevo grabbed a stick and squatted near the fire, the flames throwing grotesque shadows across his hard face. With firm strokes he drew a passable map of the nearby jungle in the ground. He stabbed the stubby stick roughly at it. 'We'll approach from here. We'll pretend to be travellers: a wizard and his companions lost in the storm.'

'What storm?' asked Hebor.

'It will come,' said Tevo. 'After passing through the magical barriers we'll request food and shelter for one night. My name will be Chalon Zim. He was a wizard: a recluse living in the mountains, found dead by my cousin seven days ago.'

'What if Flick or Zorrin knew Zim?' asked Smuddy Binks. 'If so we could get blasted to smithereens because of an unlucky coincidence.'

'As far as I have been able to find out, they didn't,' replied Tevo, scratching his head with the muddy stick. 'Even if Flick or Zorrin had met him before he retreated they wouldn't recognise him after all the years in the hills. He was clean-shaven in his early years: hairy, latterly. My beard will be a natural disguise.'

'How will we get out of Ravenscraig?' asked Grut.

'We'll find a way,' said Tevo. 'Earth, metal, wood or fire are little barrier to goblin magic.'

'Or we might have to tunnel,' said Rectoria.

Scowling at Rectoria, Tevo continued, 'After we've gained entry, you all shut up and play dumb. Rectoria and I will do the talking. We'll raid the castle when I give the word for action. Any questions?'

Rycant clapped Tevo on the shoulder. 'This plan is typical of you: bold, direct to the face of the enemy, yet cunning and deceitful. It's perfect.'

'What now?' asked Smuddy Binks.

'We wait. The storm will be here soon,' said Tevo, unpeeling Rycant's paw from his shoulder.

'We had better find shelter,' said Rectoria.

Tevo reached into his pocket and produced a dried human finger bone. He began picking his nose with it methodically. 'No. We need to be soaked by the time we get to Ravenscraig.'

With slow-burning anger, Rectoria crouched near the

inadequate fire and waited, Rycant by her side. 'He's planned it this way deliberately,' she muttered.

'What?'

'Made sure I got drenched. I hate the icy skin and deep-seated cold. My brain seems to slow down. Spiteful toad. He'll get another huge pus-filled boil on his head tomorrow. He never seems to register where they come from.'

Five hours later the rain began. At first droplets, then great sheets of rain swept in on the wind, stinging their faces, plastering fur down. Heavy black clouds blocked the weak late afternoon sun. Lightning arced over their heads: jagged, vivid. Thunder, louder than Smuddy Binks could remember ever hearing, crashed across the ferocious skies.

Cold gripped all of them, seeping through to their bones. Under the battering even the animals' normally water-resistant coats were saturated. Only goblin stubbornness kept Rectoria crouching in her place by the few flickering twigs kept alight by a spell, the cold wracking her shivering limbs.

Still Tevo waited as the relentless rain belted down from darkened skies. His beard, streaming with rainwater, was cleaner than it had been for years. Finally, he stood up. 'Now.'

Everybody got stiffly to their feet, underbellies squelching as they rose from the mud. Rectoria started to pack up the few possessions lying around on the forest floor.

'Leave them,' Tevo said. 'We take nothing but our knives. If we fail, whoever is left alive shall meet back here.'

'Reminding us that we may be about to die,' murmured Smuddy Binks to Grut. 'Great leadership.'

'Shut it,' barked Rycant.

As Rycant turned away, Smuddy Binks stuck out his tongue.

'Grow up,' whispered Ferox, the smaller of the two foxes.

'No thanks. Too painful.'

'Follow.' Tevo strode out of the clearing.

Rectoria dropped everything back on to the ground, covered it with sodden leaves, then put her hand over the pitiful fire. *'Exato flamori.'*

The fire died, leaving no spark or warmth. The dogs and wolves loped into line behind Tevo, splashing their way across the muddy forest floor. Within only a few paces their forms became indistinct blurs in the driving rain. Smuddy Binks and Grut fell in behind them, scuttling along at the back.

Lightning forked across the sky, turning the forest into a black silhouette. Between flashes very little light filtered through from the moon yet the goblins marched without faltering, their vision almost as good as by daylight. Despite their broad ugly feet neither made a sound as they walked. On such stealthy feet goblins had walked through the years, stealing, assaulting, murdering... then vanishing as silently as morning mist.

After two miles Tevo halted. The dogs and foxes by his side stopped. Both badgers were marching with their heads down, trying to prevent rain lashing into their eyes. Realising too late that they were halting, Smuddy Binks skidded through the slimy mud, crashing into the back of Rycant.

'Clumsy idiot,' growled Rycant. 'Watch where you're going, or suffer at my paw.'

'Sorry,' said Smuddy Binks, and meant it wholeheartedly – not for Rycant, but for himself. Marching in the tipping rain had been bad enough. Crashing into Rycant's rear had been worse, like banging into a smelly furry wall.

Tevo's harsh voice cut through his thoughts. 'We'll be in plain view soon. Look exhausted.' His eyes scanned the troops. 'You won't have to act: you all look appalling.' Lip curled, he turned away to murmur to Rectoria.

'What a cheek,' muttered Smuddy Binks to Grut. 'Considering that it's his fault we all look like this. It's—'

Grut stepped sideways, digging his claws painfully into the soft upper flesh of Smuddy Binks's left forepaw. Smuddy Binks had opened his mouth to protest when he heard a sneering whisper.

'Comments against our leader?' growled Rycant. 'Dissent in the ranks? Doubtless Tevo would like to hear of this. He would be pleased to know how I keep a close eye on the troops.'

Smuddy Binks sighed. 'Don't tell him, Rycant.'

The Rottweiler's voice was rich with malice. 'Perhaps I'll stay quiet this time. But you owe me. And you'll pay.' Rycant loped off into the darkness, back to the feet of his master.

'That was stupid of you,' hissed Grut, as the badgers moved away from the main group. 'You know Tevo's ears are everywhere.'

Smuddy Binks shrugged. 'I don't care. Not any longer. I don't want to fight for this evil band.'

'Why did you join them, then?'

'I thought they wanted to return to the ancient magic. I was wrong. Every particle of the goblins is evil. The problem is that leaving equals a death sentence. There'd be a blood price on my head for the rest of what would be a very short life.'

'Same for me?' asked Grut, eyes wide.

'All of us.'

Tevo stopped muttering to Rectoria, turning to face his band. 'The glorious Sword of Alwyn will soon be mine. History will forever be seared with the story of our brilliant recapture of such a prized weapon. For now, everyone play dumb.'

Under the eyes of the animals all spirit seemed to drain from Tevo. His body sagged, his head falling so far forward that chin almost met chest. His eyes glazed as the fire in them died. Wet stringy hair framed his expressionless face as he aged fifteen years, becoming a defeated wretch. With apparently leaden feet he trudged off, eyes fixed to the ground.

Smuddy Binks gazed at him, fascinated by the transformation. Tevo normally held himself like a leader: head high, shoulders square, back as straight as bamboo. If Tevo had normally looked like this, would they have believed in him so far? Would they have joined his band? Smuddy Binks watched the hunched shoulders slouching onwards. No chance.

CHAPTER 17

High up in the castle, interested eyes observed the progress of the goblin band. The first alarms were set deeper into the forest than Tevo had predicted. As they went off, Flick transparticulated to her room to check who was approaching.

'Show me the intruders,' she commanded the ice wall.

The frozen face clouded, spitting silver sparks. It cleared to display the band squelching to a halt in the dripping forest. Intrigued, she watched Tevo lecture the group then mutate into the defeated-looking creature now stumbling towards the hideout.

The act was very convincing, thought Flick. Tevo now looked as if he could die of cold or exhaustion at any minute. Or drown, she thought, watching the rain bucketing down. Not worried, she decided. They couldn't be wizards or they wouldn't have bothered to disguise themselves. Whoever they were, they had no chance whatsoever of getting through the defences of Ravenscraig.

No longer interested, she switched her crystal to look around all the rooms in the castle – splitting the screen into six to do it more quickly. Once she had finished her survey she strolled down to the kitchen to feed Myth.

As Flick left her room, whistling, the sodden band reached a clearing in the forest. Tevo stopped, the animals halting in his wake, grateful for a few moments' respite from their leaden-footed march. Tevo gazed heavenwards as if finding his bearings, while the animals shivered behind him. Catching Rycant's eye, Rectoria shrugged.

Ahead rose a steep hill littered with huge piles of stones, as if tossed around by a giant. The builders of the ancient broken city had scythed their way through the heart of the trees. Now the jungle had clawed back its territory. Strangling vines coiled round the blocks, lush vegetation cascading over broken walls, as if to suffocate the remains of the once-beautiful buildings.

Tevo methodically scanned the jungle. Something caught his eye, slightly to the north west. Following his gaze, Rectoria saw it too: a flash of brilliant pink.

'At last,' Tevo breathed.

Rycant stood close enough to catch his words, despite the drumbeat of rain on the thick leaves above their heads, but only Rectoria picked up the note of relief. Adjusting his course to the left, Tevo forced his way through the jungle, thrusting branches out of his way. Rectoria and the animals pushed through behind him without speaking. A last shove, then Tevo halted.

A thick wall of vines, cascading from a high bough above him, trailed down to tangle with the dense undergrowth. More than a dozen vast, bright flowers hung from the vine stems – each slashed open into four huge petals, their tips rolled out to display their sapphire interiors. Rain dropped from their edges like diamonds formed of the elements, falling to melt into the dirt. Only a few of the huge exotic flowers had burst open, the others still heavy swollen buds.

Smuddy Binks stared at them. 'I've never seen such flowers,' he muttered to Grut. 'Even though I've roamed Eridor for many restless years.'

'Me neither,' replied Grut.

'I wonder why Tevo is so fascinated by them. It's really odd. Normally he doesn't care about stuff like stunning colours or scents. His favourite smells are baked dung fungus and fresh blood.'

Tevo examined each bloom, touching them lightly as he peered into their gem-coloured interiors. After a minute, he swung round to Rectoria.

'This is it,' he said in a hiss, pointing to a flower slightly above head height. He grabbed Rectoria by the arm and yanked her forward, excitement overcoming caution. 'This is the key vine flower. It's exactly what Jago described: a clump of flowers, but only one with bright orange at the base of its stamens.'

Rectoria peered up into the sapphire interior. At the very highest point of the yellow stamens a band of vivid orange traced round their bases, then smudged and melted into the blue velvet interior of the petals.

Tevo grasped the vine below the signal flower and yanked firmly three times. Then he pulled the flower close to his face and, as if it were an old-fashioned speaking tube, he called into its interior.

'Roo-peart scribbley winkle, fisky doodle pleep.'

As the last syllables of the incantation fell into the silken bloom, the hill in front of them split open silently, as if it were made of two tilted sliding doors. A banana tree at the far end split as if struck by an invisible hatchet. The halves paused three metres apart, like silent sentries. Beyond the opening lay a vast courtyard – the size of an aircraft hanger – bathed in the light of a sunny day, the storm above not penetrating the magical barriers protecting the area.

Tevo dug Rectoria in the ribs and then trudged forward, the animals trailing after them. Inside the opening they halted in the sunlight and looked around.

In the centre, a fountain shaped like a thistle spouted a cascade of silver-blue water, which fell in a sparkling spray to a fish pond below. Around the edge, marble columns rose to the vaulted ceiling, their tops decorated with sculpted flowers, fruit and animals.

A heady scent wafted from lily flowers floating in the pond, waxy white petals above glossy emerald leaves. Scattered in the flower beds along the ancient walls grew a cascade of orchids, hibiscus and honeysuckle, hanging over the walls in tangled clumps. Birdsong drifted from all corners, as thrushes, nightingales and tiny parrots flew from mango trees to the wide necks of tiger lilies. Pineapples grew next to rose bushes in the liquid shade of banana trees.

Rycant growled as the mountain closed silently behind them leaving no trace, making it impossible to locate the exit.

'Relax, friend,' said Tevo, his tone false even to his own ears. 'It's only Zorrin's front door. He'll soon be here to welcome us.'

Tevo reached out his hand as if to pat Rycant. One glance at the long nails aiming for his head was enough to make Rycant duck. Tevo surveyed the courtyard, taking in the general whereabouts of where they had entered, despite it being now invisible among the plants. With battle discipline, he absorbed as much information as he could, in case they needed to escape by this route – not that it was likely to be possible. Jago hadn't whispered anything to Luke about how to get back out.

Tevo grabbed Rectoria by the elbow. 'Come along.'

Limping, Rectoria allowed herself to be steered to the heavy oak kitchen door on the far side of the courtyard. Tevo raised his hairy fist and knocked.

While the goblins had been trying to find the key vine, Flick and Myth had engaged in another round of a recurrent cold war: suppertime. Flick wanted Myth to eat green beans and Brussels sprouts but Myth loved large lumps of meat, preferably a juicy hyena steak. Flick had tried cajoling, threatening and leaving him hungry. Myth had in turn purred, growled, kicked, cuddled up to and flattened her, but still ended up with vegetables on his granite slab.

In the end they had reached a compromise. He ate a few veggies, pushed some around with his nose and spat most into the fire. If he managed to convince Flick that he had eaten quite a lot of the healthy stuff he got his favourite pudding: chocolate-covered pinglots. Tonight he had eaten a large pile of pumpkin, which earned him a double helping of treats.

Smiling at her victory in this round Flick went back to her room, followed by an equally happy Myth. She sprinkled some hail on to the mountains and dropped a jar of light breeze on to the hot plain.

'Sun out at eight p.m. tonight,' she called down to the animals as she switched on her crystal to view the jungle transformers.

To her horror she found the goblin band standing in the courtyard, gazing at their surroundings.

'The barriers have let them through, so at least one of them had to be an elemental wizard,' she said. 'But then why the transformation of the goblin?'

'Imposter. Crisis brewing,' said Myth.

As she gazed at the crystal she heard the first of Tevo's heavy-fisted knocks echoing down the corridors, the insistent thundering drawing her mind back from stunned inaction to clear focus.

'What shall we do, Myth? If we pretend to be out they'll probably attack.'

'So we fight.'

'Risky. We don't know how heavily armed they are, or the extent of their magic.'

'Then let them in. Keep them trapped. On our own territory you have many powers – potentially enough to defeat them.'

'If I get it wrong we're dead meat.'

'Get it right then. Use guile. Let's do it.'

Flick muttered a quick spell to transform herself into a ragged old woman, grabbed Myth's fur, then transparticulated them both to the kitchen.

Tevo thundered on the door again, wondering if he should try to use magic to get through the lock. Slowly the massive oak door creaked ajar, a waft of roasting meat escaping through the gap. A wizened old woman stuck her around the door's edge.

'What do you want?' the hag snapped, in a thin cracked voice.

Rycant backed away.

'What's wrong?' Hebor whispered to him.

'Self-control stretched to breaking point. She looks yummy, if a little stringy. I'm tempted to charge and flatten her.'

'You can't. Tevo will kill you.'

'I know, but I'm so hungry, I can almost feel my teeth closing round the soft flesh... taste her warm blood dripping deliciously from my lips... imagine the satisfying crunch of her neck bones.'

Closing his eyes completely, Rycant flattened himself on the paving stones and put his front paws over his face.

'Submission?' murmured Hebor.

'No, but if I can't see her neck I may not want it as badly.'

'We're lost,' said a tired defeated voice, unrecognisable as Tevo's. 'I am Chalon Zim, a wizard from the north west. My party and I have been caught in a terrible storm. We need shelter for one night.'

'Go somewhere else,' said the antique female, starting to shut the door.

Rycant partially rose, ready to spring.

Tevo rammed his foot into the closing gap. 'There is nowhere else. My goblin servant is sick. Going back into such a storm may kill her.'

The ancient face became thoughtful. 'All right,' she croaked. 'You can come in, but you must stay in the kitchen.' She wagged a bony finger. 'The guards will be very angry if I let you into the rest of the house.'

'A thousand thanks,' breathed Tevo, reaching forward to clasp the old woman's thin hand. 'Tonight you will have saved at least one life. You'll be surprised by the gratitude we'll show in repaying our debt.'

'He's giving an honest reply,' Rycant whispered to Hebor. 'His repayment will be to slit her throat.'

'Yeah, right. She'll be astonished, but only for a few seconds – until her body bleeds into a corpse.' Both dogs laughed, shutting up when Tevo turned and glared at them.

The aged woman snatched her hand away and moved aside, allowing the band to squeeze through. Tevo staggered in, supporting Rectoria as she limped across the threshold. The animals slunk in behind the goblins, crossing to the fire.

'You're safe now, Grelsnorg,' said Tevo, helping Rectoria into a chair close to the crackling blaze. He gazed up at Flick. 'We truly don't wish to cause you more work. I suppose you already have a large number to care for – what with guards, servants and animals.'

'Masses.' Flick frowned. 'More each day. No one cares about how much trouble it causes me.'

'We care,' said Tevo in a honeyed voice. He looked round at the band. 'Don't we?'

Several animals nodded as Rectoria replied, 'Such a lot.'

Flick grunted. She shuffled across to a cupboard sunk deep into the stone wall, muttering under her breath. Although empty seconds before, the cupboard now contained several loaves of bread, some cheese and a large jug of beer. Flick yanked them out and slammed them on to the kitchen table.

'Eat this. Touch nothing else,' she said, irritation tracing through every word. 'The meat is for the guards.'

'Are your masters at home? We'd like to thank them ourselves for their generous hospitality,' said Tevo.

'They are, but don't bother,' replied the old hag, shuffling towards the back door, the smell of old fish and rotting cabbages wafting along behind her. She yanked a pile of blankets from an alcove close to the sink. 'Use these. Don't leave any dirt about. Wash your plates. I'm going. Too busy to waste more time with you.' She left the room with Myth slouching along by her side, locking the door behind her.

Flick pointed to the room above the kitchen and whispered an incantation. Footsteps began to make their way across the ceiling, as an ever-growing swell of chatter and laughter filled the room. The sound of chairs being scraped back, cutlery clattering and glasses clinking filtered from above as a large crowd apparently gathered to eat.

'Keep them fooled, my little illusion,' she whispered.

'Back to your room?' murmured Myth.

'Yes, but we'll hoof it. I need to run off some of this adrenaline.'

Footsteps echoing on the flagstones, Flick hobbled down the corridor until she rounded the first corner. Then, hitching up her trailing skirts, she belted along towards her room, shedding hairpins as she ran. With Myth at her side, she blasted up a flight of stairs and raced round the final corner. Banging her hand against the opening panel she ran into her room, leaving the door open behind her. Swiftly she checked the Live Wizards List.

'The name Chalon Zim isn't there. We're right. They're impostors.'

'Send a souvent. Get Zorrin.'

On a tiny shelf in Flick's bedroom sat a round silver ball – a souvent – her memory transporter. With it in her hands she thought through recent events as vividly as she could: the goblins in the forest, their arrival, the Live Wizards List with the missing name.

The grey ball became a swirling mix containing vivid images of goblins, animals and the fortress, as it filled with the contents of her mind. Finally, she added a verbal message and then deliberately broke her line of concentration.

'That's enough,' she said to Myth. 'It's ready for Zorrin.'

Myth trotted over to place a paw on the transparent wall of her room. A hole appeared, edged by fire.

Flick balanced the ball on the very tips of her fingers. *'Aeroflux Zorrin.'*

A tunnel of wind sprang up from behind her, ripping the souvent from her hands, blasting it into the night – a silver line carved across intense darkness. Within less time than the sweep of an eagle's wing, it had gone.

CHAPTER 18

In the kitchen the goblins continued to act their part, seemingly tired and defeated. The fossilised servant of Zorrin's might have some form of seeing device – or the door could be of magical glass. They switched to speaking Siden, the ancient language of the goblins. No non-goblin now stood a whisper of a chance of understanding what they said.

The goblins and animals ate all that was there. Then, sleepy with food and beer, the animals dozed off – except for Smuddy Binks, who was too disturbed by his thoughts to sleep. Round like a whirlpool inside his head went the problem of how to break free from Tevo and his gang without it costing him his life.

He gazed angrily at the fire, the passion in its depths reflecting the mood of his soul. A log shifted and fell in the fire's heart. The sudden blaze lit up a dark corner beside the fireplace which had been in the shadow of a pile of logs. Buried in the gloom lay the outline of a door.

Smuddy Binks froze, his eyes fixed on the potential exit. In a second it had plunged back into darkness. Yet, now knowing it was there, he could still make out a faint rectangular outline etched on the wall.

The fates had offered him the escape route his heart burned for, yet would there be any point in running away? If he did manage to get out of the kitchen unnoticed he would never exit Ravenscraig alive. He'd either be killed as an invader or imprisoned by the old hag's guards. The riot of conflicting ideas in his head seemed as if they would drive him mad.

Tevo's cruel laugh cut across his thoughts. Smuddy Binks

glanced up at him. Suddenly the decision was made. Smuddy Binks hated every line of that hard face. He loathed every move, every sound that the evil wart made. Shoving aside any doubts, Smuddy Binks focused on escape. He would figure out how to exit the fortress once he was free of Tevo.

He glanced at the other animals. All were asleep, brains numbed by the heat. Yet with the slightest unexpected noise they would instantly wake, ready to do battle; with him, if need be.

His eye moved on to Rectoria, who was listening to Tevo's lecture. She was staring at the floor, motionless, face rigid.

Smuddy Binks flattened his body, fur brushing the floor as he crept towards the black outline of the door. The soft scratching of his claws on the flagstones was masked by crackling from the immense fire and the storm howling down the chimney.

'Stop,' shouted Rycant.

Smuddy Binks dropped flat to the floor. He waited, hardly daring to breathe, expecting a harsh blow to the head. None came. Slowly, he turned to look at the pack leader. Rycant lay on his side, eyes closed, his legs beating the air.

'Stop,' he muttered.

Smuddy Binks realised that he was deeply asleep, presumably chasing a dream rabbit. Tevo looked across, startled by the noise.

Cold sweat bathed Smuddy Binks. Eyes opened only a slit, he watched Tevo frown at Rycant then sweep his gaze across to the other animals. Tevo snorted, then swung back to continue lecturing Rectoria.

Nerves aflame, Smuddy Binks touched the centre of the dark outline. Noiselessly the door swung open. He slipped through the hole.

A pitch-black narrow tunnel rose ahead of him. Unable to turn round in the space, he carefully pushed the door shut behind him with his back paws. Total darkness entombed him. Blindly, like a mole searching for the surface, he scrambled up the cold passageway. Muffled by the solid stone walls, the storm had a faraway unearthly tone.

After a dozen cautious steps Smuddy Binks banged his front

paws on something hard. Trapped in a blind-ending tube, he felt as if his pounding heart would split his chest open. Bracing his back paws on the walls, he placed his front ones on to the blockage and shoved. It shifted a tiny amount, enough for a crack of light to escape from the straight edges. Smuddy Binks took a huge breath, dropped his shoulder and rammed up against the door, pushing for all he was worth.

The trapdoor gave, yawning open in front of him. Moonlight flooded his world from a small window set high on the wall opposite. Not bad so far, he thought, heaving himself out of the tunnel. He turned to look back down through the trapdoor. No furry nose could be seen following him up the shadow-filled tunnel. Seemingly, Rycant slept on and Tevo had yet to put a blood price on his head.

He swung the hatch back into place, feeling that although it wasn't much of a barrier it had delayed him for a few minutes. It might do the same if he were pursued.

The door on the far side of the room gave on to a long corridor lit by balls of fire suspended below the ceiling. Old-fashioned furniture hugged the walls at intervals: dark, sinister, but potential shelter in a crisis.

The storm crashed beyond the thick stone walls, jangling his nerves. Rain-swept trees creaked eerily under the wind's punishment. Flickering light from the overhead fires created weirdly dancing shadows like disembodied spirits. Yet even his hunter's sixth sense couldn't pick up any sign of danger. Pressing his body as low as possible to the cold flagstones Smuddy Binks slunk on, passing like a ghost across the floor.

Without warning the corridor lit up as if by arc lights. Smuddy Binks halted, one paw frozen in the air, ears straining to pick up any noise.

Lightning. His pent-up breath sighed out of him. Pull yourself together, stupid, he told himself. By the time the answering bang of thunder reached the draughty passageway Smuddy Binks had sprinted to the staircase at the far end. Up two broad flights he raced, as if the goblins had already discovered his flight.

At the top of the stairs he paused for a moment, listening for any hint of life, his sensitive paws alert to any vibration in the floorboards: a sure indicator of anyone's approach. There was none. Marginally reassured, he slunk on at random until he saw an open door. From within flowed a welcoming pale yellow light.

CHAPTER 19

Flick heard a faint scratching sound in the corridor, just audible above the muffled noise of the storm.

'*Discorpus,*' she mouthed.

Noiselessly she evaporated into a vague shapeless shadow floating across the room, rising swiftly to pass into the corridor high on the wall. She drifted over a badger crouching outside her door, staring into her room. As Flick's shapeless self slipped into the corridor he glanced up, startled. Without pausing, Flick slid slowly up the wall, remaining as thin and vague as possible. The badger's head swung round to peer over his shoulder, looking for the cause of the shadow. Clouds flitted across the face of the moon, casting many bizarre shapes on the walls. By the time the badger glanced back Flick had merged with the gloom of the high ceiling, becoming invisible.

Reassured by the moon shadows, Smuddy Binks crept up to the door. Immersed in the golden glow spilling from Flick's room, he stood immobile, gazing at a massive opening on the far side of the room, beyond which lay the jungle.

Smuddy Binks cantered across the star-patterned floor to the very edge of the hole. He paused and looked at what lay beyond.

A high jump, but probably not lethal if he ended up on the lilac bush that looked a softer landing than some of the rocks nearby. There might be a spell guarding the gap, but he didn't care. One brave jump would be escape or oblivion. Smuddy Binks took six steps back then sprinted at the hole. Eyes wide, legs outstretched, he launched himself into the air.

With a hard crack he crashed on to the magical glass floor.

Astounded, he looked between his paws to see only space despite standing on something very solid. He eased forward on bruised paws, testing the ground as he moved, wondering where the invisible barrier would end. What kind of magic could this be? Some form of trap? he wondered.

A soft hiss came from in front of him. He edged forward. His front paw banged into the transparent wall which rose straight up out of the floor to arch back to the solid walls of Ravenscraig.

Standing on his back legs Smuddy Binks reached up as high as he could, but the magical substance in front of him remained unforgivingly hard.

Leaden-hearted, he glared at the jungle, angry with the setback. Then the fighter in him cut in. He wasn't beaten. Not yet. 'Stick with it,' he hissed to himself through clenched teeth. 'I've not lost anything. I thought I'd cracked it; I was wrong. That's all.'

He turned his back on the glass wall and surveyed the room in front of him. The crystal wall silently spat sparks, its silvery depths constantly changing. Faint splashing came from the waterfall as it flowed through the floor.

The crystal wall looked very solid; unlikely to be a way out. He crouched on to his back paws, surveying the waterfall, wondering if it might have a cave behind it like some ordinary waterfalls. If so, it could be a hiding place until he worked out how to escape. He'd need to check it out before he searched the rest of the fortress.

As he crept towards the waterfall he heard soft animal noises coming from beyond a low wall close by. Flattening himself, he commando-crawled across the floor. Close to the wall he waited for a moment – not breathing, listening. His senses hadn't fooled him. Some of the animal voices were undoubtedly badger. Were they frightened or in pain? Even his extraordinary ears could not make sense of the words, masked by the waterfall flowing nearby.

Raising his forepaws cautiously on to the wall he peered over at the tiny world before him, astounded by the minute animals. Several of them gazed up at him.

'Are you real?' Smuddy Binks asked.

A rose flamingo looked at him scornfully. 'Of course. You?'

'Small doesn't mean imaginary, you know,' said a minuscule badger. 'Ants are real. Furthermore, I'm your size or,' he continued, eyeing Smuddy Binks up, 'perhaps a little bigger, when I'm outside Mondia.'

'You change size?'

'Of course,' replied the badger. 'We wouldn't all fit in here if we were normal size, would we?'

Smuddy Binks stared, horrified. 'Is that what happens if they catch you here? They shrink you down and imprison you?'

A larger blue-black badger said, 'Captured, my front paw. We're not trapped. We live here because we choose to. What kind of—'

'Who are you?' cut in the smaller badger. 'You're not one of us. Why don't you know anything about this compound? If Flick had brought you here to join us, you would know about Mondia. Come to think of it, have you even met Flick?'

They glared at Smuddy Binks with increasing hostility.

'He has now,' said a soft voice, as Flick reparticulated behind him.

Smuddy Binks almost jumped out of his fur. He peered around, expecting other bodies to appear out of nowhere.

Flick grinned. 'Don't be spooked. I won't hurt you. Come and see the compound with me. It's feeding time.'

'What do I do?' Smuddy Binks asked himself. If I bolt for the door I'll never make it. She could probably fell me with some sort of spell, like a flaming arrow or a badger-eating dragon. So say 'Yes.' I've nothing to lose. Also, I'll live for a bit longer.

'OK,' he agreed, heart pounding.

Flick reached up to the shelves beside Mondia. She selected a few jars, which looked as if they contained bits of dead animals, and placed them in a flat silver basket.

Perhaps that's her game, Smuddy Binks thought. In a second I'll be chopped up and tossed over the walls to the lions. If my body remains the same size when I'm chucked over I could feed every carnivore in Mondia for about a month. Smuddy Binks swallowed hard, but stood his ground. If she has already decided to kill me I'm lunch for the lions anyway, he reasoned.

'Where do you come from?' Flick asked, as she opened a jar of dead mice and started sprinkling some close to the vultures.

'Rantorf,' he said in a tight voice, mind running at the speed of a cheetah.

'Are you part of the Handeen group?'

Smuddy Binks stared at her, stunned. How could a human, even a wizardess, know any detail about badger tribal groups? Only four lived in that area, Handeen being the biggest. Tevo or Rectoria wouldn't have known that badgers even had tribes. 'Yes,' he replied.

'Are you from the North or South Bank?' called the smaller badger.

'South Bank.'

'Me also. Name is Sibik.'

'I'm Grolf,' called the large, blue-black badger.

'Smuddy Binks.'

'You and I played together as cubs,' said Sibik. 'I couldn't forget such a stupid name.'

'Thanks. Don't you have an older brother – Mullox?'

'Yup. Good memory.'

'When did you last visit Rantorf?' asked Flick, sprinkling the contents of a blue bottle on to the plains.

'Ages ago.'

'Hey, that's cold,' yelled a lion.

'Flipping freezing,' roared another.

Flick glanced down at the bottle in her hand. The label said Hail. She laughed. 'Sorry. Although it's a life experience for you. Everyone should feel ice some time, even wild kitty-cats like you. I've picked up the wrong jar. Should have been Hares.'

Smuddy Binks screwed up his face. Flick glanced across as she replaced the hail in her basket.

'All the food is magically produced. None of these 'animals' ever lived. I create them out of various plants and herbs. Go on: tell me about your early life.'

'All we did was play: in muddy tunnels, by the river, in piles of autumn leaves, eating fallen apples until our bellies ached.'

'Seems lovely. Why did you leave?'

'My grandfather's death. Savaged by pinglots.'

'How awful.'

'My childhood ended very suddenly. Reality struck. I left to seek justice for him.'

'Did you find it?'

'Yes, but the mental scars remain. Why are you asking?'

'Interested.'

'Like you believe I have feelings, or hope or even a brain? The goblins don't. They think I'm stupid.'

'Which makes them stupid, not you. Why did you come to Ravenscraig?'

Smuddy Binks panicked. He couldn't tell her. 'Sorry, I'd better go now,' he said, backing away.

'Catch you later,' yelled Grolf.

'Yeah… maybe. Bye, Grolf. Bye, Sibik.'

Sibik didn't reply. He lay snoring, stuffed with dandelion shoots, half buried in a lavender bush.

'See you again some time,' said Flick as she watched him bolt for the door.

CHAPTER 20

Smuddy Binks sprinted back the way he'd come with his mind wrenched in two directions at once. Unable to run and think at the same time, he stopped and lay under a chest of drawers to mull.

But I like Flick, he thought, but do I have good enough reason to side with her? I made a major mistake by giving loyalty too early to Tevo. Maybe I'm overreacting to the situation with the goblins, he reasoned. Maybe they don't really think I'm stupid. Perhaps if I go back and report information about Ravenscraig's floor plan they will respect me more. Once we've broken out of the castle I could sneak away, not trying to sever from them and Ravenscraig all in one go. Doing either will probably be fatal: doing both together will definitely be the end for me.

'Well done, Smuddy Binks,' he imagined them saying. 'You've been amazingly brave.'

Mentally propped up by the vision, he made his way to the kitchen. As he squeezed back through the hatch, the goblins and animals stopped talking. Cold eyes turned to stare at him.

'Where have you been?' shot out Tevo, the icy hardness of steel in his voice.

Rectoria crossed the room to grab Smuddy Binks by one ear. Viciously, painfully, she shook him. 'Who said you could go?'

Smuddy Binks glared back at their hostile, suspicious faces. Hatred of all of them cascaded through his mind like a shower of fire. Anger washed out reason. He opened his muzzle to yelp out a stream of abuse.

He caught Hebor's smirk. This was exactly what that filthy dog wanted: Smuddy Binks to be suffering and in serious danger. A few unwise angry words would be followed by the smell of roasting badger. Smuddy Binks's mind cleared, as if a freezing wind had blown through his head. He let his body sag, head droop.

'My ear,' he squealed, overplaying the pain. 'Please let me go.'

Rectoria shook him even harder. 'No chance. Where did you go?'

'I went to the main part of the house. Spying.'

'What, you, a stupid badger?' asked Tevo. 'Snooping? What exactly did you hope to learn?'

Smuddy Binks tried to wrench away out of Rectoria's grip. Her nails dug in harder, blood welling up where the ragged tips had cut into his flesh as he pulled away. Smuddy Binks stopped struggling as it increased the pain.

'I thought I could find out who was here and how many guards... ' His voice tailed off as he looked at their stony faces.

'Crass idiot,' spat out Rectoria, taking his other ear and shaking his whole head violently.

'Stop. It feels like my brain is banging around inside my skull.'

Rectoria continued to shake him. 'You could have blown our cover. It has cost us much to get this far. We'll not have it all thrown away by an insignificant fur ball like you.' Rectoria flung him across the kitchen, as if she were a shot-putter.

Smuddy Binks crashed into the stone wall. Agony shot through his head as points of white light floated across his darkened vision. The animals' laughter seemed to be coming from a long distance away.

He shook his head to clear his mind, but only made himself want to hurl. He swallowed hard and took a couple of deep slow breaths. Gradually his vision cleared, although his skull still felt as if it had been cut in half with a meat cleaver.

The other animals stared at Smuddy Binks. Not one had lifted a paw to help him, not even Grut. Each was probably suspicious because he'd escaped: each grateful that it wasn't them in Rectoria's firing line, he reasoned. He felt that by lying he had already betrayed the pack. This gave him a swell of pride.

A faint smile hovered at the corners of Hebor's mouth, as if he was loving seeing another animal suffer. Smuddy Binks held his gaze and let his hatred of the dog cascade through him, hardening his heart. It was exactly the spur he needed to keep his mind focused on pretending to still be loyal, although he was dying to bury his right front paw into Hebor's smug face.

Whining, he started again. 'But I wasn't caught, and I did find some information.'

'Yeah, sure. Like where to find some edible food, I hope,' said Rycant.

Everybody laughed.

It seemed impossible to believe, Smuddy Binks thought. Hours before we were comrades – brothers in arms – a team. Now, with minimal encouragement from Tevo and a faint whiff of suspicion, they are ready to ridicule me, to stand back and watch me suffer. Right. I'm on Flick's side now, but I'll be dead if they know. Keep acting.

'So what did you find out?' Tevo dropped his mirthless laughter like a mask. 'Not that it's going to help us.'

'Not very much,' muttered Smuddy Binks, keeping his face bland and stupid.

'How many soldiers did you see?' barked out Rectoria.

'None,' he replied. Instantly, he realised that this didn't help Flick. He added, 'You see, I crawled under a chest of drawers and fell asleep.' He looked round at the other faces as if seeking understanding. Stony eyes met his own.

Hebor's malicious smile deepened. 'You must be either lazy or stupid to doze off on when spying.'

'Both,' Rycant replied, laughing.

'Is that all you have to report?' growled Rectoria, grabbing his ear again like a clamp.

'Yes,' replied Smuddy Binks, allowing genuine pain to show in his face. 'I suppose it is.' He dropped his gaze, silent.

Rectoria hung on, digging her nails in harder. 'Obey or die,' she hissed at him. Letting go, she aimed a kick at Arnak and Ferox who were watching the display of emotional fireworks. 'Get out of my way. I want that spot.'

Leaping to their feet, the foxes sloped off, glaring at the badger. Smuddy Binks slunk away to a dark corner where he could lie undisturbed. He pressed one of his aching ears to the cool floor, mind in overdrive, working out how he could help Flick.

Two floors above them, Flick watched their conversation on her crystal. As Smuddy Binks lied about falling asleep under a chest of drawers she knew that he was protecting her, hiding the fact that they'd met. Could he now be her ally, ready to betray the other side? she wondered. But she couldn't yet trust him. After all, he'd probably set off round the castle spying. If he was now on her side, he might turn back again.

'Extalo.'

The crystal went blank. Flick sank to the floor and sat cross-legged, thinking. She'd seen Smuddy Binks emerging from the log store hatch into the kitchen as she had switched the crystal back on. Presumably he had gone back the way he had escaped. The opening was fairly small – but if a largish badger could get through, doubtless several of the other animals could – including the foxes, though not the goblins. She needed the door to be guarded immediately.

Swiftly she went and scanned Mondia for Benix. The white Pyrenean mountain dog lay on a lush emerald mountainside chatting to two turquoise curly-horned rams. As he saw Flick's hand reaching down to him he stood up and stretched.

'It seems I'm off.'

'No problem,' replied the older ram. 'See you later.'

From the perspective of his present size Flick's fingers seemed to be those of a particularly tall giant. The vast hand approached, blotting out the sun, throwing Benix and the goats into deep shadow. Two massive fingers dropped a small bubble over Benix, then whisked him into the sky. He felt an amazing rush, like being launched into space.

A few seconds later he landed on Flick's bedroom carpet. Flick popped the bubble, reversing the weightlessness spell; Benix sprang to full size. Waist height, solid muscle, he leapt at Flick, knocking her flat. Planting his feet either side of her, Benix licked her face with his great wet rasping tongue.

'No time for a cuddle,' said Flick, failing to push the ninety-kilo dog away. 'This is an emergency.'

'Excellent.'

She wrapped her arms round his warm soft neck to pull herself back up to sitting. 'I need you savage, not friendly.'

'How's this?' He bared his teeth, planted his feet, his tail straight up. From deep inside his barrel chest rose a menacing growl.

'Perfect.'

With a snap of her fingers his silky white fur changed to spiky dark brown and his eyes became red. Benix sloped across to the mirror. As he admired himself, Flick explained about the goblins, including how a badger had already gained access to the main house.

'Guard the log chute. Let no one escape through it. I'll show you the target.' She instructed the crystal wall, 'Pictal kitchen.'

The silver-blue crystal clouded, flickered silver sparks – then cleared, displaying an empty room.

Horrified, she called urgently, 'Pictal intruders.'

The screen split into several pictures: Tevo aiming for Zorrin's study; Rectoria running towards the basement; the other animals scattering as they crept softly round Ravenscraig.

Flick felt as if her heart had fallen like a brick into her stomach. 'They've escaped.'

'Didn't you lock them in?'

'Yes, but only with a key. Their magic must be more powerful than I'd thought.'

She took his muzzle in her hands, holding his face close to hers. 'The situation is grave. The goblins must be stopped at all costs. I'll tackle the goblins: you deal with the rest. Trap but don't kill the badgers. One may be on our side. Find Myth.'

'I'll work alone. Keep the kitty.' The massive dog bounded off.

'I need Myth. The battle has begun.'

CHAPTER 21

At Makusha, black clouds hung in thick banks, chucking out snow and hail. Bitter wind slammed around the side of the mountain, flinging splinters of ice into the faces of the group struggling up from the modo. Craggy slate-grey rocks jutted out of the deep snow, razor-sharp edges clawing at the sky. No sheltering tree broke the landscape. Zorrin's use of the word inhospitable was proving to be a massive understatement.

Alex trudged with his eyes screwed up against the wind, his field of vision down to narrow slits. Even so, his eyeballs stung unbearably, as if they were rough metal marbles rammed into his head. His ears felt like frozen lumps of flesh attached painfully to his skull. Yet his body remained warm, thanks to Zorrin's magic. Unfortunately Zorrin hadn't been able to make a seal round their heads, as they would have suffocated.

'Alive and cold,' he'd said as they set out, 'Is better than warm but dying.'

Stating the obvious had earned him a thump on the shoulder. The retaliatory cuff on the head had nearly started a war as Myth piled in, until Tariq had pointed out that they were trying to save Eridor – so shouldn't they get going?

Setting off from the Modo had been awful, but the further they'd climbed up Makusha's flank, the worse the conditions had become. Within a half-hour's trudge, the wind had stiffened up into a blizzard.

Beside their narrow path the ground fell in a sheer cliff on to vicious pointed rocks hundreds of metres below. On the other side, the mountain face rose steeply.

'See that ledge above us?' asked Skoodle.

Yup, transferred Alex.

'Packed with snow.'

Yup.

'Ripe for an avalanche.'

Which could be set off by sound. Which is why I'm not talking.

Oh. Something funny, by the way. Check out Zorrin.

Pulling his foot out of another deep snow hole Alex paused and glanced across to Zorrin, whose long hair was tumbling down his back encased in ice as if it were a frozen waterfall. *Too cold to laugh.*

Sherpa. Sherp quicker or we'll freeze.

Snail pace is max. Want to walk?

Thanks, but no.

'This is not so bad,' said Ikara from the ground near Alex's feet.

Alex halted and stared at her. *How anyone could describe this as anything less than horrendous?*

No wind at snake height: heated snow proof cap; great spells from Zorrin, returned Skoodle. *Not so terrific for us.*

Some reptiles get all the luck, replied Alex, as hail hammered on to his head.

And food, Skoodle added, as a fat snow beetle veered into Ikara's path. *That stupid creature will make a tasty snake-snack.*

Ikara's tongue snapped out and coiled around the beetle, but the wet tip of it froze to the ice. As she yanked to rip it away, the force of her contraction whipped her body forward. She landed sprawling on the side of the path. The beetle slid from beneath the loop of tongue and scuttled off behind a rock.

'Help me,' Ikara said. 'My tongue ith thtuck.'

Zorrin stopped and looked back. *'Relashio velk.'*

The tip of Ikara's tongue began to steam then flew off the ice, whipping backwards like released elastic. There was a small crack as tongue met teeth at speed.

'Death to all beetles,' she said, pushing her cap back in place with her tail. 'And if any of you laugh… '

'No. Serious business,' said Zorrin, the creases at the sides of his eyes deepening. Tariq turned round with Keeko to stare at the landscape. Alex bit his lip hard. But in Alex's pocket a hamster lay on his back kicking his legs and whooping with laughter, tears streaming down his furry face, thoughts suddenly blocked.

'Onwards,' said Zorrin. Alex could have sworn that there was a smile buried in the long wizard beard, but his tone was serious.

Ikara glanced suspiciously at him, unsure whether to believe the serious tone of his voice or the lines beside his eyes. Pursing her lips in irritation, she set off at a fast slither. Raising his eyebrows and grinning back at the others, Zorrin walked off after her.

Skoodle's voice floated up to Alex. 'Thtupid thnake.'

Trudging onwards, Alex leaned into the wind, trying to keep to Zorrin's tracks. At each step, he sank up to his knees in the snow. Each leg had to be wrenched out before he could attempt another achingly slow pace forward.

We may not make it, Alex transferred to Skoodle. *I'm exhausted.*

You've dealt with more difficult stuff, like running from crocodiles.

Marginally worse. Must lie down for a bit. Halting, he transferred to Zorrin, *Can we rest for a bit?*

Deeply unwise. We'll freeze to death if we stop moving, despite the spells.

But the snow looks so soft and comfortable… it might be warmer than you'd think. I'll try it out for all of us.

As Alex's knees started to sag Zorrin cut in, *Keep going. There's a cave ahead. We'll shelter there. You're getting a soggy brain. Snow fever.*

Sharp hamster claws dug into him. *Keep walking or I'll savage you.*

Alex lifted a heavy leg, staggering forward, mind slightly focused by the pain of eighteen claws. Five minutes later they found the cave. They stumbled through the tall oval entrance into a wide tunnel. Icy wind roared past the opening but could not touch them. Alex leaned against the cold rock wall, eyes closed, panting. The lack of hail stinging his face and head-freezing ache felt blissful.

'Follow me,' said Zorrin, lighting a small fire in the palm of one hand. 'We'll move down the tunnel, then I'll make a hot drink before we go back out.'

The relief that Alex had been feeling blew away in a sudden rush of irritation at the whole wizarding world. Why did it have to be so tough? He'd done nothing bad, yet now he had to fight to save his and his friends' lives. Why did they all have to wade through a spine-chilling blizzard? It was ridiculous that the Xo force stopped them transparticulating into the mountain. There had to be another way. Anything had to be better than tramping through this horrendous storm.

Zorrin reached into his robes and brought out a large steaming mug of hot chocolate.

'Looks terrific,' said Keeko, snatching it from Zorrin.

Feeling even more irritable at Keeko getting hers first, Alex took the next one and drank deeply. At the first gulp he could feel warmth cascading through his body, like a warm balloon bursting inside him.

'Snow fever gone?' asked Zorrin, handing out drinks to the others.

'That desire to lie down, whatever the cost? The foul mood? Yes, both gone. How did it happen?'

'Your brain got cold. It happens more to humans than other animals except toads, which have been known to lie down and die in relatively mild hailstorms.'

'Yummy,' murmured Ikara. 'Frozen toad.'

'No. This must be better,' whispered Skoodle, voice thick with contentment. 'Chocolatably wonderful.'

'Fabulous,' Keeko murmured, licking chocolate off the fur round her mouth.

'Ice,' said Alex, relaxing.

Zorrin raised his eyebrows. 'Steaming hot? Warm?'

Wrapping his fingers more tightly around his cup, Alex replied, 'About seventy-five degrees Celsius.'

'Seventy-one, but close,' said Zorrin, taking a long drink.

'Whatever.' Alex couldn't argue. All the fight had gone out of him. He felt like a boneless body bag, unable to think or reason, capable only of the sensation of molten pleasure.

Zorrin waved his free hand in an arc, murmuring a few words, then sat down on air.

Mug in hand, Keeko scampered across and sat next to him. 'Clever,' she said.

'Basic structural spell, which is one of the five divisions of magic.' Zorrin pointed to the air next to each one then added, 'Go on, sit down. Now you've all got a seat.'

Alex sat, finding the air solid yet soft – like a cushion, but warm. Ikara curled up, head lolling over the edge of her pillow, drinking from a low wide bowl on the ground in front of her.

'Tongue OK, Ikara?' asked Zorrin, a half smile playing on his lips.

'Fine,' she replied, licking her mouth. 'Pity none of you bothered to grab that insolent insect. It would have gone well with this: beetle dunked in chocolate.'

After a few minutes Alex found that the ice in his hair was melting, trickling down his neck. He leaned forward and put both hands in his sandy blond hair, scruffing it up, shaking out the water like a dog.

'Hey, stop,' said Skoodle. 'You're getting me wet.'

'Sorry. It works fine on the beach.'

Skoodle shook his head. 'Location malfunction.'

Zorrin rose, holding his cup flat on the palm of his hand. He raised an eyebrow at it. The cup vanished. From inside his robes he pulled a long yellow parchment and smoothed it flat on to an air table. With a leather-clad finger, he pointed at the map of Makusha. 'We're at this point. Following this narrow path, we need to get a kilometre further around the mountain.' Zorrin indicated a thin dotted line. 'The rock sides above and below us will be vertical, but we'll probably be safe.'

'Probably is not comforting,' said Skoodle. 'How about definitely or undeniably?'

'Take your pick. Both are wrong.' Zorrin folded the map. 'Onwards.'

Involuntarily, Alex shuddered.

'Not you, Alex, nor Keeko,' said Zorrin, placing a hand on their shoulders. 'We'll go on alone and collect you on the way back.'

'No way,' Alex said, getting to his feet. 'I'm part of the expedition too. I'm coming.'

'And me,' said Keeko, standing up on her cushion and glaring at Zorrin. 'I'm going to the centre of this mountain or dying in the attempt.'

'It's better that you don't,' said Zorrin, his tone gentle. 'You're already weakened and exhausted. If Alex gets snow fever again it will be a disaster. The others will be fine. Tariq is built for these conditions; I have made Ikara impervious.'

Keeko started hopping up and down. 'But—'

'No buts. It could wreck the whole expedition. There's no point in taking the risk, Keeko. It'll be safer if we remain in groups.'

'Alex and Skoodle are a group,' said Keeko. 'I'm coming.'

'It's better that you stay, Keeko,' said Tariq, crouching to place an enormous arm around her shoulders. 'If we needed an extra fighter we'd take you – but this is only information gathering: speaking with stone, gossiping with granite, reminiscing with rock.'

Keeko looked into his deep brown eyes. 'You sure?'

'Never been more positive.'

'Nor more negative about the weather. Odd combo,' commented Ikara. 'Totally positive plus totally negative. That makes you an emotional blank.'

'Watch the compliments,' said Tariq, rising, 'or I may never get my swollen head back out of this tunnel. Ready, Ikara?'

'Suppose so. I'm so going to keep this spell once we're off this living rock brain.'

'It's a very difficult hex,' said Zorrin, as he glanced over at the snow drifting at the end of the tunnel. 'It took some time to make as well as a wad of mental effort. Enjoy it while it lasts.'

'Or while I last,' she said. 'We may yet die on this mountain with its meteorological black curse.'

Tariq grinned. 'Optimism will get you everywhere. Ever tried it?'

'No. I'm giving it up.'

'You can't give up something that you've never tried,' said Tariq.

139

'Watch me. Learn a life lesson. Welcome to ultra-cerebration theory.'

'Theory is fine. What about practical applications?'

'Practical ultra-cerebration? Look, if I'm inventing something I'll make up what I like. I didn't create a practical bit.'

Tariq set off towards the mouth of the tunnel, Ikara beside him. 'Let's define ultra-cerebration... '

Alex felt a surge of loyalty as he watched his friends forcing their way into the storm, tackling this elephantine task: protecting Keeko, Skoodle and himself, yet not making a big thing out of it. The credit-rating of favours lay heavily against him. He'd have to do a whole heap of rescuing them all to get even.

CHAPTER 22

Once the others had vanished into the swirl of white Alex felt suddenly deflated. All the adrenaline of fighting had evaporated, wiped out by inactivity. A valve seemed to have opened in his head, draining all positive emotion. Was he being weak? Should he have insisted on going? But if Zorrin was their leader, shouldn't he listen to him?

Hands sunk deep in pockets, he kicked a stone along the tunnel, stubbing his toe. 'We've got to do something. We'll go crazy otherwise.'

Skoodle curled up on his air cushion. 'Nothing to do.'

'OK. Crazy it is.' Alex sat on the cold stone floor, back against the tunnel wall, waiting.

Eventually they heard Zorrin via the orgreeb. 'We've reached the main cave, thank the stars. What's that, Ikara? No, I agree, it's not exactly dry – but at least it's out of the storm.'

They heard Zorrin clearing his throat, then his voice rang back clearly in their orgreebs. 'I am Zorrin. Speak to me please, Makusha.'

Silently they waited but there was no response.

'Come on, Makusha,' hissed Skoodle. 'Answer the wizard, like a nice mountain.'

'Makusha, I beseech you. Give me a sign that you hear,' called Zorrin.

'Why doesn't he answer?' Alex asked, pacing up and down the tunnel. 'There's nowhere else to go to find out what we need. He's got to speak.'

'Makusha – can you hear me?' called Zorrin.

Keeko sat with her back to the wall, playing with her tail. 'Not having fun.'

'This mountain has made idiots of us,' said Skoodle. 'It's either only a lump of stone or, if it's alive, it's sulking. Or do mountains sleep?'

'Makusha,' shouted Zorrin, Tariq and Ikara calling with him. 'This is a disaster. No answer means we're dead meat. Witch fodder.' Alex banged his fist into his hand, body rigid with frustration. 'Makusha, listen to us,' he yelled.

The floor of the tunnel began to tremble until the whole mountain seemed to be moving. Boulders crashed to the floor, missing them by inches. A long chasm opened in the roof immediately above their heads, pouring out a heavy shower of small stones which battered their heads and shoulders.

'What's happening?' shouted Keeko.

'Rock rage,' Alex yelled back. 'Makusha must be furious. We've got to get out or we'll be crushed.'

He rammed Skoodle into his pocket and grabbed Keeko, pulling her to his chest. Pounded by a hail of pebbles, he clambered over rubble, dodging the bigger rocks. Keeko gripped him tightly round his torso as Skoodle muttered to Uncle Toomba.

Into the earthquake boomed a deep low voice, seemingly coming from all directions at once. 'I am used to being addressed with respect, not irritation.'

'I'm sorry, sir,' shouted Alex, halting. 'But Zorrin had called you and you didn't answer.'

'Zorrin is with you?'

'Yes,' shouted Keeko, nodding frantically, not knowing if the mountain could see her.

The boulders stopped falling. Clouds of grey dust rose from the piles of freshly-hewn rock littering the cave. Alex pulled his shirt over his mouth to avoid inhaling the thick air. Coughing, Keeko grabbed a fold of material and held it over her nose – her eyes above it wide.

Before Alex had had a chance to stop coughing long enough to speak again, Zorrin's voice echoed back. 'Makusha, I call you.'

'I can hear you now,' the mountain growled back. 'But your voices are very faint. Zorrin, welcome.'

'Thank you. We have brought gifts for you: a staff of light and fire, Queen Rak-hi-eda's wedding pearl and some cabivitrim.'

'I need no such gifts. It's kind of you, but please keep them. Why did you come here?'

'We need information, knowing your memory is without equal. But before you tell us anything – could you be heard outside these caves? Our enemies might be close.'

The great rumbling voice came again. 'It's not possible for evil ones to penetrate here. Should they try to enter, the Xo force would attack them like a tornado. Flung back out into the storm, limbs shattered, they would die like dogs in the blood-freezing snow. The only danger is from one who might change sides in the future. If there is no potential turncoat among you, I can speak plainly.' The shuddering echoes of the deep voice died away.

'All my companions are loyal,' replied Zorrin. 'Each has a reason to hate the evil forces. Tariq, Ikara and Keeko fought loyally for our side during the Battle of Gelforth. Alex and Skoodle helped them rescue me from Karlan.'

'Then I can speak freely. What do you need to know?'

'Why would Virida be prepared to kill to get the Sapphire of Akan? Where can we find it?'

Alex paused just inside the mouth of the tunnel, close enough to feel the icy blast of the wind. 'We'll hang on here,' he murmured. 'But be ready – I may yet jettison us out into the storm if the earthquake restarts.'

'The sapphire holds the power to command nature: the wind listens to its owner, as do the seasons. Its true resting place is here, deep in my heart. About a hundred years ago, a wizard stole the sapphire.'

'How did he get in?' asked Zorrin. 'What about the mighty Xo force?'

'Tarver's mind had been pure when he entered my walls, so he escaped the Xo. He had intended to use the sapphire to bring a halt to the devastating hurricanes which were sweeping Eridor at that time – destroying homes, farms, creating a famine. Yet the sapphire's power of corruption is so great that it warped him within hours, the power eating his soul. Few may handle the stone and live: Tarver died within weeks of stealing it.'

Fascinated, Alex forgot the bitter cold of the wind in his face and the pain from his torn hands. 'But why would possession of power make you die?'

'From the greed that comes with it: the loss of all true core values such as loyalty, honesty and trust. In the power struggle that invariably follows, faithful friends turn against each other, becoming the bitterest of enemies. Brothers turn against sisters, children against their parents. Inevitably, murder follows. The stone has passed down through the years on a river of blood. Very few have lived more than two or three years in possession of the sapphire; some only hours. All have kept it a deep secret.'

'Why all the secrecy?' asked Skoodle. 'Why not boast about it? I'd tell the world if I had found the sapphire.'

'Then you'd be attacked by powerful alchemists, evil wizards and great warriors. Secrecy is security. Over the years almost all those who have seen it have died, so that now most believe it to be only a legend; a tale told by white-haired old men over an evening fire.'

'Amazing story,' Keeko said, yawning.

'Yet a prophecy says that one day the stone will be returned to its true cradle. Then the deep magic will keep the stone undisturbed forever. Nature will then be free to return to her natural cycles. The wind would once again blow in response to the cloudy heavens, not to keep me incarcerated and alone. Didn't you think it odd that there's a snowstorm so close to the jungle?'

'I suppose it is strange,' said Zorrin. 'However, it's been like this for so long that I didn't question it.'

'This blizzard has lasted for over a hundred years. The keepers of the sapphire keeps it this way, so reaching me is almost impossible, thus stopping anyone getting my help in finding the stone or even confirming its existence. No mortal could have made it to my head without a powerful wizard.'

Tariq's voice cut in. 'We've made a pact with Virida to hand the stone over to her. If we don't, she'll kill us.'

The rumbling grew louder again. Enormous tremors rocked the stone walls.

'Then you must die. If the witch obtains the stone, massive bloodshed will follow,' growled Makusha. 'You must find the sapphire then bring it to me. Preventing such major destruction will far outweigh the loss of your few lives.'

'Great,' said Skoodle. 'Injury, pain, freezing and near death – and now we're going to die anyway. Today really isn't turning out well.'

'I accept that I must die,' said Tariq, voice calm. 'I'll do all I can to regain the sapphire – but for the forces of good, not for Virida. The others may dissolve our pact now if they choose. They needn't fight to regain the sapphire knowing they'll die. I can undertake this quest alone. If they want to find it to save their skins by giving it to her, our pact must be dissolved, our paths must separate.'

'The pact stands. I fight with you whatever the cost,' stated Ikara.

'And me,' said Keeko.

'Slight problem here,' murmured Skoodle. 'When we made the pact, staying alive was a possible option. Bit of a no-win situation now.'

'I'm not going to give the sapphire to Virida. My parents fought against her; possibly died fighting,' said Alex. 'The group can count on my loyalty and, presumably, my death.'

Skoodle sighed. 'Then me too. Otherwise it's a waste of an episode of near freezing. Uncle Toomba, prepare for a reunion.'

Makusha began speaking again. 'The stone is with the serpent Hypnos, who lives in the Caves of Desdea. One wizard alone has ever managed to map these caves and return alive: Brinstaller. The only possible way to get to Hypnos is to find the single remaining copy of his ancient map.'

'Where is it likely to be?' asked Zorrin.

'At Ravenscraig, sent there many years ago for safe keeping. Our ally was killed on the mission but he had taken steps to ensure that the map ended up in your possession, whatever his fate. Being so heavily disguised, you would not have recognised the map for what it was.'

'We'll return at once. One more question before we go. An evil force possesses my cat. Can you tell me how to overcome the force within him without killing Clawds?'

'The smooth white rocks on this chamber floor will cut off an evil power flow or divert it. They may save your cat. Call on one of the jagged black ones if you need my help. I'll do what I can. Take some of each.'

'A rock to call for a rock. Seems reasonable,' muttered Skoodle, as Alex started gathering rocks and stuffing them into his pockets.

'Also, the small blue flowers that grow in the meadow beyond the snow will heal any injury while life is still present, if used by one who has the healing force. Flick is such; one of you may be another.'

'I hope it's me,' whispered Keeko.

'As you leave, an eagle – Fernando – will land close by. Take from his wings two feathers, no more. They will aid you.'

'What will the eagle feathers do?' asked Tariq, passing rocks to Zorrin for storage.

'The magic is variable, but help will appear in some form. Some advice: in future call me from where the monkey stands, in my hearing area, not from where you are now.'

'Any more info about finding the map or the sapphire?' asked the silky voice of Ikara. 'Presumably each is well hidden. Wild guess... probably right.'

'I can't help with either. You must rely on your own wit and powers for this quest.'

'Thank you, O Great One,' said Zorrin. 'We must leave at once.'

'It's you who are the powerful one,' the deep voice replied. 'I have mass and memory. You are great in magic, deed and courage. I salute you.'

'Until we meet again, goodbye,' said Zorrin. He looked around the cavern, a flickering torch above his head. 'Everything's just fallen into place. The great white columns at the front; the slimy floor beneath; the flat red rock stretching backwards, disappearing back like a slide. We're in the mouth of the mountain. The others must be in the ear. I must modify my map.'

The journey back down was deeply punishing. On the way up they'd had a purpose carrying them through the snow and driving hail. Now, although they had achieved what they had set out to do, the mood was funereal: all hope shattered. The death sentence could never be lifted.

After a long weary tramp they dropped low enough to reach the treeline. A few straggling evergreens appeared; scrawny branches bowed under the battering of the wind.

'These trees look dead,' Skoodle said to Alex. 'Like we'll be fairly soon.'

'Not helpful.'

'Just planning my short future. How do you think she'll kill us?'

'Thunderbolt? Poison? Chucked to a pet shark?'

'No chance of gorging ourselves to death on chocolate?'

'None.'

After a while the temperature began to rise – the visibility clearing, the snowdrifts melting into thick sludge. Sheltered by the thicker trees, the group was no longer battered by the wind.

'Look. The blue flowers.' Keeko jumped off Tariq's back and ran towards the clumps of flowers, which glowed with an inner light.

'Everybody pick some. Alex and I will store them with the stones,' said Zorrin, reaching for a largish group.

High above them a golden-bronze eagle hovered on an updraught, sky riding, gradually circling lower. The broad wings held him suspended on the thermals until he finally landed on a grey granite rock, cruel hunter's talons outspread.

Skoodle squealed as Zorrin walked towards the immense bird with its long curved beak.

'Greetings, Fernando,' Zorrin said. 'Makusha told us to request two feathers.'

The eagle nodded. Zorrin took a step closer, keeping eye contact with the magnificent creature. 'Are you able to tell us the secret of your feathers?'

'They have many secrets,' said Fernando, his voice deep and melodic. 'All of which you'll have to discover for yourselves, for in no one's hands are they the same. My advice is this: whenever you're in dire need, call on the feathers. Their powers will aid you somehow.'

With care Zorrin reached forward and plucked two feathers, choosing ones which were slightly longer than the rest, standing out from the eagle's wing.

'You have chosen well. There are troubled times ahead. Yet we will meet again before peace returns.'

'Is that hope or an ability to predict the future?' asked Tariq.

The eagle gazed at the bear, a half smile on his face. 'If anyone believed that I could read the future, my freedom would be in extreme danger. When we do meet again, it will be an amazing coincidence.'

Turning his beak to the wind, Fernando stretched upwards. Wings extended, he caught an air current, rising majestically. Climbing into the cloudy blue skies, he beat to the north.

'So handsome,' said Keeko, watching him go, a wistful look in her eyes.

Thanks, transferred back a deep voice. *Also married.*

CHAPTER 23

Pounding down a scree slope, the group was carried by momentum, each footfall creating small rock slides. On a high, they finally halted on a large plateau at the base of Makusha.

Alex bent over to brace his arms against his thighs, dragging air into his aching lungs.

'An hour's walk to the modo,' said Zorrin, gasping. 'Blast the Xo force. Wish we could disparticulate now. You hungry?'

'Ravenous,' said Skoodle, climbing out of Alex's shirt.

'From all this pocket-riding exercise?'

'No, from mental exercise. All the time you're only charging around, I'm thinking.'

They all sagged to the ground. Alex rolled on to his back, arm across his eyes. 'What a foul day. I'm still no closer to finding out about my parents and now I never will be.'

Skoodle scrambled up to sit in the middle of Alex's forehead, forcing him to close his eyes or go cross-eyed. 'Negativity's a mental mudbath. It'll suck all happiness in. Do something. Jive. Eat. Don't dwell.'

'How long have you had a degree in psychology?'

'About four minutes. Self-awarded for particular brilliance.'

Zorrin seated himself cross-legged on a mound of air, holding his hand over a flat stone. Pale lilac fire sprang up from the rocky surface, crackling and hissing. Zorrin pulled a stick from inside his shirt, placing it over the fire. It popped open into a wok. From a pocket he produced a bag of what appeared to be green candyfloss and threw a tuft of it into the pan. A fountain of thick green liquid spurted up from the bottom, filling the wok to the brim.

'Cream of vegetable soup? Or something else? Carrot?' Zorrin waved his hand across the pan. The soup turned bright orange.

'Beetroot, maybe?' asked Keeko, swinging down to sit beside him.

The contents of the pan turned deep purple. With no real desire for anything different, but wanting to see it change again, Alex suggested tomato. In a snap, the soup changed to brilliant red.

'Perhaps all of them?' Zorrin motioned his hand once more. The pan now held four colours in gently bubbling quarters, multicoloured steam wafting from its surface.

'We'll need something to eat with it.' Zorrin glanced at some pods on a nearby bush. 'These look about ripe.' He raised an eyebrow at them.

The pods started to swell. After quadrupling in size, they burst open with a little pop. At the heart of each was a small, warm loaf of bread.

'Pick some,' Zorrin said. 'They'll be delicious.'

Cautiously Keeko put a paw out for one then put it to her nose, sniffing. 'It smells fantastic.'

'Clever,' said Ikara, reaching out her tail.

Zorrin shrugged. 'Easy. Wizard-cub stuff.'

In minutes each had a bowl of soup and a few rolls. Alex could feel strength pouring back into his tired limbs as warm purple liquid coursed down his throat. Finally full, he pushed his bowl away and lay flat on his back in the thick grass.

An irritating whistling noise, getting louder each second, broke the contented silence. A silver ball propelled by a column of air blasted through the leaves, aiming straight for Tariq.

'Look out,' yelled Alex.

As Tariq hit the ground, the ball swept sharply over his head in a neat S bend. The air stream died, depositing the missile at Zorrin's feet. Intrigued, Alex sat up.

'It will be from Flick. Only Ravenscraig uses souvents. It must be urgent.'

Zorrin yanked the wok from the fire then flung the ball into the blaze. Out of the core of the flames rose a dramatic series of images: a dramatic pageant of what had happened recently at Ravenscraig.

'Why can't we see Flick?' asked Keeko.

'Everything was recorded through her eyes and ears, replayed by her memory,' replied Zorrin, eyes fixed on the images before him. 'That's why we can hear her voice more clearly than those of the others.' His face looked grave as the scenes continued. 'I recognise that evil goblin, Tevo.'

As the image of the Live Wizard's List appeared they heard Flick's voice, 'The situation is critical, Zorrin. Come now if you can.'

Zorrin sprang to his feet, his mood streak sparking red. 'Back to the modo. Run.'

'The black stones,' said Tariq, grabbing Zorrin's shirt. 'They might harness or overcome the Xo so we can transparticulate back to the castle.'

'Worth a go,' replied Zorrin. He pulled one of the pebbles out of an inner pocket. 'Hold on to my shirt.'

Each grabbed a handful of black silky cloth, Ikara grasping a fold in her mouth.

'Disparticulate us to Ravenscraig,' Zorrin told the rock.

The grassy plateau began to fade. Elfin music, like distant high-pitched pipes, filled the air. A turquoise mist engulfed them. The trees nearby grew shadowy, the ground less solid – until they were suspended weightless in space. Slowly the haze cleared as they appeared in the front hall of Ravenscraig. Their feet came to rest on cold stone. Alex started to pull away.

Zorrin grabbed his arm. 'Don't move yet. If you interrupt reparticulation you may remain always partly in shadow. Many ghosts are not the dead, but the result of such interruptions.'

The high-pitched music faded to a whisper, then vanished as they became totally solid. Zorrin replaced the rock inside his cloak, pulling up his sleeve to reveal his wrist crystal.

'Show me Flick.'

The crystal revealed Flick sprinting along the corridor outside the dungeons, black and gold hair streaming out behind her.

'Alive, by the stars. Show me the invaders.'

Several pictures emerged: Rectoria prowling in the underground labyrinth at the east end of the castle; Tevo creeping up the main stairs, heading for the study; Benix growling at Grut, who lay cowering under a chest on one of the second-floor landings; Smuddy Binks in a bedroom above the kitchen; the foxes Arnak and Ferox padding along a corridor, as Hebor aimed for the laboratories.

'We need to split up. I'll get Tevo,' said Zorrin. 'Ikara, can you take on the badger in the bedroom?'

'Certainly,' hissed Ikara. 'A badger against a snake – no contest.' She slipped from the room.

'Keeko, go and help Flick. Tell her Rectoria's location. Help her neutralise that vicious she-devil of a goblin.'

'Excellent,' said Keeko, jaw set. 'She tried to kill Tariq at Gelforth. It's payback time.' She loped after Ikara.

'Tariq, can you deal with the dog near the labs? If I'm right, it's Hebor. He has no magic, unlike Rycant, but he's a fierce fighter. Kill if you have to.'

'Consider it done,' said Tariq, rising to stand upright: solid, muscular, menacing. He sprinted out, claws bared.

'That leaves you with the foxes. OK?'

Alex nodded, throat dry, palms sweaty, wondering how to deal barehanded with angry warrior foxes. He set off at a run, aiming towards the west corridor, a rhythmical thudding against his leg from the box in his pocket. Then it sank in. Cabivitrim: potential weapon. He stopped.

'What are you doing?'

'Getting armed.' Alex pulled on the golden glove.

'Nothing more vicious than a fighter with a hand warmer.'

'It's all we've got.'

'We've also got my vivid imagination and currently I see the foxes ripping into your neck then blood gushing down your chest as your life flows out of you.'

'Where will you be while I'm dying?'

'Floating in a fox's stomach acid on the way to Toomba.'

'Bite the fox for me as you go down his throat. Might distract him.'

Glove in place, Alex sprinted on, feeling it was best to get the fight over with whatever the result. Rounding a corner, he came upon Ferox standing in the centre of the hall, teeth bared, snarling. Alex stopped, focusing his mind.

The fox was much bigger than Alex had assumed, standing about the size of a husky. Cabivitrim now seemed inadequate for the job – and a double-edged sword. If he got stuck to one of the foxes he'd be ripped apart.

Keeping eye contact with the fox in the hope that showing no fear would delay an attack, Alex edged open the box, his palm sweating inside the golden glove. He took out one green ball. Warm, squishy and disgusting, it smelled like pond slime.

Ferox stood, head up, body taut – as if his muscles were on standby. Alex took aim and threw.

The fox ducked. The green squidge whistled past his shoulder to land on the carpet some feet beyond. Ferox didn't turn his head to see where the missile had ended up, keeping his eyes on Alex.

Grabbing another jelly ball, Alex recalculated where to aim. Lower down the body would make the glue less easy to dodge. With a quick snap of his elbow Alex hurled the next cabivitrim at Ferox.

'Missed by less,' said Skoodle, chin on the edge of his pocket. 'Almost encouraging.'

With focus born of desperation Alex recognised a pattern to the animal's movements. As the first ball had spun at him the fox had flattened to the floor slightly then sprung back. For the second missile he had twitched to one side. Each time he'd used minimal movement to avoid the problem then instantly recoiled to his original position.

Alex reached into the box for a third cabivitrim, sweat trickling down the back of his neck. He had already missed twice. Ferox's snarling became louder, tail waving, presumably waiting until Alex faltered.

Mind in cold battle calculation mode, Alex took aim. His arm rocketed forward as if to throw, but he held on to the glue. The fox ducked. As Ferox sprang back to his attacking position Alex hurled the cabivitrim. It hit a front leg.

Ferox glanced down at the shimmering green ball. Growling, he scraped his front paw on the floor. As soon as the green slime touched the carpet, it stuck. Ferox yanked his foot, screaming as he tore skin and fur. The cabivitrim held.

'Devil-cub,' Ferox yelled at Alex. 'What evil magic is in this? Arnak, come.'

Another fox appeared at the far end of the corridor, much larger than the first. After a fleeting glance at Ferox, Arnak sprinted forward, his eyes fixed on Alex's throat.

'Crisis,' yelled Skoodle. 'Run.'

'He's faster. We fight.'

As Skoodle dropped to the bottom of his pocket, Alex reached into the box for the last cabivitrim. Two misses at a standing fox. One ball left for a sprinting animal.

Alex's tiny target had to be the border of one of the front paws, the only body part that definitely would touch the carpet. Absorbing the rhythm of the fox's gait, Alex threw. The green slime hit the front paw, but too high to stick to the floor.

The fox sprang, jaws wide. In desperation, Alex hurled the box at the fox's head. Too late to dodge, Arnak took the blow full in the face. Stunned, he lurched sideways. The cabivitrim hit the carpet and stuck. The fox clawed at his fixed paw, sticking down both.

'Snot-ball,' Ferox shrieked. 'Cowardly yellow-livered dungworm. I'll claw you to shreds for this.'

'I'll rip your throat out, you stinking pool of putrid pus,' yelled Arnak.

Skoodle appeared at the pocket edge. 'Yeah, maybe.'

Peeling the hot glove off his hand, Alex threw it to the floor. He'd won. Relief flooded through him. Buzzing with adrenaline, he surveyed the field of battle: his trapped enemies, bloodstained, surrounded by ripped-off skin and fur.

'We were brilliant,' said Skoodle.

'Too right. Now we need to find the others.'

'It's probably half-time by now. Will they have oranges?'

'No. Be serious. This is a battle.'

'I am serious.'

CHAPTER 24

As Alex sprinted for the narrow gap between the foxes and the wall, the tip of one of Ferox's claws found his flesh. Alex felt ripping pain, then blood running down his leg. Alex ignored it, not bothered at all. Blood on both sides, but he had won.

He rounded the next bend and stopped. A vast black dog was pounding towards him down the corridor. The dog's muscles rippled under black wiry fur: a killing machine double Alex's size.

'Reverse,' yelled Skoodle.

Alex wheeled round and bolted back past the foxes.

'Kill him, Rycant,' shouted Ferox. 'Rip that evil human spawn apart.'

'Willingly,' growled the huge dog, sprinting past.

Alex ran flat out, yet the pounding canine feet got closer with every pace. With the snarling only yards behind him, Alex ran into a room, swinging round to slam the heavy door shut.

It was too late. Rycant's salivating muzzle thrust through the gap. Alex flung his whole weight against the door. Wood splintered on to skull with a loud crash. Howling, Rycant smashed the door open, flinging Alex across the room, blasting him into a table. The enormous dog stood facing Alex, growling, taking his time now that his victim was at his mercy.

Trapped, weaponless, Alex wondered whether he'd have time to throw himself through the closed window. Death by falling several floors in a shower of splintered glass might be better than having his throat torn out. As Rycant sprang, Alex grabbed a large object from the table and cracked it on to the dog's head. Head bleeding, the Rottweiler staggered sideways.

'It's Clawds,' yelled Skoodle.

Glancing down, Alex saw that he was holding the statue of the cat. The dark sculptured wood glowed intensely, as if from an inner light. It rapidly got warmer; within a couple of seconds it was too hot to hold. With a grimace of pain, Alex dropped it.

It landed upright, the cat perched on his hind paws as he had been when lignified. Some extraordinary force seemed to be surging through Clawds, like a thousand-volt electric charge. Wood began to melt into fur, the lifeless paws returning to flesh. The statue expanded rapidly as it turned back into a living cat. Within seconds a nine-foot monster stood near Alex, howling. Growling, Rycant hauled himself to his feet, hair bristling.

The great cat's jaws opened, so wide that it seemed his head would rip apart. A hand appeared out of Clawds's mouth, followed by a second.

The two hands yanked at the giant cat's back teeth as the being tried to haul itself out of the immense feline. Yowling, Clawds wrestled to close his jaws against the clawing fingers, his still-lignified forepaws hanging uselessly by his sides.

After a grotesque minute a man's head appeared, a ragged slash down his cheek. Bulging eyes stared out of their sockets. His neck veins were engorged like fat purple ropes as he strained. Then, for a moment, the facial muscles relaxed as the figure inhaled a lungful of air.

'Karlan,' gasped Alex.

Spurred into movement, Alex took two steps towards Clawds. The dog leapt forward, snarling, teeth bared, paws braced. Alex moved back a few inches. The growling subsided. The dog clearly wasn't frightened of the face appearing. Karlan must be one of his allies.

Karlan started struggling again, overbalancing the cat. Clawds's head hit the corner of an oak chest. He lay still, eyes closed, motionless.

Leaning on the blunter teeth at the back of the mouth, Karlan forced the cat down his body inch by inch. Black-clad shoulders and chest appeared, covered in lumpy slimy stomach contents. In a few seconds the wizard stepped out, kicking Clawds to one side as if he were an empty sleeping bag

Stiffly, the wizard raised himself to his feet. 'You and your stupid friends released Zorrin,' he said to Alex. 'You're directly responsible for this outrage.' He touched the ragged wound on his face and indicated his stinking shirt. 'You'll die to pay for it.'

His tone was cold, clinical – as if he'd passed a death sentence so often that it was neither interesting nor negotiable; just fact. Skoodle scrambled round to the back of Alex's shirt as Karlan started to brush some of the foul matter from his clothes.

Alex could feel Skoodle climbing down his back, scratching his skin through his thin shirt, then scurrying down his leg.

Karlan looked up again. 'You'll not escape this time,' he said, spitting his words out like bullets. 'I'll teach you a lesson. Luckily for you, you'll not remember it, as corpses have no memory.' He turned to the dog. 'Rycant, is Tevo also here?'

'Yes.'

'Bring him to me.'

Karlan watched the dog lope out of the door. Out of the corner of his eye Alex saw Skoodle scurry across the floor to the cat, then bury himself in his tabby fur.

So he has not run for help, thought Alex. He's abandoned me, getting clear of the death bolt. It doesn't matter. In a minute or so nothing will matter to me ever again.

Playing for time in case Zorrin might track him, Alex blurted out, 'Your escape was astonishing.' He forced admiration into his voice. 'How did you get out?'

'It's interesting to see that somebody as young and feeble as yourself appreciates powerful magic when they see it.'

'I'm fascinated,' Alex raced on, brain trying to keep up with his words. 'You were totally trapped, weren't you? You should have been helpless.'

'Yet, as you have seen, I wasn't. Never underestimate the power of the evil forces. Not that you'll have much time left to make further judgements on anything.'

'Even so, how did you do it?' asked Alex, pushing on, throat as dry as the Sahara. The hammering of his heart was so loud inside his head that he almost expected blood to start spurting out of his ears. 'Did you send a beam of magic to the dog?'

'No,' replied Karlan, sounding irritated. 'I couldn't transmit any messages anywhere. Zorrin's spell had dealt with that. Rycant is a magical creature. When my trapped power met him with such force, the fusion of two enchantment zones shattered the spell binding me. Unfortunately, it also strengthened that blasted cat, so he did not die as he should have done. In fact,' Karlan added with a thin smile, 'I suppose I ought to be thanking you for this rescue. Think, as you die, of how you have cost your friends their lives.'

Alex blundered on, words spilling out at random. He waved his hand around airily. 'Do you think this room will do for a meeting place with Tevo? Has it enough magical vibrations to help your mental energy flow?'

Idiot, he thought. How could I say something so stupid? Karlan is bound to realise that this is aimless rambling.

It seemed, however, not to be so stupid. Karlan's gaze swept around the room taking in the pale stone fireplace, the scarlet silk curtains, the portraits of elderly wizards, the sparse oak furniture. He inhaled deeply, filling his lungs with the mixed aroma of wax polish, old wood and the electric scent that invariably follows a storm.

'I suppose so.'

Alex backed away a step. Only a couple of yards separated him from the open door, but at this moment even two paces was a terminal distance. 'Why do you hate Zorrin?' he asked, as the wizard looked back at him.

'History. If you knew his life story, you'd hate him too. Enough of this. I have given you longer than you deserve.' His bony arm rose from under the long, stinking shirt. The executioner's finger pointed straight at Alex's heart.

CHAPTER 25

Inching back towards the door, Alex felt no longer frightened, merely angry. He had played the game and lost. So close, so finely judged, yet he was to die anyway.

His gaze flicked up to the window behind Karlan. 'Zorrin,' he yelled. 'Thank the stars.'

Karlan swung round. The panes were empty. Only his own furious expression was visible. Beyond hung impenetrable black night. Though he had no chance at all of making it through the door, sheer survival instinct drove Alex to bolt.

A scream ripped through the air, a terrible inhuman sound of mortal agony. Glancing over his shoulder, Alex saw Karlan arching backwards, howling, knees buckling beneath him. Behind the wizard Clawds reared up: nine feet of fighting feline, blood glistening on the tips of his outstretched claws. Face contorted with pain, Karlan swung round, his deadly finger aiming directly at Clawds: his slashed, bleeding back towards Alex, his ripped shirt in tatters.

Clawds's paw hit the wizard's arm like the crack of a baseball bat. In agony, Karlan stared down at the broken limb. White-faced, he lurched forward, landing in a senseless heap on the floor, arm sticking out at an unnatural angle.

Shaking from his adrenaline surge, Alex looked up at the immense cat. 'Clawds, that was amazing.'

'Thanks.' Clawds wiped his bloodstained claws on the wizard's shirt. 'Who saved me?'

Skoodle stuck his head out from behind a chair leg. 'Me,' he squeaked.

Vast yellow eyes swung towards the hamster. 'You, tiny one? How?'

'The flower from Makusha. Stupid to trust a lump of granite. But I thought… maybe… there was a chance… ' His voice tailed off under the unwavering gaze of the immense cat.

For a moment Clawds stood looking down, head to one side, frowning. Finally he spoke. 'Pax. Never again will I eat any hamster, or indeed any rodent, if that's what you desire.'

Whiskers quivering, Skoodle pulled himself up straight. 'You can stuff yourself with rats, but if you would be so kind as to avoid hamsters and mice – other than the ones who are disguised wizards – that would be very nice, please. Or is it thank you?'

'Done.' Reaching down, Clawds held out his paw, which was the size of a table tennis bat. Skoodle reached up with his own minuscule one. The two solemnly shook hands.

Running footsteps approached. Alex and Clawds turned to face the door, ready to fight. Skoodle ran behind Alex.

Myth at his heels, Zorrin sprinted into the room, finger drawn at the ready, face set. For a moment he stood surveying the scene before him: the gigantic cat, the unconscious wizard lying twisted on the floor, Alex bloodied but still standing, Skoodle behind his left foot.

'Do you like the new size or should I go back to the portable version?' asked Clawds.

'Big is great,' replied Zorrin, grinning. 'At least until this battle is over.'

Clawds nodded. 'No problem.' He pointed at Karlan. 'What are you going to do with this pseudo-mouse? He's likely to wake in a minute.'

'Trap him.'

Zorrin held his hand out flat. A bubble appeared on his palm. Enlarging rapidly, it floated over to the broken figure on the floor and landed with a small pop, enveloping Karlan totally.

'Bubble prison. He'll live, assuming we can get back in time to allow him more air. If we don't… ' Zorrin shrugged.

'So if his friends kill us, he dies. Seems fair,' said Skoodle.

'Back to battle,' Zorrin said. 'Follow me.'

The group ran out of the room, the rhythmical fall of Alex's trainers echoing softly down the hall.

'Silence needed,' whispered Zorrin, throwing some violet pellets ahead of them which landed in a shower of deep purple and silver sparks. As Alex ran across the smoking embers, his footfalls became completely silent and springier, as if he were running on air bubbles.

Round the next bend they came to the foxes: stuck, heavily scratched, tufts of fur lying around them.

'Sons of poisonous wart-bellied toads,' yelled Arnak. 'Release us at once or Tevo will slash your heads open and dunk his bread in your brains.'

'You did do well,' Zorrin said to Alex.

'Pond waddlers,' shouted Ferox. 'Die, orange slug bottoms.'

Alex shrugged. 'I had to use four.'

'Purple rat's droppings,' shrieked Arnak.

'Not a bad hit rate. I don't suppose you've had much practice throwing cabivitrim.'

'Correct,' said Skoodle. 'But he had a good coach. Me.'

'Four-toed yellow buzzard flies,' bellowed Ferox, pulling hard on his stuck tail. It came away with a loud rip, leaving fur stuck to the floor and the tip completely bald.

Zorrin pointed at the foxes. *'Via dungato.'*

The floor beneath the foxes became hazy then disappeared altogether. Grabbing uselessly at the evaporating edges, Arnak and Ferox fell into molten blackness. As the screams of the foxes died away, the floor moulded itself back to normal.

'Cool. Where did they go?' asked Skoodle.

'Dungeons. They'll be trapped until Flick or I release them. We can decide later what to do with them.' He pointed at the spot where the foxes had vanished. *'Relaschia cabivitrim.'*

'That sounded like a sneeze,' said Alex.

'It unlocked the cabivitrim.' Zorrin picked up the box and glove from the floor and put them in an inner pocket.

A ferocious volley of barking filled the corridor. Rycant's heavy form rounded the corner, thundering towards them, saliva dripping from his blood-hungry jaws. The golden-furred form of Tariq appeared sprinting three steps behind him, tree-trunk legs powering the massive bear along.

'Run,' yelled Tariq.

Zorrin pointed at the ground immediately ahead of the dog. *'Via dungato.'*

A hole appeared. Rycant tried to stop, front paws slammed on the floor, legs outstretched. Carried by his momentum, the dog disappeared over the edge, barking furiously. Tariq stopped inches from the hole, which resealed itself silently in front of him.

'What happened?' he asked, staring at the floor.

Alex grinned. 'Dungeon express.'

'Tevo is already imprisoned with several others,' said Zorrin. 'We need to find Flick and Keeko. They may need our help.'

As Zorrin checked his watch crystal, they heard a soft rhythmical scraping sound approaching from around the bend. Repeatedly, a longish rustle followed a short sighing. Zorrin aimed a spell at the junction of the two corridors.

'Visage,' he mouthed.

A mirror appeared on the wall, showing Ikara with her tail coiled tightly around a large unconscious badger. She was slithering along a few feet then stopping to contract, dragging the heavy animal behind her. From the rigidity of her facial muscles it seemed that only sheer cussedness kept her going. She didn't appear to be aware of the watchers, as there wasn't any break in her rhythm when the mirror appeared.

'The mirror is invisible to her,' Zorrin mouthed in answer to Alex's puzzled frown.

They ran to join her.

'Finally. The badger police,' she said, loosening her grip. 'That was almost as tiring as dragging a human from a mudbath.'

Alex grinned. 'Don't worry. I haven't forgotten. I'm still grateful.'

'Keep it that way,' replied Ikara, stretching. 'My muscles are on fire, but I couldn't leave him. If he'd woken up he might have become a nuisance again.'

Zorrin pointed at the floor near the badger.

'You'll like this,' Alex told Ikara.

'Via dungato.'

The floor melted, dumping both badger and Ikara into a hole.

'Unfortunate,' said Zorrin, adding, *'Expelo serpentus dungato.'*

The ground melted once more. With a whoosh Ikara was launched out of the yawning gap, landing in an untidy heap.

'Most amusing,' Ikara hissed, untangling her coils. 'A little more focus next time, please.'

'Sorry. The last loop of your tail must still have been around the badger. At least you got to see a part of Ravenscraig that very few visitors do.'

'A photo would have been fine.'

'Good tip.'

Flick reparticulated behind them, breathing heavily and holding Keeko, her waist-length black and gold hair looped up into a ponytail. 'Keeko knocked out one of the badgers. Crashed a suit of armour over him.'

'Flatted and splatted.' Keeko hopped to the floor and started doing a victory dance with Skoodle.

'And Rectoria?' asked Zorrin. 'Is she still free?'

'No. She's in the dungeons, but dealing with her was tougher than I'd expected.'

'Ravenscraig is temporarily safe but it's vital that we find the hidden map,' said Zorrin, running a hand through his mood streak.

Skoodle sighed. 'So that we can tackle a massive aggressive lizard-wizard monster?'

'Exactly.'

CHAPTER 26

In the study, Zorrin sat hunched over his desk. Skoodle lay nearby in a half-eaten plate of cookies while Keeko flicked raisins at him from the cloud sofa.

'It's got to be somewhere in Ravenscraig.' Alex sat tearing paper into shreds, tossing bits on to the floor. 'We need to think laterally.'

Ikara was draped around the top of a hatstand, her head supported by two pegs. 'Same as for the last six hours. It's been a real riot,' she replied, yawning. 'Especially when we belt off round Ravenscraig each time we think we've cracked the puzzle. Such good exercise. Although those mice I bravely tackled on the third floor were extremely tasty.'

'You knew they weren't evil before you ate them,' said Alex, lounging back in his chair. 'Zorrin had already told you.'

Ikara licked her lips. 'Still brave. He could have been wrong. Wizards sometimes are, you know.'

'Undoubtedly,' said Zorrin, rising to pace the floor, Myth at his heels. 'Let's think it through again. We've checked the charts and maps.'

'All normal,' said Tariq from a sofa, where he lay cleaning the last of Rycant's fur from between his front claws.

'We've searched the labs and stables.' Zorrin stared into space, as if looking at a mental blueprint of Ravenscraig.

'Normal,' said Alex. 'Or as normal as it gets at your pad. We've been into the dungeons, the kitchen and every one of about a hundred other rooms. We've prodded at paintings, lifted carpets and scavenged in cubbyholes. You've had a go at transforming almost everything, including zapping the wallpaper.'

'All we have ended up with,' said Ikara, 'are several smoking black holes in the decor. Although when you got angry and set fire to a table lamp, that was very funny.'

'I wasn't cross,' said Zorrin. 'I was… '

'Frustrated?' suggested Tariq, watching a particularly large bloodstained tuft drop to the floor then vanish as the result of an automatic cleaning spell.

'Impatient, irritated, exasperated, at the end of your tether? Out of ideas?' asked Ikara. 'Cerebrally blank? Zip inspiration? Kaput neuronally?'

'All right, brainbox, it's your turn.' Zorrin threw a bag of paperclips at her. 'You tell me where the map is.'

Ikara reached her tail out for a cookie to the accompaniment of the soft metallic clatter of falling clips. 'I didn't say I knew.'

'I'm hungry,' said Keeko.

'Stomach triumphing over catastrophe?' asked Skoodle.

Zorrin's white streak was spitting red sparks in his frustration. 'We'll give it another twenty minutes. If we haven't thought of something by then, we'll go and eat.'

'Eagle stew?' asked Ikara. 'Rock cakes?'

'Let's start from the beginning,' suggested Tariq, his tone so calm that even a Zen practitioner would have been proud of him. 'We're looking for something that came into this house about sixty or seventy years ago. Maybe it materialised here.'

Zorrin shook his head. 'Not possible, owing to Ravenscraig's security.' Red, blue and purple sparks dropped from his hair on to the desk, starting several paper fires.

Tariq batted them out as Skoodle wandered out of the danger zone.

'It may seem a stupid question,' came a dry hiss, 'but could this ancient object be something with an irritating habit of disappearing?' Ikara waved her tail at the astromometer, which was gradually rearticulating.

'By the Great Warthog's beard, you could be right.' Zorrin leapt up and shot across to the hazy instrument. 'One of my father's friends, a wise old wizard called Brinstaller, sent it. He disappeared shortly afterwards.'

'That's the wizard who made the map. I've cracked it,' crowed Ikara.

Zorrin muttered a few words and pointed at the astromometer. Apart from a flash of green and gold light as the spell hit one of the violet glass phials, nothing happened. He tried several other charms, which in turn produced a cross-looking elephant and a shower of footballs which he disparticulated. The next attempt produced a small tornado that smelled like rotting cheese. Choking, they all ran from the room while Zorrin directed the foul gust out through the cloud door, a chunk of cloud sofa held over his mouth to stop him inhaling the stinking air.

'Did anything else arrive at the same time?' asked Tariq, poking his head back round the door. 'A leaflet on how to use it, a tag... a letter stating where it came from?'

'Genius. Yes, a book of instructions. I've got it here somewhere.' Zorrin reached deep into the cloud sofa and rummaged around. Triumphantly he produced an extremely large book in smoke-grey leather entitled 'The Astromometer: A Guide'. Zorrin pulled it open as the others wandered back in to crowd round him.

The text appeared to be a straightforward aid to interpreting the stars. It listed the meaning of changes in the depths of the various coloured liquids, followed by sections on star movements and advanced astrophysics.

Zorrin leaned back with a sigh. 'It would take months to get through this, even if I knew what I was looking for.'

'Is there a section on what to do when things go wrong?' asked Ikara as she slid gracefully back up the hatstand.

'You're becoming inconsistent,' said Skoodle. 'That was a helpful comment.'

Ikara stuck the full length of her tongue out at him. 'Don't wind me up, mouth-watering rodent.'

Skoodle turned his back on her as Zorrin flicked through the text to find the troubleshooting section. The fat chapter described how to make adjustments in case of equiviscous evaporation, in a Torvian leap year, or with interference from hyper-blackmagnetism. Tariq and Alex leaned over Zorrin's shoulder, scanning the bewildering text.

After an hour of reading no one had been able to spot any words seemingly out of place, misspelled, a spell – or anything else offering a clue to whether this book could be the key to transformation. Dark gloom took over Alex.

'The astromometer can't be the answer,' said Zorrin. 'Something else must be the hidden map. Let's go and eat, then start again in half an hour.'

Ikara let go of the top of the hatstand and landed in a neat coil on the floor. 'Another dead end. Complete disaster. We don't know when Virida wants her stone by, but she doesn't strike me as patient. This is getting dull.'

The band trooped down to the kitchen to find Flick wearing black goggles and a fuchsia-striped overall, with long turquoise hair held above her ears in bunches. On the kitchen table sat rainbow-coloured jars and beakers, the gloop inside bubbling and making small frequent explosions. A test tube near her spat out two globs of yellow gunge, then the rest of the sludge turned mud brown.

'Fludzi ploop. Not enough rhinoceros toenails.' She sprinkled in some mid-brown powder. With a bang the mess returned to yellow, bubbling fiercely despite the lack of a flame beneath it. 'How are you getting on?' she asked, peering at the molten gunge.

'Dreadful,' said Ikara, coiling herself into the fruit bowl, engulfing an apple. 'It's seriously aggravating to spend so long trying to solve a puzzle when – if we succeed – we all get killed, anyway.'

Flick pulled off her goggles and reached up to a shelf for mugs. 'Don't be so negative. Too much thinking about death is depressing. Coffee?'

As she made drinks, Zorrin outlined their theory about the astromometer.

'Certainly, it has potential,' said Flick, opening a box of what looked like flat purple bananas and offering them round. 'Couldn't you make it transmorph?'

'No. The instruction book is vast, so we homed in on the section on troubleshooting. Irritatingly, there were absolutely no words that even half resembled a transmorphing spell.'

Flick finished off a sticky mouthful and licked her fingers. 'That's easy. Fifth line down, backwards from the middle.'

'Why do you think that would work?' asked Zorrin, as a stray hair spark lit his third banana. Without bothering to blow it out he crammed it into his mouth.

Flick watched him, wrinkling her nose. 'Never eat anything that's still alight. Remember Nanny Orlink's rules, Zorrin. The fifth line bit is the code I had with Pops. It's a great little spell. When you read the words forward they say something ordinary like, 'Warty toads are delicious in soup'. Yet when you read them backwards the words transform into an enchantment. But you have to find the exact middle of the sentence to start.'

'You never told me this before,' said Zorrin, wisps of purple smoke drifting out of his nose.

'Why would I? It was a secret between Pops and me. The only other wizard who knew was my godfather, Brinstaller.'

'Dancing terrapins. It's got to be the answer,' shouted Zorrin, leaping from his chair and rushing out, the others behind him. On arrival in the study he grabbed the instruction book and began counting the letters on the fifth line of the problem section. When Zorrin had found the exact middle he started to read backwards. The words came out as mumbo jumbo. Five times he tried it, with no success.

He slammed the book shut. 'This is frustrating.'

'Maybe it's not in the troubleshooting section,' said Tariq, reopening the book at the front. 'Try the beginning of the main text.'

With a sigh, Zorrin found the fifth line and started counting the characters. Marking the place with his nail, he began to read backwards. The words that came from his mouth bore no relationship to those written on the page, backwards or otherwise.

As he reached the end of the line the astromometer disappeared with a small bang.

Zorrin gazed at the space where the instrument had been. 'We've found a spell, although not the one we wanted. Now I've lost my astromometer, probably forever. It was really useful. Blast all childhood wizard wheezes. We'll have to—'

The place where the astromometer had stood started to fill with soft pale blue mist. It became rapidly more solid until, wall to ceiling, stood a vast map of an underground labyrinth. Across the very top, written in green flames, was 'Caves of Desdea'.

Keeko cheered as she cartwheeled across the floor. Skoodle jived on the desk as Zorrin, Tariq and Alex whooped and danced round the map.

Ikara rolled on to her back, stretching, displaying her glossy gold underbelly. 'Ice,' she murmured.

Zorrin stopped, mid-whoop. 'Everything was great till then. That word.'

'Get over it,' laughed Alex.

'You can't fight fashion,' said Skoodle.

'Watch me.' Zorrin turned to the map as Keeko rolled her eyes behind his back.

Ornate, curly writing marked the cave of Hypnos. The cavern contained a large lake surrounded by a complicated mesh of tunnels.

'That's interesting,' said Zorrin. 'Hypnos is shown as being in the very centre of the lake. It's probably because he's an aqualate.'

'A what-alate?' asked Ikara.

'Aqualate. An amazing creature: front part lizard, back half snake. It has gills, so it's capable of living under water. On land it's astonishingly fast, owing to its muscular legs. Under water it uses its tail for power. In either environment it's deadly. I've got a picture of one somewhere.'

He reached into the cloud sofa and produced a large book entitled 'Weirdities', subtitled 'Species of Eridor: from Alcanates to Zyrons'. Zorrin flicked rapidly through to Aq. The aqualate displayed was a revolting-looking creature, its moss-coloured skin mottled and scaly as if camouflage. A huge ugly lizard head with blazing red eyes and vicious flesh-ripping teeth sat on a squat neck above its powerful body and four legs, beyond which a long muscular snake's tail curled away.

'The front end looks horrible,' said Ikara, 'but I expect the back half's a distant relative of mine.'

'How big are aqualates?' asked Tariq.

'Variable. Depends on age. Hypnos is probably over a hundred years old, so he could be twenty metres by now.'

Alex had a sudden vision of a whole nest of them. 'Could there be more than one down there?'

'I doubt it,' replied Zorrin. 'Hypnos left the main colony of aqualates many years ago. He travelled alone to Desdea to be an apprentice to Saranak the wizard. No one knows what happened in those dark caves long ago, but Saranak disappeared. All attempts to trace him have failed.'

'Probably lunch. Two slices of bread, one wizard; yum,' said Ikara.

'Who was Saranak? Was he one of our people?' asked Tariq.

'No, although once he had been true and noble. However, something corrupted him, eating his soul. The more power he acquired, the more he craved it.' Deep pain clouded Zorrin's eyes, tracing through his voice. The sparks in his hair died. 'Still, he doesn't concern us. If Hypnos has the sapphire he's not going to let it go easily. He has enormous magical power and is physically a fearsome creature. No one has emerged from Hypnos's cave alive in the last twenty years.'

'Is this a pep talk? I'm feeling so positive already.' Ikara slid on to the floor near Skoodle and formed herself into a question mark, using the hamster as a dot. Her voice dropped into deep melodrama. 'How are we going to get into this mountain of doom?'

Zorrin pointed at the lower region of the map. A beam of light blazed from his finger. As the beam travelled, each section appeared in three dimensions, rising into the air, performing a Mexican wave in response to the light.

'Through the jungle to the south of the caves. The north coastal side falls like a flat wall of sheet metal hundreds of metres down into the sea. There are no caves or cracks to force entry through. The mountains to the east and west are even worse than Makusha.'

'Count me out,' said Skoodle. 'I've made a pact with myself to avoid life-threatening experiences until I get killed by Virida.'

'Can't we materialise inside the caves?' asked Tariq.

'No,' replied Zorrin. 'This map may not be self-updating. We could appear immediately in front of Hypnos or in the middle of a stone wall. Either would be a painful death. We'll reparticulate in the jungle, then approach via one of the tunnels leading to the central cave.'

'I suppose you want us to start instantly,' said Ikara. 'One hundred per cent mental effort, then full-on physical.'

'I think not,' said Zorrin, turning towards her with a smile. 'Tomorrow at first light will be soon enough. We need to be refreshed to meet the challenges of Desdea.'

'Frankly,' said Alex, tossing a grape to Ikara, 'I'm in no rush to meet Hypnos, even if the back end might be a half-brother of yours.'

Ikara caught it in her mouth. 'Front half aqua, back bit late, as we might be tomorrow; late departed. Also you're coming, rodent.'

'Write "Gone to lunch with Toomba" on my gravestone,' said Skoodle. 'That's if anyone can find enough bits of me to bury.'

CHAPTER 27

The jungle was dark and sinister, its vegetation dense. No bright flashes of colour broke up the shades of green and brown enmeshed with black. A rich earthy smell mingled with the musty aroma of leaves that had been crushed on reparticulation.

'Can you feel evil here?' Tariq asked Alex.

'Yes, very strongly.'

Zorrin raised an eyebrow at Tariq.

'Alex has the power of predor.'

'Unfortunately you're right, Alex. I can feel it too,' replied Zorrin. 'However, I don't sense a strong magic field. There will doubtless be powerful defences, but it seems that an enchanted wall is not one of them.'

They set off in a straggling line, Zorrin navigating by his watch crystal, which now held a copy of the map.

As they strode deeper into the jungle, hairs rose on the back of Alex's neck. His palms grew sweaty and his pulse raced, as if he were a hunted animal. Yet there was no obvious threat. Colours shifted in the dappled light of the weak sun, which struggled to break through the dense canopy above. Long black vines entwined themselves in strangleholds around the branches then cascaded on to the forest floor. Great droplets of condensation quivered on the ends of leaves, dripping chillingly on to their faces as they brushed past.

Keeko clung tighter to Tariq's chest. As they moved through the thick curtain of vines she reached up to push one out of her way. 'It's a snake.' Looking around, she screamed, 'They all are.'

The jungle writhed into life. Serpents dropped to the jungle floor, coiling themselves around the limbs and bodies of the invaders, enveloping them in cold moving flesh. The world became a sea of black muscle, blazing red eyes, flickering tongues.

'Volta,' shouted Zorrin.

An electric bolt shot through Alex's body. Jolted rigid with pain, he couldn't breathe. The snakes arched backwards as the shock surged into them, then fell motionless to the ground. Instantly more snakes twined around him, bodies like flexible steel cables, hard, tight, painful.

'Transparticulate us,' shouted Ikara, wrestling with a snake twice her size.

'I can't,' Zorrin gasped, almost suffocated by a snake around his face stifling him, another clamped round his chest. 'We're not close enough together. *Volta.*'

A shaft of white-hot pain seared up Alex's leg followed by warmth as if he was bleeding, then numbness. 'My ankle's been bitten,' he yelled.

'Squeeze your thigh to stop the venom spreading,' Zorrin shouted back.

It was too late. Alex felt light-headed, hot and sweaty, as poison raged around his body. Skoodle scrambled out of his top pocket.

'Don't move,' Alex muttered. 'The snakes will get you.'

Undaunted, the pinprick of feet travelled upwards. Alex's legs were starting to buckle, his arms hanging uselessly, his breathing heavy.

Through swimming vision he could see Skoodle's face only inches away, a blue flower held in one of his front paws, the open mouth of a snake immediately behind him. The teeth started closing in on the hamster.

'Skoodle,' Alex said, mouth muscles tight. 'Behind—' The numbness of his lips stopped any further words as his muscles stiffened in the final agonising phase of paralysis.

There was a dull thud by Alex's ear. A small-pronged fork pushed into his mouth. It must be a snake tongue injecting venom deep into my core, he thought. He tried to spit it out as his eyes started to close for the last time, but his mouth was too weak to work. Everything lay hidden in a thick mist as blackness moved in. There was no more pain in his body. The paralysis must now be complete, he thought. They would all die together: Skoodle eaten, the others poisoned or suffocated. Alex felt totally calm for there was no more fight in him, no further struggling to be done.

'Volta.'

As the weight fell away from his body Alex found he could move. Two glistening eyes were staring straight into his. Instinctively his hand rose to pulverise the snake that had eaten Skoodle but his reactions were still slow. The sluggish hand missed.

'What are you doing?' squeaked an indignant voice.

'Sorry,' he croaked, throat tight. 'I thought you were the snake that had eaten you.'

'Nobody ate me. Keeko fixed him.'

As sensation returned Alex became aware of Keeko wrapped round his chest, blood on her foot. At his feet lay the unconscious body of a snake, bleeding from a gash on its head.

'She kicked the stuffing out of him.' Skoodle's voice rose in terror. 'Hide me.'

Another snake's head reared into Alex's vision, sweeping rapidly down towards Skoodle.

Alex rammed Skoodle inside his shirt, hand over the top. The snake's teeth tore into his shoulder.

Grabbing the serpent behind its head Alex squeezed with strength born of anger. 'Can't get me. Blue flower protection.'

The jaws opened as the snake gasped for air. With no pity, Alex squeezed the life out of him, ignoring the other snakes wrapping themselves around his limbs and body.

'Volta.'

The snakes fell back, stunned. The pile of unconscious bodies lay a foot deep. Yet still more came to attack, dropping from trees, slithering over their unconscious comrades to get to their victims. Alex flung the snake's body on to the pile.

Tariq's voice scorched across the gap. 'Save yourself, Zorrin. There's no sense in all of us dying.'

'No. I'm not leaving you,' yelled Zorrin as he wrestled with an enormous serpent which had wound its way up through his long curly hair, its body round his throat. 'Without the shock we are seconds from death. *Volta.*'

'The eagle feather,' shouted Tariq. 'Call on it.'

Zorrin reached into an inside pocket, getting to the feather seconds before a snake clamped his arm to his body.

'Help us, feather,' he bellowed. 'We're in mortal danger.'

Alex hoped that the snakes would evaporate or explode. Little else would help. Even with an entire rainstorm of swords they couldn't hack their way through the mass of snake heads that came in waves. Like the Hydra, where one fell two took its place.

'Feather, do something. We're minutes from death,' cried Zorrin. '*Volta.*'

The adrenaline rush of battle spurred on both attacked and attackers. The fight grew fiercer: the snakes fuelled by the smell of blood, sweat and fear; Zorrin's group by anger, revulsion and terror.

'Something's happening,' choked out Ikara, her senses infinitely more acute than the others'.

Then they all heard it: a rhythmical beating noise like the wind, rapidly increasing. Seconds later, Fernando tore through the canopy of leaves above them, wings folded, neck outstretched in a full dive. Behind him, in a V-shape, six more eagles rocketed straight at them.

'Quickly. I'm being strangled,' croaked Alex. 'Say volta.'

'No,' said Zorrin, his voice husky as he clawed at the snake around his throat. 'The timing must be right. We must disentangle as the eagles arrive or we'll take the snakes.'

The body clamp around his chest stole Alex's breath. Another squeezed his abdomen. Through dimming vision Alex could see Tariq slashing with his razor claws at the half a dozen wriggling snakes encircling him. Only a hair's breadth of time separated the eagles from the victims below.

'*Volta,*' shouted Zorrin.

A rustling of wings above Alex: a rush of air on his face. Fernando grabbed him across the shoulders with his talons, hoisting him up. Keeko lay motionless against Alex's chest: no flicker of life in her staring eyes, no heart thudding against his own. An eagle swooped in to pluck her from Alex.

'Not the monkey,' screamed Skoodle. 'She goes with us.'

The eagle nodded, then diverted to help the two largest birds hoist Tariq.

Skoodle's hand forced Keeko's lips apart to cram some small blue petals into her mouth. Alex looked down at the still face. It doesn't work on the dead, he thought, mind awash with pain.

Wrenching the flower back out of Keeko's mouth, Skoodle pulped it between his front teeth. He shoved the mulch back into Keeko's mouth. With a small paw he ground juice into her gums. 'It's got to work. Breathe, Keeko, breathe.'

Despite no response he worked on, small claws scratching open her gums to reach blood.

A deep shuddering breath shook Keeko's body. With a jolt her heart started – erratic, but a definite beat. The cold face became infused with warmth. Keeko's eyes remained closed. Her lips moved slightly.

'Don't spit it out; swallow it,' Skoodle shrieked, his words almost ripped away by the wind.

A tight metal collar seemed to be constricting Alex's throat. Treacherous tears fell as he clung tightly to the small furry body, willing Keeko to absorb his warmth, his life force. 'Skoodle, you're a hero.'

A tiny shudder vibrated against his chest. Sobs wracked Skoodle's body as he stroked Keeko's face. 'I'd do anything for her,' he wailed. 'No matter what.'

Keeko's long tail coiled round Skoodle. 'OK. Teach me to jive,' she whispered as she drifted off to sleep.

'Any time.' Skoodle buried his face into Keeko's shoulder, weeping.

Alex wrapped his arms tighter around Keeko, grateful to feel movement in the tiny chest.

The eagles swept over the edge of the jungle, heading for the coast. The temperature dropped dramatically as they climbed higher.

With the added wind chill factor, Alex felt frozen to the core. He pulled Skoodle and Keeko closer, sharing his falling body heat.

He raised his head to look at his surroundings, then wished he hadn't. Half a mile below, the jungle looked tiny. If they slipped from the eagle's claws they would fly as well as a bowling ball; death by being pulverised on the ground. He closed his eyes, hoping that the wave of nausea would subside and not lead him to chuck, covering Keeko, Skoodle and his rescue eagle with his entire stomach contents.

Onwards they flew, the powerful beating above them reassuring despite the unpleasantness of the ride: the nausea, the hard talons in his shoulders, the bone-chilling cold.

Zorrin, we're freezing, Alex transferred. *Can you do something?*

Oh, sorry, replied Zorrin. *Wasn't thinking. I don't feel it.*

A small pearly bubble sped from Zorrin's hand, enlarging as it flew. Reaching Alex it encased him, Keeko and Skoodle. The wind disappeared, the temperature rose.

Better? asked Zorrin.

Much, replied Skoodle. *I wish he'd had the sense to ask sooner.*

Like you couldn't have asked? asked Alex.

Stop it, both of you, murmured Keeko. *I need to sleep.*

With a glare at Alex, Skoodle put on a thought-block and closed his eyes.

After a while the eagles began to lose height. A small cove came into sight, with several indistinguishable black dots scattered around its sea border. As they began to descend, the dots came into focus as a boat and three small houses. The eagles landed on the beach, releasing the group.

'Our heartfelt thanks for saving our lives,' said Zorrin to Fernando, bowing deeply.

'You've got my feather, so I must rescue you,' said Fernando. 'What an amazing coincidence that we've met again.' He winked at Zorrin, then swung back up into the skies, the other eagles falling into a line behind him. Aiming inland, they flew towards the jungle.

Alex placed Keeko on to the sand, then outlined what had happened. Zorrin gently examined her.

'She's fine, if a little fragile. It's lucky that Skoodle got to her so fast and that he has the power to heal with the flower.'

'It shouldn't have worked. Her heart had stopped beating,' said Alex.

'Reversible if within three minutes, like humans. Any longer...' Zorrin shook his head.

He started a fire on the smooth sand, using some driftwood and a few muttered words. They huddled around it, shivering from cold and the aftermath of terror, which had left them feeling like empty shells.

Zorrin looked like an ancient Druid, sitting near the flames with tumbling black hair, shadows flickering on his sculpted face. 'Are you fully all right now, Alex?' he asked.

'I'm fine, but I don't understand why they didn't poison all of us. Skoodle would have been eaten long before he made it to the rest of you with the flowers.'

'Greed,' replied Zorrin. He threw some lime green powder on to the fire, making it blaze higher. 'A weakness of theirs, which saved our lives. The deadly chemical in their venom makes you inedible. Squeezing you to death is different. They must have thought it was feast time when several hundred kilos of fresh meat wandered in.'

'Thank Jupiter for their filthy carnivorous stomachs,' said Ikara bitterly. 'They were going to kill me as well. Cannibals.'

Tariq lay on the sand, curled around Keeko. Ikara slid over to lie on his other side, making it look as if the bear had a greeny-gold streak down his back.

'Why did you get the eagles to bring us to this cove?' Tariq asked. 'Are we going to disparticulate from here back to Ravenscraig?'

'No. We'll approach the caves again, this time from the sea.'

Ikara shook her head. 'We've just been so close to death that we could count his nasal hairs; that was on using the easy route. How near to him do we get with the tough route?'

'Probably closer, but anything has to be better than returning to that bit of the jungle,' replied Zorrin, leaning back in an air armchair. 'Here's my plan.'

CHAPTER 28

Two hours later *Phaedea* sailed out of the harbour, crewed by Yidgit and Figstaff. She was an elegant old-fashioned schooner, with her tall sails swelling gracefully above dark wooden decks.

'Odd to have a frog and a man-rabbit combo in charge,' Skoodle had muttered, as he transparticulated on board.

'Everything on Eridor is bizarre. Chill. Get used to it,' replied Alex. 'It's good to see Yidgit.'

'It's so funny to see how the two parts of him work,' said Skoodle.

'Isn't using an ordinary sailing boat a bit limited?' Alex asked Zorrin. 'A speedboat would be quicker.'

'Probably not,' replied Zorrin. *'Ventus.'*

A stiff breeze blew up, whizzing them towards the cliff, a tall bow wave fanning backwards.

'How do you manoeuvre this thing, Zorrin? It has no steering wheel or ropes,' asked Ikara, looking round.

'Arm movements from the captain,' replied Zorrin, waving an arm to the right. The boat swung to starboard.

'Fantastic,' said Keeko. 'Can I steer?'

Zorrin nodded. 'If Yidgit or Figstaff don't mind.'

Figstaff shrugged as the rabbit said, 'No problem.'

Zorrin muttered a spell, then said to Keeko, 'She's all yours.'

'Whoopee,' yelled Keeko, spinning round, arms flung out.

The boat whipped round in a circle. Ikara slid rapidly towards the sea. Alex grabbed her tail, hanging on to the mast with the other hand.

'Unlucky,' said Zorrin from his knees, clutching on to the railings. 'Remember you're steering.'

'Keep going round in a circle,' Skoodle told Keeko. 'Mountain avoidance technique.'

'What if I did a cartwheel?' asked Keeko.

Zorrin pulled himself upright. 'Don't try it. Capsizing is cold.'

'Steer sensibly or the frog gets the job,' hissed Ikara.

'Bossy snake.'

'We need to aim towards the midpoint of the mountain's flank,' said Zorrin.

Wiggling closer, they could see dull grey stone falling in a sheer drop straight to the sea: no cave or landing point was visible. Once the boat had sailed to within a few metres of the mountain Zorrin handed control back to Yidgit.

'How are we going to get in?' asked Tariq.

From his top pocket Zorrin took the red enamel box which had sat on his desk.

'Time tears,' said Keeko.

'Correct. One will transport a lump of rock back to a different time zone. I hope I can throw it as far as the mountain.'

'I throw javelin,' said Alex. 'Shall I do it?'

Zorrin nodded as he pulled a glove out of an inner pocket. 'Put this on before you touch it, or you'll end up in another era.'

Alex pulled on the silver glove, the finely-woven metal mesh cool on his hand. Taking the box, he removed the small clear ball. It lay in his hand reflecting the clouds above it like a soap bubble.

'Wish me luck.' Alex flung the time tear at the mountain.

A jagged black line cracked through the cliff face, etching out a vast piece of rock. Then the stone fragment vanished, leaving a hole in the side of the mountain.

'Brilliant,' yelled Keeko.

'Thanks,' said Alex, shoving the box and glove in his pocket. 'Wherever it landed, they'll assume it's a meteor.'

Skoodle shook his head. 'They won't be assuming anything. They'd be lying dead under it.'

The ship sailed through choppy water into the massive dark cold cavern, which extended one hundred metres towards the mountain's heart. The sides of the hole dripped water as if the rock face was bleeding brine. They sailed slowly past the mouth of several tunnels, which straggled away from the newly-gouged out channel. After a few minutes Yidgit moored against the mouth of one of the larger passages.

'I'll stay and help look after the boat,' said Skoodle, looking through the gloom at the dark sinister hole. 'I don't do cave and aqualate combos. Childhood fear. Sorry.'

'You get to choose,' said Ikara. 'Walk or I carry you. In my gullet.'

'You're a big bag of sympathy, aren't you? A real pussycat,' replied Skoodle.

'Cuddles is my second name.'

Zorrin lead the way on to the floor of a damp tunnel, the rock strata visible in the lamplight from *Phaedea*'s decks. 'Sail back to open waters and wait for us there,' he instructed Yidgit. 'We'll transparticulate back to the boat when we can.'

'Can you disparticulate from inside an aqualate's stomach?' asked Skoodle.

'Possibly, but you might bring the contents with you.'

'*Ventus,*' said Figstaff.

A swirling breeze blew up, filling *Phaedea*'s sails and swinging her round to face the sea. The wind straightened to propel her into open waters. The tunnel became gloomier as her light grew distant.

'This is cold, but a hundred times better than a mass of blood-poisoning snakes,' said Ikara, her voice echoing into the shadows. 'It's a pity it wasn't our first option.'

'There was a good chance it wouldn't work. I'm a wizard, not a fortune teller.' Zorrin unrolled a map, copied from the one in his study. He pulled out a stubby yellow stick and tapped it twice on the wall. The tip exploded into flame, illuminating the tunnel brilliantly. He tapped it once more and the fire reduced to a warm glow.

'Ice,' said Skoodle.

Zorrin groaned. 'They recycle dead hamsters into finger puppets, you know.' He pointed to one of the black lines in the labyrinth criss-crossing the map of Hypnos's lair. 'Our locator dots are here. We'll follow this tunnel through to the central chamber, but we must be careful: Hypnos may pick up our scent long before we make it to his inner sanctum.'

Zorrin opened a small velvet bag, inside which lay some scarlet orgreebs. 'Take one each so we can communicate without Hypnos hearing. To use it, whisper. The sound will be transmitted to all the other orgreebs.'

As they followed the glow from Zorrin's stick, the reassuring sound of the sea behind them grew fainter. In the gloom Alex missed his footing, sending a stone ricocheting into a wall. The sound echoed down the tunnel, seemingly forever. Breathlessly they waited. Yet after an agonising few minutes no ugly snout, no lacerating teeth had appeared in the damp air. Exchanging a glance with Alex, Zorrin moved forward.

'Wish you'd paid more attention to your 'How to walk like an Apache' classes at school,' whispered Skoodle via his orgreeb.

'And me,' added Ikara.

'Thanks,' whispered Alex. 'Shoe. Stone. Mistake. The end.'

'Yeah, for all of us,' whispered Skoodle.

Zorrin murmured. 'The tunnel terminates just up ahead.'

'So do we,' muttered Ikara.

In another few metres the tunnel opened into a vast high-vaulted cavern, lit by the glow of an illuminated lake in the centre. As the surface of the water rippled in the slight draught, light danced and shimmered on stalagmites and stalactites. The glow from the central lake didn't reach the walls, where deep shadow pools held their secrets. In awe, the group stared at the dark majesty of the cathedral-like cavern.

'It's all fine and hunky-dory getting here,' whispered Ikara. 'But where on earth do we start looking?'

'In this central cavern,' murmured Zorrin. 'Hypnos would want to keep the sapphire somewhere close to him, so he could protect it. I suspect that he uses the tunnels purely for getting out to catch food.'

'Tasty morsels like us?' asked Skoodle. 'He'll think it's his birthday, with us all coming right to him. Hold the glowing stick high, so he'll think there's a candle-lit cake.'

'Hush, gloomy guts,' said Keeko.

'This cave is gigantic,' pointed out Alex. 'It will take hours to check. Furthermore, he would hardly leave it lying around on the floor.'

'Nooks and crannies in the walls may be a likely hiding place,' suggested Tariq.

'Think he'd have put it in that thing?' Keeko pointed to a high ledge many metres above the ground on which stood a dirty turquoise cup-shaped object, its upper edge jagged as if it had once been a whole oval. Further along the narrow ledge opened the mouth of a tunnel.

'Could you climb the rock face below it?' Zorrin asked Keeko.

Keeko looked at the glistening wall running with water. 'No. It's too slippery. Too few handholds.'

'How about getting to the ledge from further along the wall? Looks a bit less steep and damp,' suggested Skoodle.

'No chance,' replied Keeko, shaking her head. 'Suicide bid. I'm too pretty to die.'

'There is another way,' said Zorrin. 'Give me a moment.'

Staring hard at the stalactite in front of him Zorrin stood completely still, then transmorphed into a small orange and blue parrot. He soared over the edge of the cup, perching for a moment to tap it. After flying around the mouth of the tunnel Zorrin swooped back to the ground. With a squawk, he transmorphed back to a wizard.

Dusting a few orange feathers off his shirt, Zorrin said, 'Unfortunately there's no sign of the sapphire. The cup is empty but the inside surface is beautiful, shiny like an opal. We'd better split up and start searching the walls.'

'How?' asked Ikara. 'Even a snake's eyes aren't that good. It's pitch black over there.'

'Dip your heads in the lake,' said Zorrin. 'Being fed from a tributary of the River Ohm, the lake is self-illuminant.'

'What?' asked Skoodle.

'Creates its own light.'

'Fantastic. Hamster with a halo. Dip me first,' said Skoodle, hopping up and down.

Alex lowered Skoodle into the lake by his back legs. Righted again, Skoodle's head glowed as if each hair was a tiny fluorescent tube. Droplets of water cascaded down his back like runway lights.

'Ice,' said Keeko. 'Me next.'

Zorrin groaned. 'Even in here? Ice?'

'Yup. Defrost, language-challenged one,' said Ikara.

Other than Zorrin, who chose to use his light staff, they all dipped their heads. Ikara dipped her tail as well then wriggled across the floor, leaving a fluorescent trail as if she were an elongated snail.

'I'll start over there,' said Zorrin indicating the back cavern wall. 'Tariq, can you begin—'

The surface of the lake started hissing and bubbling. From deep in the water came a roaring, rapidly increasing like a jet taking off. Something dark loomed in the depths, enlarging every instant. With a crash like a thunderclap, the surface of the lake exploded.

The monster Hypnos erupted from it, towering ten feet high, scaly arms outstretched, vicious claws ready for ripping. Instantly, Alex sprinted towards the boat tunnel, pounding across the hard unforgiving ground. The roars of Hypnos echoed off the cavern walls, filling his head with noise. Out of the corner of his eye he caught sight of Tariq running to a nearby tunnel, Keeko clamped to his chest.

Vaguely aware that Zorrin hadn't moved, Alex flung a glance over his shoulder, hoping not to see Hypnos's snout just behind him. Zorrin was backing away slowly, calmly facing the gargantuan beast who was hesitating, looking round as if choosing a victim.

Alex stopped and swung round. 'Run, Zorrin,' he yelled. His voice echoed round the cave, poor competition for the mighty bellows issuing from Hypnos.

Zorrin's voice came to him through the orgreeb. 'Keep going,' he said urgently. 'I haven't gone mad.'

'You sure?'

'You heard the wizard. Hit it,' yelled Skoodle.

'I'm OK,' insisted Zorrin, although his voice sounded tense.

Alex picked up speed and sprinted as if all the demons on Earth were after him.

'Faster,' yelled Skoodle. 'Run while your legs are still attached to your body.'

'That's strangely motivating,' returned Alex.

Hypnos focused on the closest figure: the wizard. After another moment's hesitation, Zorrin pelted for the blackness, his light staff held in front. Hypnos sprinted after him, an avalanche of muscle and teeth, his claws clattering on the spiky rocks.

'*Ventus,*' called Zorrin.

A slipstream of air picked him up, zooming him into a tunnel. The aqualate surged into the confined space, every horrific sound magnified in the echoing void. Zorrin hammered along just in front of the serpent's flickering tongue, only millimetres from the jagged rock walls.

A gust of heat on the back of Zorrin's neck gave him a fraction of a second's warning that Hypnos must be a fire breather. A blast of flame shot forward, scorching the rock behind him.

'*Centra,*' Zorrin shouted.

An invisible shield particulated behind Zorrin, deflecting the inferno. Hypnos screamed as the flames rebounded into his face.

Enraged by pain, Hypnos drove on faster – gradually inching closer as Zorrin surfed the air, weaving crazily. Zorrin's mind was racing: max speed, but losing ground. He would have to transparticulate soon. As every second passed, the danger of wizard tag increased. Yet if he disappeared, Hypnos would turn back to the central cavern.

An idea sparked into his mind. If Hypnos thought he was still ahead, the monster would charge on, buying them time. Zorrin checked his map. Six feet away a tunnel ran parallel to this one. Rounding a sharp bend Zorrin transparticulated into the tunnel next door, sending the fire torch ahead on the air stream as a decoy.

Zorrin reappeared in total blackness. Hardly daring to breathe, he stood for a moment and waited, listening.

CHAPTER 29

In a stone cell in the heart of the mountain, a prisoner sat slumped, head drooping forward almost to his chest. Restlessly, pointlessly, he twiddled a rat bone in his fingers, as he had done for many empty years. Despair had long ago left him. Cold, all-consuming anger and lust for revenge were the only emotions he now felt. His filthy grey beard straggled down to the waist of his tattered robes. The starving man didn't notice the disgusting stench of his personal filth, mingled with the stink of rotting rodent carcasses.

Rats roamed freely at his feet. In the beginning he'd beaten them away as they gnawed at his disintegrating boots, but when they'd become his only source of food, he had allowed them to stay. With the ache of hunger wrenching at his guts, he'd smash one against the wall, then cook it with the small amount of magic he still retained. Rat-tails, skulls and bones littered his cell.

The receding clatter of Hypnos's claws sounded in the air. Yet something was different. In the lined and filthy face, the eyes glittered through the darkness, hungry for vengeance. He leaned his head to one side and concentrated.

The roaring became fainter. The trembling in the ground beneath Zorrin's feet subsided. Igniting a tiny fire in his hand, he listened for a few more seconds, then increased the light. The tunnel lit up, its craggy stone walls scorched where Hypnos had bellowed out his anger over decades.

'Hypnos has gone for a bit,' Zorrin said aloud to the others through their orgreebs. 'Return to the main cavern.'

Before he could summon an air stream, the croak of a barely human voice reached him.

'Zorrin.'

Thunderstruck, Zorrin halted and looked about. No one was there. The walls were solid, containing no chink or hole from which someone could have called him. But a voice had spoken; one he had not heard for a very long time.

'Saranak?' he asked, taking out his orgreeb.

'Over here,' called the voice from behind him.

Zorrin wandered back down the corridor, until he came to a very small slit in the stone, through which seeped the pungent smell of rotting flesh.

'Are you in here?' he asked, peering into the blackness, but unable to see anything.

'Yes,' Saranak replied, voice thin and hoarse from disuse. 'Let me out, Zorrin. I can help you.'

Zorrin frowned. 'You help me? How?'

'I know how to kill the creature.'

'Then tell me quickly. Otherwise my friends and I may die.'

'It's not that easy. You must let me out. Then I shall assist you.'

'A good try, but with your past history of treachery, I'd rather face Hypnos alone.' Zorrin turned away, relieved to be leaving the stench.

'No,' croaked Saranak. 'I swear to help you, on the Rod of Gethsite if I must. I need to be free, so that I can kill that traitorous monster by my own hand.'

Zorrin turned back. 'You remember what will happen to you if you break an oath sworn by the Rod?'

'Yes, I know too well. But note this: I'll not swear to fight on your behalf always. Just today. It'll be enough.' The voice began to sound stronger as hope filled Saranak.

'Deal done. Vow.'

Saranak coughed hoarsely then said:

'By the power of the Rod, at this moment I swear:

In Gethsite tortured find me, if breaking oath I dare.

189

Till midnight tonight Zorrin's ally shall I be,
Those who fight against him are enemies to me.
Revenge will be mine; though it cost my living breath,
By the power of my hand, Hypnos shall meet death.'
The last words echoed softly down the tunnel, a chilling refrain.
Zorrin nodded. 'It will be binding. Stand back.'

He put his tiny fire on the floor, then held out his arms towards the wall, not quite touching it. Hands aligned with the slender fissure, he murmured. *'Nactras vobe.'*

The gap started to widen, creaking as the rock groaned against the powerful enchantment surging through it. Yet, despite his efforts, the gap remained too small for even the wasted frame of Saranak.

'Nactras vobe,' Zorrin repeated, sweating profusely, his mental processes pitted against intricately-woven magic.

The spell gave with a loud crack. A jagged fissure appeared in the grey stone wall. Through the crack limped a pitiful creature, physically broken. Yet his eyes blazed with the passionate fire of hatred, giving dangerous life to his thin face.

'Thank you. This allegiance, albeit brief, should be to the advantage of each of us. Perhaps you would dim your flame. It's painful to my eyes after so many years in the dark.'

'You have suffered, Saranak,' said Zorrin, reducing the brightness of the fire as he picked it up.

'Hypnos tricked me. I, who had taken him on as an apprentice when no one else would. I who spoke to him of hidden magic, taught him dark spells that few dare to use, roused demons that fewer still can muster. Yet it was me he turned against when his knowledge became great enough. The student overthrew the master.' The filthy bent wizard propped himself against the wall as he spoke, his reedy voice cracking.

'Why did you allow him to learn enough to overcome you?'

'I didn't teach him that. He stole my books and papers. He's an evil one. Yes, I see you smile. I'm evil in your eyes because my path differs from yours, and many of the Dark Sciences are well known to me. Yet I am not a traitor to my associates. Now he'll pay the penalty of all traitors: death. Let's get on with it.'

His bowed figure set off at a limp, his breathing ragged after only a few steps.

'Have all your powers gone?' asked Zorrin.

'Not all, but few remain.'

'Since we're at present allies, I shall assist you.' Zorrin pointed at Saranak. A burgundy hooded cloak appeared over Saranak's filthy rags.

'Better.'

'*Ventus.*'

An air stream whisked them towards the central cavern.

'Good spell,' Saranak murmured. 'Almost civilised.'

'Do you know where the Sapphire of Akan is?'

Saranak drove a hand through his dirty grey hair. 'Hypnos has it. He stole it from me.'

'Where does he keep it?'

'I don't know.'

'How can you kill him? What's his weakness?'

A faint smile appeared on Saranak's face. 'In our newly-formed allegiance, you'll have to trust me. You'll find out a minute or so before he dies. For years I have plotted his death. Revenge must be by my own hand.'

The wind stream deposited them in the main cave. Saranak gazed around the cavern, screwing his eyes up against the cold blue light of the lake.

'You remember this cave well, I take it?' asked Zorrin, putting his orgreeb back in.

'Faultlessly. I kept my sanity by taking a mental journey around this labyrinth. At the end of each dream, I triumphantly reached out and crushed him.' Saranak grimaced, malice oozing from the cruel mouth. 'I'll go now, but don't worry. I'll do my part.'

He made a mocking bow to Zorrin and set off for the dark north west side of the cave.

CHAPTER 30

Ikara and Alex wandered out of the shadows.

'Who's he?' asked Ikara, watching Saranak stumbling away.

'Temporary friend. He returns to the other side by dawn.'

Ikara spat after him. 'We need no such friends.'

'Unfortunately we do. He may know a way to kill the monster. Now that Hypnos knows we're here, it's either his death or ours. Shortly he will realise that I'm no longer ahead of him and return.'

'We'd better get looking,' said Tariq, shambling into the light, Keeko perched on his shoulders.

'Shouldn't we go?' asked Keeko. 'He'll kill one of us next time. It was lucky he chose you, Zorrin.'

'No, it wasn't,' said Alex. 'I saw Zorrin wait, deliberately making himself into bait. Hypnos chose the closest victim; the one who didn't run.'

Zorrin shrugged his shoulders. 'I was sure I could escape, so it wasn't a big deal.'

'Rabbit droppings,' said Skoodle. 'If I'd done it, I'd make sure you were eternally grateful to me.'

'Or rather, to your memory,' replied Ikara. 'No one except Zorrin would have survived.'

A roar of warm air belched out of a tunnel. The ground beneath them began to tremble as the heavy lizard thundered towards them, the scrabbling of claws growing louder.

'He's coming,' squeaked Skoodle. 'Run.'

'We'll follow Saranak, help him kill Hypnos, then get the sapphire. *Ventus.*'

The spell picked them up on an air cushion floating about a foot above the ground, as if they were on an invisible surfboard.

'This is great,' said Ikara, whizzing along behind Zorrin. 'If I have to die, I might as well do it comfortably.'

Noise blasted from the end of a tunnel. Hypnos burst into the cavern, mouth dripping green slime.

'Faster,' shrieked Keeko. 'He's seen us.'

Hypnos drew a vast lungful of breath, ready to blast out another fireball.

'*Centra,*' Zorrin yelled.

The fireproof screen solidified behind them a second before the first bolt of fire hit. Zorrin flicked a glance backwards, hoping to see Hypnos receiving another reflected fireball in his face. The reptile ducked to avoid the rebound inferno, which rolled over his head.

'Zorrin, Zorrin, he's our wizard. He will kill that ugly lizard,' chanted Skoodle.

Tariq looked back at the enormous monster charging along behind them, glowing reptilian eyes fixed on his target. 'Skoodle has a point. Can't you annihilate Hypnos? Or are you holding out to get info about the stone?'

'I can't kill him,' replied Zorrin as he accelerated the air cushion. 'I can't even do him much harm. His magic is too great.'

Ikara sank down, tail over her eyes. 'Tell us earlier next time, if there is a next one.'

'At least it will be quick,' said Tariq. 'Perhaps better than at Virida's hand.'

'If you two would shut up about the merits of various types of death, we could have a go at working out how to avoid being bumped off,' said Skoodle. 'Can't we escape down a tunnel?'

'No,' replied Zorrin. 'We could end up trapped.'

'Then disparticulate us,' said Alex.

'Not possible up here. It's taking all my energy to keep us and the shield moving at this speed.'

They closed in on the thin figure of Saranak, limping across the cavern floor.

As they drew level with him, Zorrin held out his hand. 'Grab on,' he yelled.

Saranak's bony hand reached up. Zorrin clasped him by the wrist, yanking him up off the rough stone floor on to the air stream.

Saranak indicated north west across the cavern with a spindly finger. 'Get me to that tunnel mouth. Split the air cushion: shield me and distract Hypnos.'

Pointing to the floor, Zorrin muttered a few words. The air cushion parted. Saranak swung a few degrees to the right in the air.

'Fugato non visare decime,' muttered Zorrin.

'He's vanished,' said Alex, looking at where Saranak had been only a second before. 'Double-crossed us.'

'No, he hasn't. I have made him invisible for a short while so Hypnos will chase us, giving Saranak a chance to make it across the cavern.'

'Good trick,' said Skoodle, stamping his foot on Alex's shoulder, arms crossed, whiskers trembling. 'Perhaps you would care to do the same for the rest of us. We've been your allies for longer than two minutes.'

Another firebolt hit the screen, filling the air with the acrid smell of scorched earth.

'Seems he's heard that hot roasted snake is terrific,' said Ikara, climbing Tariq to get away from the centra screen.

'Look out,' shrieked Keeko. 'Wall ahead.'

'Follow Saranak,' yelled Alex, eyes fixed on the solid stone only seconds away.

'No. If he gets killed, we all die,' replied Zorrin. 'Hold on. We're going over.'

The air cushion twisted, wrenching them through 180 degrees, heading back the way they'd come. Ducking under the ragged cave ceiling, they cleared Hypnos's fiery mouth by only centimetres.

Hypnos belched out another fireball, engulfing them in the smell of spent gunpowder. Suddenly they were falling, accelerating towards the row of slime-covered teeth. Keeko's tail, outstretched in terror, entered the cavernous throat. She screamed at the touch of Hypnos's burning tongue.

'*Deshira,*' yelled Zorrin.

The group rocketed up before Hypnos could snap off Keeko's tail.

'What happened?' asked Tariq, arms wrapped around the terrified monkey.

'In the twist, the heat shield slid above the slipstream,' said Zorrin ignoring the angry roar echoing around the cavern. 'The fireball destroyed the air cushion. I've reversed them. The heat shield is now below us.'

Hypnos bellowed. A bolt of flame flashed upwards. Instinctively everyone braced, Keeko burying her face in Tariq's chest. Warmth soaked through to the bases of their feet. The ball of fire bounced away, leaving the new air cushion stable. Alex breathed out.

'It's good that he's angry,' said Zorrin, looking down at the enraged face.

Ikara stared at him. 'Explain.'

'He's acting like an ordinary serpent: raw rage is driving him. Once he calms down he'll think like a wizard. Then we'll be in serious trouble.'

'It would be a shame to go from this minor problem to a really difficult situation,' said Skoodle.

'I'm afraid it's true,' said Zorrin as the air cushion blasted them through the dark air high in the cavern. 'I can protect myself against his spells, but to make sure that all of you are safe too would be close to impossible. Let's hope that Saranak acts quickly. We had better provoke Hypnos; keep him angry. Going down.'

The air cushion dipped sharply once again, rolling steeply towards the monster's gaping jaws.

'Sizzling snakes,' gasped Ikara, holding on to Tariq's leg.

As soon as he saw his victims falling, Hypnos reared up on to his back legs, clawing at them, jaws snapping, tail lashing.

'Animal still,' said Zorrin. For several seconds they hovered above the savage throat, taunting the serpent, tantalising him, close enough for them to smell the fumes of burning.

Hypnos's tongue tip flew upwards as fast as a bolt from a crossbow, bearing straight towards Alex's legs, snapping out like a leather whip.

'*Gulino,*' yelled Zorrin.

Deep cold gripped Alex's lower abdomen and legs, as they turned into steel. His whole lower body felt dead. The poisoned tip clanged against metal, unable to penetrate to his flesh.

Hypnos lashed his tongue around Alex's legs and yanked, dragging him down. Tariq and Keeko grabbed Alex, hauling hard. Yet even with the bear's massive strength it was no contest; Hypnos would win.

'*Tukata.*'

The steel legs began to grow spikes: in seconds, hundreds of sharp points pierced the enveloping tongue. Hypnos's scream ripped through their heads as his tongue untangled and fell loosely away.

'*Desamori,*' Hypnos growled, his deep rasping voice echoing round the cavern.

'Twisted toads,' said Zorrin. 'Wizard now. That's the shield gone permanently. My show of magic must have made something click inside his head.'

Hypnos took a deep breath, ready to launch the fatal fireball.

'*Tempestua,*' shouted Zorrin. A massive sheet of water appeared below them, meeting the ball of fire head on. The two opposing elements exploded into a thick cloud of steam.

'Don't inhale,' yelled Zorrin.

Everyone stopped breathing. As the steam wrapped itself over them, every particle of their skin started itching, as if millions of termites were crawling over them. As the seconds ticked past, the oxygen levels in Alex's body plummeted. He fought against the screaming demands of his chest, not daring to inhale. If the pain of his skin felt appalling, the agony inside his lungs would be a thousand times worse.

Zorrin seemed to be constructing a spell, waving his arm in a swooping gesture. The pressure in Alex's chest built to almost unbearable. His ears felt as if they would burst.

'It's OK,' called Zorrin. 'Clearing spell.'

Alex closed his eyes and sucked in air, relieved to be breathing, the ache in his chest subsiding.

The temperature plummeted as if an air stream direct from the Antarctic were blasting through. The current below them sparkled blue and silver, the water droplets turning into tiny crystals of ice.

'Crisis: a full freezing spell. I may not be able to keep us alive.' Zorrin started muttering under his breath, yet the temperature continued to fall.

Within seconds, ice had formed in Alex's hair. Every breath out froze into delicate white clouds, falling from their nostrils to shatter on the ground far below. Cold bored through to their bones.

'My body's stiffening up,' said Tariq, sitting down on the air stream. 'It's hard to move.'

Zorrin nodded slightly to acknowledge that he had heard but continued to murmur, face rigid with concentration.

Ikara will be gone the soonest, thought Alex, looking down at the stiffening body at his feet. Cold-blooded; a disaster in polar frost. Already her eyes had glazed and she seemed to have stopped breathing. As his mind roved over this thought, the blood in his brain was flowing so slowly that he felt no sadness, nor could he think of anything to do to help.

Tariq picked up Ikara. She came up rigid, like the branch of a tree. His movements achingly slow, Tariq placed her up against his chest and wrapped his great furry arms around the icy body. Brave move, thought Alex. Choosing to embrace a block of ice while freezing to death, in the faint hope that the minimal heat he had to share would keep Ikara alive.

Below them Hypnos waited, knowing he'd won. No further fight was needed. He watched his victims dying slowly, painfully.

The temperature dropped further. Every breath that Alex took became tougher, as if his lungs were made of iron. The air felt thick, like treacle. His whole body ached. Tiny sparkling lights engulfed his vision. Unconsciousness could not be far off.

Zorrin's lips were still moving, but slowly. He's failing, Alex realised. We'll all soon be dead. This icy entombment would be an appallingly painful end: more torture than he could have believed sheer cold could produce.

No longer the focus of Zorrin's concentration, the air stream had been gradually dropping and slowing. Hypnos waited, poised for attack, until his victims were within reach.

At last he leapt. The whole of Alex's visual field filled with a vast cavern of a mouth, smoking black throat beyond. There was the hiss of steam as Hypnos's hot breath met ice. Alex cried out, but too late. The jaws were closing.

CHAPTER 31

A wall of sound bellowed out of Hypnos, wrenching his jaws apart. The howl echoed around the chamber, terrifyingly reverberant. The temperature began to rise. Alex's mind started to clear as Ikara began to breathe.

A long ragged gash was carved across Hypnos's underbelly. Blood gushed from the wound, staining the rocks beneath him crimson. Crazed with pain, Hypnos clutched his side with a scaly claw.

High above them, Saranak stood on a ledge, stringy grey hair swirling in the wind from the tunnel behind. He held the turquoise cup triumphantly above his head, a small fragment of it in his other hand.

'Hypnos,' he called in a cracked voice. 'You know what I'm holding? Your death.'

Hypnos spat fire. 'You, Saranak? Released by your enemies? They were fools to trust you.'

'Not so, it seems,' murmured Ikara. 'Go on – kill the aqualate, turncoat wizard.'

A high maniacal laugh rang from the gaunt figure on the ledge, burgundy cloak billowing behind him. 'As I was to trust you for so many years. How much did you learn?' He snapped his thin fingers. 'Enough to trap me by betraying my trust, but not enough to be safe from such a small party of invaders. If you had learned your lessons properly these filthy marauders would be dead by now. Yet Zorrin still lives – a problem for me tomorrow – but then you always were a lazy student.'

The aqualate's head swayed in anger. 'Is lazy not better than cruel and twisted?'

'Got a point,' whispered Ikara. 'Someone hand me a monkey to warm my tail on.'

Keeko moved forward to sandwich Ikara between her body and Tariq's.

Saranak's face broke into a humourless smile. 'I have little emotion: that is true. My life has been a tortuous path, sometimes touching the darkest voids. Yet it is I who now stands victorious.'

'A wound is not a victory,' thundered the monster, grasping his bleeding side. 'The shell belongs to me. Replace it and you'll go free.'

A bitter laugh screeched out of Saranak. 'I am free. No thanks to you, however. Loyalty meant nothing to you. I was an innocent man, condemned to starve alone in darkness.'

'You were a cruel master, Saranak. You had no love for me. Yet I agree that now you have the upper hand.' The serpent's glittering eyes left Saranak's to fix on the turquoise cup. 'So I'll once again be your servant, bound to you by an oath of the deeper magic. Together we will cast out this crew.' He waved a scaly front leg at Zorrin. 'Likewise we'll destroy all who cross our paths. In full power together, we shall be invincible. All Eridor shall bow to us.'

'No,' cracked out Saranak, voice growing stronger with every passing moment. 'Once I have crushed you, my powers will return to me in full. I have no need of you now. I was wrong to have trained you, to have shared my knowledge, for two can never have the total focus of a single mind.'

He held the cup high up above his head.

'Don't,' yelled out Hypnos, the word almost consumed by the massive ball of fire exploding from his mouth.

'I really don't want to do this,' said Saranak, ragged turquoise cup balanced on his fingertips. 'I have waited for so long… dreamed so often of the moment of your death. In a few seconds the pleasure of anticipating your death will transform into a wonderful memory.'

'Why kill me, when you could harness my forces? This way makes no sense. Bind me and let me live. It's better for both of us that I serve you than die.'

'A good speech. Yet that silver tongue has cost me many years of pain and darkness. I no longer want to hear what it has to say any more. Goodbye.'

Saranak's skull-like face lit up in the passion of his victory, sunken eyes staring like a madman. His hands clasped the cup, relishing the intense joy of touching the pinnacle of his plans and dreams. Then he threw the cup towards the cavern floor. Hypnos screamed as he leapt forward, tearing the wound in his side wider. Blood pumped from his stricken body as he plunged through the air.

The cup smashed on to hard stone, shattering into minute fragments. With a thunderous crack, Hypnos splintered into a thousand shards of fire. Particles of his body fell like burning rain on to the lake, hissing and spitting as they sliced through the surface.

Alex grinned at Tariq. 'So the bad wizard really could kill him. Explosive result.'

'I'll change your legs back, Alex. Can't stay metal forever,' said Zorrin. '*Gorflork.*'

High on the ledge, Saranak was undergoing an extraordinary transformation. The outline of his bony body became full as his crooked back straightened. Straggly grey hair thickened into a rich chestnut mane falling down his back. Tattered rags morphed into luxuriant dove-grey robes cascading to his feet. The flesh of his face became strong in the glow of the lake.

Saranak looked down at his changing form as energy pulsed through him. 'Now I reap the fruits of my revenge.' He drifted down to the cavern floor on an air slide. The others floated back to the ground to join him.

'What was the cup?' asked Zorrin.

'The shell from which he had hatched: prized above all other possessions. When I began to suspect that my powers were being drained I enchanted it, so I could ensure that its destruction would destroy him. He knew, but could not disentangle the spell.'

'Stupid of him to leave it lying about,' said Skoodle.

Saranak glanced at the rodent. 'He didn't. He stole it from me then concealed it. However, once he'd stripped me of my magic and imprisoned me without food in a doorless chamber, he believed that I was no threat. So he returned it to its perch. He gloated about it many times when he came to see if I'd starved to death yet.' Saranak looked down at his new robes and brushed off a minuscule speck of dust. 'The master turned slave has once again become the master.'

'I do not recall you telling me that your powers would return on Hypnos's death,' replied Zorrin. 'I doubt if I would have released you if I'd known.'

The two wizards faced each other, handsome young faces oddly similar, eyes locked as if trying to read each other's mind.

'I don't recall you asking me the question,' replied Saranak. 'In fact, from the way I feel, I believe that his powers have been transferred to me as well. Two wizards in one. When I'm no longer your ally, I'll be a mighty enemy. Tomorrow will be an interesting day for you.'

A new voice filled the cavern, familiar, terrifying, echoing from a ledge high above them. 'Hypnos exploded. Saranak rescued and empowered. You have done well.'

Zorrin's head whipped around. 'Karlan. You were trapped. How did you escape?'

A figure stepped out of the shadows to stand beside Karlan, head high.

'Flick,' breathed Zorrin, body rigid. 'Why?'

'Difficult to believe her change in loyalty, is it? Tough.' Karlan glanced across to the slender figure beside him. 'People will do anything for love – won't they, dear?'

'Of course,' said Flick gazing at him with open adoration.

'Yet Flick understands that in battle sacrifices may need to be made.' He pointed at her heart. 'If any of you try to resist, she dies. It seems that I hold all the power: my ally Saranak released and restored to double his full power, Hypnos destroyed, the love of your sister, the loyalty of Tevo's troop… '

As he spoke, there came crunching of feet on rocks. Out of the shadows enrobing the high ridges stepped Rectoria, Tevo, Rycant and all the warriors who had so recently invaded the castle. The final figure stepped forward, elegant and slender in a full-length flowing navy dress. Waist-length black hair fell in a sleek cascade around her beautiful face. Her cold ebony eyes swept over the group on the floor.

Karlan took her hand and lead her to the edge of the ledge. 'I believe you have all met Virida, although not perhaps in this form.'

Keeko gasped and clung tighter to Tariq. Skoodle vanished back into Alex's pocket, small body trembling against Alex's chest. Taking Virida's and Flick's hands, Karlan stepped off the ledge on to an air slide. They drifted down to the cave floor, landing in front of Zorrin.

Zorrin ran his hand through his mood streak, which was spitting red sparks. He addressed Flick. 'You released all of them?'

'I did,' she replied, lifting her chin.

Alex stared at her, unable to believe what he was hearing.

'I'll kill her,' muttered Ikara. 'Just give me half a chance.'

Addressing Karlan, Zorrin said, 'I assume all of this was a set-up designed for me to get this far, then for you to sweep in and take the sapphire.'

'Correct. I would not have risked my life against that monster. Many have died trying to get past him. Your powers and wit are superior to most, so I felt that somehow you might succeed, although the release of Saranak was, of course, an unexpected bonus. I didn't know he was still alive.'

Saranak raised an eyebrow. 'I trust that if you had realised you would have spent time searching for me.'

'Undoubtedly,' Karlan replied, his eyes steady on Saranak's own.

'The kidnap at the Redwood? How did that help you in this plan?' asked Zorrin. 'I'm struggling to piece together the whole story.'

'It didn't. At that point imprisonment was intended purely to disempower, until I could work out how to kill you. It was only when I heard Alex trying to enlist your help to seek the sapphire that I realised that a delicious new twist had entered. I would tag along, let you destroy Hypnos, and then take the stone for myself.

If you were to die in the attempt that would suit my purpose almost as well.'

'You're making that up,' said Alex angrily. 'It's a pile of lies. You couldn't have heard us talking. You weren't even there.'

Karlan looked down at him. 'As it happens, I was. Do you recall a dazed field mouse in the upper room shortly after you released Zorrin at the Single Redwood? It was me. I had decided that transformation would be a better option than a direct attack. Although naturally I had recovered well from our tussle, I wasn't fully up to strength. I was intelligent enough to know that Zorrin, being angry and forewarned, would be a powerful enemy. Once I knew your plan, I turned myself into a crocodile. You hospitably flew me to Ravenscraig.'

'You also threatened to kill me on the boat,' said Alex.

'Correct. Though you tediously escaped without giving me any information.'

Alex was seething inwardly. He'd faced Karlan twice and won. Now, because of Flick's treachery, he was back in Karlan's power. He would know exactly how this had happened. 'How did you know that I was even on the boat?'

A snort greeted this comment. 'That was easy. I'd been waiting for you. At some point your parents' research was bound to fall into your hands. It was predictable how you'd attempt to get to Eridor as there's only one direct entrance from your world, also only one boat a week to Tikopia. I only had to wait for a few boats before you turned up. Yet if your parents had told me where the netbook was before I disposed of them none of this would have been necessary.'

'Disposed of them,' yelled Alex, stepping forward, fists clenched. 'What did you do to my parents?'

'What was needed,' said Karlan. 'As it is necessary to kill you now, Zorrin.' He pointed a finger at Zorrin's heart.

'We agreed that he wasn't to die,' said Flick in strangely flat measured tones.

Karlan half turned to her. 'Yet he must die. Surely you see that, my dear? He'll do everything in his power to prevent us from getting the sapphire. We have come so far. We cannot fall at the final hurdle.'

'But we agreed,' said Flick, frowning.

'The agreement is broken.' Karlan turned to face Zorrin, ready to launch the death spell, finger unwavering.

Zorrin looked at his sister. 'I love you,' he said. 'Goodbye.'

CHAPTER 32

'Touching,' sneered Karlan. *'Mort—'*

Flick's hand slammed down in a karate chop, breaking Karlan's wrist. Face contorted in agony he grabbed his arm, knees buckling. Flames appeared at Flick's feet. As the inferno licked up her body, her foot lashed up, kicking Karlan in the chest, sending him flying backwards. A second kick smashed Virida on to the ground, splitting her scalp, concussing her. The fireball travelled up Flick, leaving her untouched.

'It's the spell combusting,' whooped Zorrin. 'It wasn't love. He'd hexed her.'

'Kill them,' yelled Tevo.

The cavern filled with noise. Hollering furiously, Tevo's warriors abseiled down the walls. The angry pack charged at the small group in the middle.

'Death or dishonour,' screamed Rectoria.

Without a glance at Karlan's agonised figure, Flick ran across to join Zorrin and the others. 'I'm so sorry.'

Zorrin hugged her. 'Already forgotten.' He pointed at Karlan and Virida. *'Inertia wizii.'* Pale ropes spun round their feet, binding their arms to their chests. 'Guard them,' Zorrin called to Saranak. Nodding agreement, Saranak pulled them to sitting, using their bodies as a living shield, sheltering him from the goblin pack.

Tevo's troops surged forwards, hunger for blood in their eyes. Zorrin's group swung to face the oncoming marauders.

'Aliano,' shouted Zorrin.

The group was wrenched upwards, high above the angry pack. Snarling wolves and foxes screamed at them in fury.

'The goblins will use crossbows or throw some axes. We'll need these.' Zorrin muttered a few words under his breath. A bow and some arrows materialised in front of each of them.

Tariq shot into the pack of wolves below. With a yelp, one of the wolves keeled over and lay still. The roar from the enraged pack doubled.

'Tariq one, wolf pack nil,' yelled Skoodle waving his tiny bow in the air.

'Duck,' shouted Alex.

As Zorrin's body dropped, an axe whistled past inches from his left ear.

Taking aim, Keeko shot an arrow into Tevo's shoulder. The goblin fell to his knees, clutching his body as blood seeped through his fingers, saturating his shirt.

'Attack,' he screamed as Flick grabbed another arrow. 'It's only a flesh wound. Fight the filthy sons of tainted earth.'

'*Deflecto,*' called Karlan from where he lay, barely conscious.

Flick's arrow took a right-angled bend from its flight path towards Arnak's heart, landing on rocks nearby. Alex took aim at Rycant.

'There's no point,' said Zorrin, grabbing his arm. 'They'll all miss now.'

'*Deflecto,*' Flick shouted.

Two crossbow shafts heading for Tariq veered away, ricocheting off the roof above him, clattering to the floor.

'Kind of Karlan to remind me of that spell,' said Flick.

'What now?' asked Keeko.

'The feathers,' replied Tariq, as an axe flew past Alex.

'No. The eagles won't help us here. It's too dark and enclosed for them,' said Zorrin.

'We're in a mountain. Call on Makusha,' said Ikara looking down at the angry hoard below the air cushion. 'Use a stone.'

Zorrin pulled a black stone from his pocket and held it on his open palm. 'Makusha, we need you.'

Ikara felt it first, her snake's senses so much more acute than any goblin or human. Her inner ear sensors detected the changes in air pressure as the first of the tremors vibrated through the cavern, building rapidly. Within milliseconds they could all feel it.

The vibrations in the rock sent spasms through Tevo's impaled shoulder. 'What's happening?' he asked, struggling to rise.

Rectoria pushed him back down. 'Stay still, otherwise the arrow may shift and kill you. A corpse cannot be a leader.'

A small earthquake was surging through the mountain. Enormous fissures slashed across the walls of the cave as the ground groaned and shifted. A vast split appeared in the cavern ceiling, zigzagging down the wall, extending crazily across the floor to the very heart of the lake. Boulders cascaded from the raw edge of the fault as it gashed its way through the body of the mountain.

The animals crouched, terrified. Unsure whether to fight or run, they stared at the goblins for guidance. Tevo lay still, white-faced, jaw muscles clenched, clutching his wound, offering no lead.

'We'll get crushed,' cried out Keeko.

'Hunch over to protect the smaller ones,' called Zorrin, as deadly jagged rocks cascaded from the ceiling.

'No. Get us down. We need to run for it,' yelled Alex.

Zorrin swung towards him, glaring a warning. Though not understanding, Alex formed a scrum with Tariq, Flick and Zorrin.

'I'll pretend to try and make a spell,' whispered Zorrin, his voice normal through their orgreebs. 'Once I announce I've failed, then bolt, but go no further than the dark shadows.'

Zorrin raised his head and cast his arms about wildly, shouting bizarre words. His waving and gesticulation became increasingly frantic. Alex and the others watched him, sweating. From the floor of the cavern Rectoria stared – the animals by her side trembling, hair on end.

'It's not working,' screamed Zorrin. 'Get out. Save yourselves. Meet in the forest.'

The air cushion dropped to the floor. As soon as their feet touched down, they sprinted for the walls.

'Retreat instantly. Meet at base camp,' barked out Rectoria.

Without hesitation the animals bolted for the tunnels. Only Rycant stayed by her side.

'Well?' asked Rectoria, glaring at the dog.

'How are we to move Tevo?' growled Rycant. 'If he stays here, he may die.'

'If we move him, he will definitely die. I will remain with him. If the fates have it that Tevo or I are saved, we shall meet you again in the forest. If not, you must take over and lead our band to victory. Now go.'

Rycant barked once, then galloped away through the hail of boulders, treacherously hoping that both goblins would perish. The thundering rhythm of his paws seemed to say, 'New leader, new leader.'

'So you do love me,' said a weak but triumphant voice from the floor. 'Despite the present mortal danger, you still stay by my side. Such is the stupid heart of a female.'

'You misjudge me. I remain here to make sure that you do die. The arrow missed your heart and lungs. You bleed now from an artery whose flow could be stopped quite easily. Your breathing grows tight because of blood in your chest, not because of any piercing of the lung.' Rectoria's tone was unemotional as she squatted beside him, ignoring the rocks falling around them.

'Why do you let me die?' asked Tevo, struggling to rise. 'The band needs me to lead them.'

'Rubbish. They need a leader, certainly, but not you. I'll head the band superbly.'

Tevo groaned. 'Tell me where to press. Give me some chance that I might crawl out of here like a dog, yet alive.'

The crack in the roof forked and extended above them. A huge boulder landed inches from Tevo's head, throwing up a cloud of thick dust.

Coughing racked Tevo. 'If you stick to this course, we'll both die. Help me, and we both may yet be saved.'

'Perhaps I should do something for you.' Rectoria reached across Tevo's chest. 'I'll shift the arrow.'

Beads of sweat stood out on Tevo's white face. As she grabbed the shaft, his body stiffened, but he remained silent.

'Your bravery does you credit. This will be worse than horrendous.'

Both hands wrapped round the wood, Rectoria leaned on the shaft with all of her body weight. Tevo grasped his battle axe convulsively as white-hot agony scorched through his chest.

Rectoria let go. 'That's better. It should bleed more freely now. You'll die more quickly.'

'You malicious harridan,' spat Tevo through clenched teeth. 'I curse you. May your own death be painful and drawn-out. May your every plan turn to dust.' He paused for a moment, then spoke slowly and deliberately, emphasising each word. 'May you lose your most beloved possession.'

Rectoria gasped, horror-struck, blood pounding through her system. 'Not Tarran. You can't curse him. He's your son also.'

'Even so. Yet I would have him join me in death. Losing him would cause you such… ' But he had no more words. He lay still, sightless eyes on the crack elongating above them.

Rectoria stood up, shaking, as Rycant reappeared out of the dust.

'Why are you here?' she asked sharply.

'Worried about you. Why are you shaking?

'Tevo's dead.'

'And you mind?'

'Not about him. He invoked a goblin's curse. Tarran will die.'

'So will we if we don't leave. Get to the tunnels. Tell me more in the forest.'

Hunched over, back battered by rocks, Rectoria ran to the tunnels. Close to the floor, concealed in pools of darkness, several pairs of eyes watched her and Rycant sprint for safety.

CHAPTER 33

Running footsteps gradually faded. For several minutes the cave remained filled only with the noise of falling stones, gradually stopping. Zorrin rose and padded to the centre of the cavern, followed by the others.

'We'd better redip our heads,' said Alex as they met at the edge of the lake. 'Dry seems to equal no light.'

'That's going to be difficult,' said Tariq. 'The water level's falling.'

Zorrin picked up Keeko by the legs and dunked the tip of her head in the lake. 'The crack must have extended across the base of the lake. Luckily we'll get light from the wet sides. Nonetheless, I'll mark our tunnel.' Pointing, Zorrin shouted, *'Flamate Orbitus.'*

A huge ball of fire appeared hanging in mid-air, hovering above the entrance to the tunnel. White and silver flames danced and flickered as it rained blue shafts of light.

'Stunning,' said Keeko.

Flick lit a palm fire. Lavender light shone through her fingers, casting shadows on the ground like fat lilac snakes. 'We'd better get searching.'

The task looked hopeless. Although the tremors had subsided, the colossal cavern remained filled with rubble, the air thick with dust.

'If Hypnos wanted to hide the crystal in a place almost impossible to get to, don't you think he would have hidden it in here?" asked Ikara, sliding the tip of her tail into the shimmering water.

'Brilliant,' said Zorrin, watching the gradual fall of the water level.

'Where better to hide a blue crystal than in water? Even if someone had worked out that it was in the lake they would never have found it.'

The last of the water drained out, leaving a vast irregular crater lined by a thin coating of shimmering damp, a jagged fissure carved across the base.

Zorrin squatted down to peer over the sides. 'That may be why Makusha caused the lake to crack and empty. He may have guessed that the sapphire could be there. Keeko, you'll need to go down first. The sides are too steep for anyone else. We'll lower Ikara to you once you've reached the bottom.'

Keeko vaulted over the side. Agile hands soon found a route down the wall. She paused on a ledge. 'I can take Ikara from here,' she called back up.

'This is not only a bad idea, it's a seriously mad idea,' said Ikara as Tariq picked her up by the tail.

'Remember Virida's curse,' said Alex.

Ikara sighed. 'On my way.'

Lying flat on his stomach, arms fully extended, Tariq dangled Ikara over the edge until she hung just above Keeko.

'Drop,' shouted Keeko.

A shimmer of green and gold plummeted downwards. Keeko caught Ikara's head, but the weight of falling snake flattened her. They landed in the sprawl of red-tipped brown fur and golden-green scales.

'Thanks a whole heap,' said Ikara, gingerly stretching her neck. 'My head is safe, but I bruised my tail, and there's a lot of it.'

'My body is totally crushed. I'll see if my tail's still attached once I can find it.'

'I can't see any blood; good sign. You go left, I'll go right,' said Ikara, as she unwrapped herself from Keeko.

They squelched stickily through the silt that had collected on the rocky bottom over many years. Hundreds of small slits fissured the rocks, interspersed with masses of tiny pools.

'By the way,' called Keeko to Zorrin. 'What exactly does it look like?'

'No idea,' he replied. 'Could be any size or shape: free or even set in something, like a ring or dagger handle.'

'Helpful,' murmured Ikara.

'We'll carry on looking up here in case our lake theory is wrong,' said Flick.

Footsteps retreated from the edge as the pair worked in silence, Keeko poking under rocks and in pools of glowing water. Ikara, less patient, swept mounds of silt aside with her tail. Finally they met at the opposite side, empty-handed.

'With my luck, it'll have gone down the central crevasse,' said Ikara, washing herself off in a large puddle.

'Maybe,' said Keeko, sitting down on a rock covered in bright orange weed. 'However, what I know for sure is that we aren't destined to find it.'

'What do you mean?' asked Ikara.

'That legend. We have to assume it's true if we believe that the stone exists. It said that a human would find it, not a snake or a monkey.'

'Mutt head. You could have said something earlier. We need Alex,' said Ikara, looking perkier than she had all day.

'Why bother?' asked Keeko, tossing pebbles into the crevasse. 'He couldn't scale the sides. Neither you nor I could catch him. It would take a whole raft of monkeys and snakes to give him a soft landing.'

'I can get him.' Ikara closed her eyes and concentrated. She started to swell until she was almost as large as Hypnos had been.

Keeko stared at the enormous snake. 'Awesome. I didn't know you could do that.'

'Only found out myself a few months ago.' Ikara slithered around to the far side of the lake then slid her head over the top edge.

'Alex,' she boomed.

'Why didn't you puff up when we were fighting Hypnos?' asked Tariq, wandering across to her. 'You could have defeated him single-handed. Or even no-handed.'

The vast green eyes surveyed him coldly. 'First, it takes time. We were a shade short of that. Also, Hypnos wouldn't have stuck to strength only in serpent-to-aqualate combat. A few spells and I'd have been a pile of minced snake, although an impressively large one. Now listen.' She explained what Keeko had said.

Alex looked at the steep, jagged sides falling to the silty bottom far below. 'You're joking, right?'

'It'll be simple,' replied Ikara. 'Slide down me. When you've finished the heroic finding thing, I'll hoist you back up.'

'Any other choice?'

'Nope,' said Skoodle.

Alex placed a hand on Ikara's head, ready to climb on.

'Hang on. Leave me behind,' said Skoodle, scrambling out of Alex's pocket. 'No point in me going down there. A hamster's not destined to find it. Legend fact.'

'OK.' Alex held Skoodle out to Zorrin.

Zorrin made no move to take Skoodle. 'No, he should go too. He's proved valiant and resourceful. Another set of eyes might help.'

'Great. Flatter me into submission.' The small cream body slid back into Alex's pocket, tiny claws holding tightly on to the edge of the cloth. 'But don't crush the valuable one.'

Alex swung a leg over Ikara's neck, mounting her like a horse, encircling her with his arms, hanging on tightly. He closed his eyes for a second to steady himself, then took a deep breath and loosed his grip.

'Too fast,' yelled Skoodle. 'Slow down.'

'Can't. Mudslick.' Alex shot off the end of the tail, landing face down in a pile of silt. 'You OK, Skoodle?'

'Filthy and I smell of stagnant mud. Otherwise fine.'

Brushing down his bruised body, Alex got to his knees.

'Start fulfilling the legend, human. Get looking,' Ikara rumbled from above them.

Alex scrambled his way round the base of the lake, scraping around in the thick silt, almost suffocated by the smell of rotting fish and bits of dead animals. He rooted beneath bushy green pond plants, dug in small pools, checked behind hundreds of rocks, looked under a clam shell, dug underneath several sheep skulls and peered into fissures – all to the accompaniment of a constant barrage of advice from Skoodle and Keeko. After a complete tour of the lake bed he'd not found the crystal.

Alex peered over the edge of the deep chasm carved through the bottom of the lake. A ghostly light, cast by shimmering water at the bottom, lit the sides. Nothing was caught on the ragged edges. 'After all that, it's not here.'

'It can't be very large or set in a dagger or anything biggish, or it would have been very difficult to pass it on secretly so often,' said Skoodle, brow furrowed. 'Yet if it's fairly small, any currents from Hypnos swimming around might have swished it away. He would have had to put it somewhere secure.'

'Like where?' asked Alex.

'The clam shell on the other side of the lake. Clams don't live in fresh water but Hypnos might have brought one in from the sea if he'd needed one.'

Alex half ran, half stumbled round the irregular sloping wall of the lake until he reached the clam shell wedged between two rocks.

'Put me down,' whooped Skoodle. 'I want a clear view of history being created. Open it. Prove I'm a genius.'

Placing Skoodle on the ground, Alex picked up the shell. 'Looks disappointingly ordinary.'

'Maybe so. Get on with it.'

Alex flicked it open. Cushioned in the pearly interior lay a blue crystal, lit by a supernatural internal fire. 'We've found it. It's stunning,' he yelled.

A cheer rose from the others.

Tariq arrived at the edge of the lake first. 'Quick, bring it up,' he called. 'Let's see it.'

'Come on, Skoodle,' said Alex, reaching down.

'Give me a minute. There's a puddle here. I'm dry as a desert.'

Skoodle scurried to a small pool and began to drink.

★

The crystal felt oddly warm in Alex's hand. As he gazed down into its magnificent depths he began to feel very strange: palms sweaty, his head dizzy. He felt invincible. I've found it, he thought. So it's mine. Why should I hand it over?

Into his brain leapt a passage that Zorrin had read out from his parents' netbook. 'The essence of the Sapphire of Akan steals into the mind, stealthily taking over free will and reason. It eats the soul, leaving a hollow shell.'

'It's getting to me. I've got to get rid of it,' he yelled at Skoodle. 'I'll come back for you.'

He bolted across to Ikara, who swung her head down.

Alex climbed astride the vast nose, eyes closed to avoid staring into her huge green ones, clutching the sapphire in one hand. Ikara swung him upwards. Sliding off the scaly head, he walked unsteadily across to Zorrin and held out his hand. The stone lay on his palm, spitting light.

'There's no doubt it's the Sapphire of Akan,' said Zorrin, as he reached forward to take it.

A blow, like being hit by a tree trunk, flung Alex backwards in a sickening, wrenching fall.

'You're forgetting the pact with Virida,' said Karlan, tone heavy with pain but triumphant.

CHAPTER 34

Karlan's voice seemed to be coming from a long way away as it seeped through the fog in Alex's stunned brain. Alex tried to raise himself a few inches off the floor. Agony gripped him, muscles feeling as if he had been crushed by a bear. Each breath he took sent shafts of pain through his chest as the raw ends of broken ribs grated against each other.

Karlan rose unsteadily to crouching, blood flowing from his chest as he moved. A trail of red marked where he had silently crawled to the edge of the lake, arms tightly bound.

Virida's eyes blazed. 'You fool, Zorrin. All this for nothing. The pact remains intact. Give me the sapphire or die.'

'Think again,' replied Zorrin. 'The agreement does not bind Flick or me.'

'I'm aware of that,' spat out Virida. 'Nevertheless, I know you would not let them die like rats, tortured in agony, when you could save them. Release me so that I may collect my crystal.'

'No,' shouted Tariq, voice echoing around the cavern. 'Do not release her.' He walked forward to stand in front of Zorrin. 'We've agreed to die, all of us. We will never let her have the sapphire. If she becomes mistress of it there will be mass destruction. Thousands of lives will be lost.'

'Tariq is right,' boomed Ikara. 'We've agreed not to concede to filth such as her.'

'Exactly,' said Keeko through her orgreeb.

'I'm prepared to die,' said Alex, hoarsely, gripped by agony so severe that he felt there could be little life left in him anyway.

'Me too,' stated Skoodle, voice angry as he shouted into his orgreeb. 'Uncle Toomba, I'm definitely on the way this time.'

'It's a brave deed you do for Eridor this day,' said Zorrin, his voice resonating round the cavern. He stood proud: sculptured face resolute, black hair cascading down his back, mood streak spitting blue sparks. 'You'll be remembered in song and legend. Your families will be honoured.'

'Their deaths will be slow and agonising. Perhaps watching them suffer will change your mind,' said Virida to Zorrin.

'I sincerely hope not,' said Tariq. 'Yet if I'm to die, I'm taking one of you with me.'

With a massive swipe of his paw, he belted Karlan in the back. Screaming, Karlan plummeted over the vertical edge of the lake.

A cry seemingly from Virida's soul tore through the cavern. 'Save him.'

Zorrin pointed at the falling man. *'Letharto.'* Karlan stopped dropping, hanging helpless in the air, like a boneless cat.

'The spell is mine, Virida. It cannot be overridden by you. Is there any reason I should not let him die?'

Virida flung herself forward on to her knees, terrified eyes fixed on the figure suspended in space. 'For mercy's sake. For respect of another wizard.'

'Not good enough. You didn't show mercy to me. You'll have to do better than that.' Zorrin dropped Karlan another two metres.

'Wait! I'll break the curse. Your companions will go free if you return Karlan safe to me.'

'Agreed,' said Zorrin, as he allowed Karlan's body to rise. 'Although I'm astonished. I didn't think that such a generous spirit was to be found in the evil forces. Why swap him for the power of the sapphire?'

The witch flung back her hair, head held high. 'He's my husband. The loss of the sapphire is like a knife in my breast, but is nothing compared to the anguish I'd suffer on losing his life.'

Karlan's limp figure was dropped into an awkward heap beside Virida.

'What will you do with us now that the stone is yours?' she asked, bending over Karlan, long black hair brushing his face.

As Zorrin paused, a soft voice cut through Alex's dazed thoughts.

'Let me help you up,' murmured Saranak. 'For you're too weak to stand alone.'

He held both hands out to Alex, who instinctively reached up to him. Saranak's hand closed round his arm, nails digging painfully into his flesh. With a sharp crack he broke Alex's wrist, wrenching the stone from his hand. A wave of pain crashed through Alex's body as he landed on his crushed ribs, fractured arm flailing. Twinkling lights filled his darkened vision.

Saranak held the sapphire aloft. 'The stone is mine and all its power with it. You're all defeated. It is justice: having broken the pact by such a foul trick, you shall die anyway.'

'You pledged to be my ally till midnight. Don't you fear breaking your oath?' asked Zorrin.

Saranak smiled mockingly. 'Possession of the crystal far outweighs the power of any oath, even that of the Rod of Gethsite. Breaking it cannot affect me now.' Saranak strode across to Virida. 'Touch Karlan,' he said. 'The power will revive you both.'

Virida leaned to touch Karlan's leg as Saranak put his hand on her shoulder. A surge of life shot from Saranak's arm into the crumpled figures before him, as if an electric cable were pouring energy into them. Their backs arched in spasm as the power surged through them. The magical bonds fell off; Karlan's wounds dried and healed. He rose to standing, head high and proud. Youth infused Virida's face as her hunched shoulders relaxed, the sagging back strengthening.

'Why didn't it help me?' Alex croaked to Zorrin, his throat tight with pain.

'You have no magic, unfortunately.'

'These bonds could be more use elsewhere,' said Saranak, pointing at the ropes binding Virida.

The magical webs flew through the air, landing to form a tangled mass of threads around Flick's and Zorrin's bodies, clamping their arms painfully to their sides, yanking them on to their knees, binding them to the ground.

Saranak's face glowed in triumph. 'Only the owner of the sapphire can release those bonds. You are permanently – terminally – trapped. Your magic is frozen. Useless.'

The goblin band stepped out of the shadows, Rectoria at the front. She brandished her sword at Zorrin. 'Not so clever after all, are you? None of you appeared at the jungle exits so we turned back, luckily in time to enjoy your downfall.'

Saranak held the crystal up to the ceiling, palm open, so that all could see his trophy as it shone its brilliance into the cold cave air. 'With the help of these warriors, victory over Eridor is mine. Zorrin, you are entirely overcome. You have no more weapons.'

'Wrong,' said a voice from behind him.

Before Saranak had time to turn round, Smuddy Binks launched himself straight at the wizard. His heavy body crashed into Saranak, flattening him. The crystal flew from the wizard's hand, spitting cold blue fire. It fell in an arc towards the edge of the lake. As everyone stared, it disappeared into the depths of the crater.

'It's fallen down the crevasse,' screamed Keeko from the bottom of the lake. Nothing can save us now.'

The evil wizards rushed to the edge of the crater and looked down. Keeko stood on the glowing mud peering into the void while Skoodle sobbed nearby, face in hands. The unearthly light of the blue sapphire would have blazed out from wherever it had landed. Nothing showed against the faint shimmer of the silt lining the lake.

Alex shifted to try and see for himself but intense pain blasted through him, leaving him breathless, rigid in agony, unable to move. Yet the look on the three evil wizards' faces proved that Keeko was right. On one was disbelief, on another rage, on the third terror.

Saranak screamed, an unearthly cry of agony, as his body shrank, becoming old and wizened. His robes fluttered in rags round his bent body. Grey skin tightened over his skull, like a corpse, peeling off his arms in sheets of dry scales. His hair turned thin and stringy.

'The oath,' he yelled. 'Quick, give me a task, Zorrin. I need the chance to show you loyalty.'

'Too late for that,' said Zorrin grimly. 'Nothing can save you now.'

'Kill me, Karlan. Don't let the Rod take me alive.'

As Karlan's finger rose, the cavern floor beneath Saranak split. Saranak fell into the fissure, screaming. Karlan's spell bounced off the cold granite in an explosion of purple sparks. The ground closed, leaving only a cloud of dirt where the wizard had stood.

CHAPTER 35

A sob escaped from Virida as she stared at the dust cloud. 'Gethsite,' she whispered, hand over her mouth. 'Eternal agony.'

White-faced, Karlan put his hand on Virida's shoulder. 'We have lost a powerful ally.' He pointed at Smuddy Binks. 'Your punishment is death.'

As he drew breath to annihilate the badger, a whistling sound cut the air. Karlan and Virida vanished.

'What happened?' asked Flick, struggling uselessly at her bonds.

'Time tear,' said Alex, pulling off the glove of Mazal with his teeth. 'I still had one from the boat.'

Rectoria laughed, harsh and strident. 'There's some justice in that. That's how Karlan disposed of your parents.'

Alex stared at her, his mind trying to absorb this monumentous news. Not dead? Alive, but in another time zone? Maybe he could he get there too. Tiredness evaporated. He wasn't going to give up now. However hopeless things were, he would fight to his last drop of blood to get back to his parents. First, he somehow had to save Zorrin. He began to crawl towards Rectoria, every movement white-hot agony.

'Using time tears shows more persistence in Karlan than I would have believed,' said Zorrin from his knees. 'They're not easy to find.'

Rectoria snorted. 'He would never have carried out such a menial job himself. He sent Olip to seek them at the falls of Fernacia, but that's not important now.' She looked at Flick, who was muttering spells and wrestling with her bonds. 'Only the sapphire or Saranak could have broken the cords that hold you now. Since they're both eternally lost, nothing can release you.'

From the scabbard by her side she pulled out a sword, its blade echoing the silver light of the fireball floating above the tunnel. She brandished it above the helpless figures of the two wizards.

Smuddy Binks rocketed forward. Snarling, Rycant leapt at him, felling the badger with a single blow of a massive front paw. The badger's head hit the floor with a dull crack. Smuddy Binks lay still, blood trickling from the corner of his mouth. The dog stood snarling over his victim, teeth bared.

'I'm ready to take my place in history as the one who executed Zorrin. If any of you move, Flick dies too.' Eyes alive with battle fury, Rectoria glared down at Zorrin. 'No more will you be the scourge of our people. I'll carry your severed head back to them, proof of my victory.' Gloating, she held the sword aloft, revelling in its cruel beauty.

'What about me?' shouted out Keeko from the top of the crater, Skoodle on her shoulder. 'What of my fate if I pledge allegiance to you now?'

Lowering her sword, Rectoria turned to view the monkey, her lip curled. 'Why would I want to be associated with a turncoat like you, so puny, so little to be trusted?'

Jaw set, face rigid, Keeko dumped Skoodle on the ground. He scurried away as Keeko squared up to Rectoria. 'I saw exactly where the stone fell. I could climb down and get it. Then you would have more power than any goblin in history.'

'What are you saying?' said Ikara, tone low and dangerous. 'You can't mean this.'

Keeko's face screwed up with anger. 'Why not? Loyalty never kept anyone alive. All I've had from sticking with you lot is pain and terror. I want to be on the winning side. You taste death for me.'

'We trusted you, Keeko,' hissed Ikara. 'Makusha asked about a turncoat among us. I bitterly regret how strongly Zorrin denied such a possibility.'

Keeko shrugged, then turned back to Rectoria. 'Well?'

Sharp claws dug into Zorrin's ankle. He looked down to see Skoodle by his side, his back to Rectoria. Sitting on his haunches

Skoodle smiled, first with a twitch of his lips then fully. Blue light poured from his mouth.

A surge of hope pounded through Zorrin as Skoodle disappeared behind him. Keeping his face blank, he looked back at the confrontation between Ikara and Keeko: Ikara furious, body rigid, eyes glittering with cold light, the sides of her neck winging out. Keeko defiant, mouth a grim line.

Something wet and hard dropped into Zorrin's hand. Warmth and power surged up his wrist. With minimal mental effort his wrist bonds severed. Flexing his shoulders lightly, all the others fell away.

He held the sapphire up high. 'The stone is now mine,' he called out.

The sapphire flashed blue and silver, shards of light cutting into the air around his hand.

'Your bonds have broken,' said Tariq. 'It's definitely the Sapphire of Akan.'

Rectoria swung her sword at Flick's neck.

'*Acier clarus*,' shouted Zorrin.

The blade rocketed towards Flick's throat as she shrank away. With a loud clang it hit an invisible obstruction, throwing Rectoria's stocky body backwards. Screaming, she looked down at her sword hand, now swollen and distorted.

'You've broken it, ogre brain.'

Face marred with pain, Rectoria grabbed the sword with her left hand and lunged at Alex, who lurched backwards. A dull resounding thud echoed round the cavern as the sword bounced off his chest. Rectoria staggered back with a howl, sword dangling.

'A useless move,' said Zorrin. 'The sapphire doubles and redoubles my powers. The acier clarus spell protects my entire band. None of you can harm any of us now.' He reached down to touch his sister's shoulder. Her ropes fell to the ground, releasing her.

Rectoria backed away. 'You have won this round,' she said, hate etching deep lines into her face. 'One day we shall meet again. Then I will be the victor.'

She pointed her sword at the ceiling. From the tip shot a shaft of green light; the ceiling started to crumble. Within seconds a barrier of rock separated the goblin band from Zorrin.

Her muffled voice could be heard shouting, 'Flee. Meet at the forest rendezvous. Everyone for himself.'

Zorrin turned away from the avalanche. Stony-faced he addressed Keeko, seemingly oblivious to the chaos of falling rubble and choking dust around him. 'So you want to change sides, do you?'

Wide-eyed, Keeko faced the furious wizard. 'I… sorry, but—'

'The sapphire flew into the crater,' said Skoodle breathlessly, as he ran to Alex. Without pausing in his tumble of words, he pushed a flower into Alex's mouth. 'It landed close by me, so I shoved it into my cheeks. Any hamster can easily store a lump that size, with almost nothing showing.' He pulled the flower out by the stem. 'Cut the sucking-a-lemon face. Be grateful, or I'll let Toomba have you.'

'I am, truly,' Alex whispered hoarsely.

Skoodle shoved the flower back into Alex's mouth, creating a mulch of spit and flower juice. As the pool of bitter fluid slid down his throat, Alex felt an outpouring of power passing through him, warm, blissful. The pain in his wrist and ribs died. The deep slash on his arm healed instantly, leaving a livid red weal. Alex touched it, amazed.

'Late-onset birthmark,' said Skoodle. 'Anyway, Keeko pretended to have seen it fall into the crevasse. I sat on the ground playing the part of the sobbing rodent, nothing visible in my mouth. Then Keeko invented the traitor speech as a distraction while I got to Zorrin. She's a great actress.'

'Played a little too convincingly for comfort,' hissed Ikara. 'In future I'll have difficulty believing anything that Keeko says.'

Alex sat up, strength flowing back, no longer in pain. An ominous rumbling began. Tremors shook the mountain as the unstable mass of stone shifted. An avalanche of rubble tumbled from the fresh ceiling crack.

'Back to *Phaedea* before the whole cavern collapses,' shouted Zorrin above the roar of the rock fall. 'Ikara, get up here. Shrink.'

'We must take the badger,' yelled Flick, pointing to where Smuddy Binks had been felled. 'He's buried among those rocks.'

As Ikara swung herself up to the lip of the crater, the others ran to where the badger had last been seen. They wrenched rocks aside, heads pounded by a hail of small stones.

'The badger can't be alive after being buried under so much rubble,' said Skoodle. 'We're digging for a corpse.'

'Maybe not,' replied Alex, grim-faced. 'Dig on.'

'I see the tip of his tail. Out of my way,' yelled Tariq.

As the others fell back, his powerful paws ripped away the last of the rocks.

The badger lay bloodstained, one ear badly ripped, back left leg at a bizarre angle. Flick sank to her knees by his side. She put her ear on his chest, then smiled. 'He's alive.'

'Skoodle, get this flower down him,' said Alex, thrusting one into a tiny paw.

'Save him as we go. The roof could collapse in seconds,' said Zorrin.

Tariq scooped up the badger, hoisting Skoodle up with the other paw. Skoodle was stuffing a blue flower into Smuddy Binks's mouth as Zorrin yelled, 'Ventus.'

They were swept towards the fireball-lit tunnel, arriving inside the mouth as the central ceiling collapsed, obliterating the cavern of Qua forever.

CHAPTER 36

Almost midnight. Fifteen minutes ago they had been standing exhausted in the tunnel, listening as the last of the tremors died away and the earth settled again. A few muttered words from Zorrin produced the now-familiar coldness and distant elfin music as they transparticulated to *Phaedea*, moored off Desdea.

'There's so much I don't understand,' Alex began once his body had passed through the hazy stage, his limbs becoming solid.

'Eat first, then talk,' said Flick, sweeping an arm over the galley table.

A magnificent feast appeared: bowls of hot soup, chicken pie, fruit, cake, juice. They all dropped into chairs and started eating as Zorrin pointed to a huge ripe pineapple. With a shower of sparks it began to peel itself, the skin unwrapping in one long curl. For a moment it hung in the air, motionless, then began to twist itself into the outlines of various jungle creatures. The snake formed quickly, but it took several seconds to create a passable elephant.

'Easy,' hissed Ikara. 'Rhino?'

Zorrin waved a finger. A charging rhino bore down on Tariq, who half rose to attack it. It became a monkey. Tariq sat back, laughing.

'Tell me, Flick. How exactly did you manage to get enchanted by Karlan?' asked Zorrin.

'Stupidity,' she replied, stabbing a hefty wedge of roast yam. 'As soon as Karlan had flown into the stables, he changed back into a man. Scheming, vengeful, back to full magic power, he crept to the main part of Ravenscraig, leaving a hexed drink for me. On finding a goblet of gorgeous-smelling juice in the kitchen I drank it, believing it to have been left by either you or Viskar. Unfortunately, as I was distracted by relief at your sudden appearance and concern about Tariq, I didn't register that it was magical, despite it being irresistible.'

'This food's irresistible. Is it enchanted?' asked Keeko, ploughing her way through her fourth mango.

'Only enough to make it yummy. Once I had drunk Karlan's vile potion, I had no choice but to obey his orders.'

'Good spell. I must get the recipe,' said Zorrin.

'No chance. Subsequently, Karlan transmorphed into a mouse to eavesdrop on your plans. Yet Clawds has such a highly-developed sense of predor, he recognised him to be evil. Once you had gone, on Karlan's orders, I released him from his bubble and took him down to the dungeons to talk to Tevo.'

'But why didn't you say something to us? Give a hint?' asked Ikara.

'I couldn't, owing to the hex. Yet his influence had been radically weakened by being lignified. That's why I could send for you when threatened by someone other than him, like Tevo. I couldn't directly contradict his orders, but I could do some things that he'd not expressly forbidden and he'd not banned me from sending a souvent.'

'How would he have known that souvents exist?' asked Zorrin.

Flick's face broke out into a huge gin. 'Exactly. He didn't.'

'But why did you imprison Rectoria?' asked Alex.

'She wasn't working for Karlan at that time.'

Tariq picked up another hunk of warm fresh bread. 'So under his orders you released the goblins from the dungeons and let the whole pack of them out of Ravenscraig?'

'Yes, and even led them to you. Yet even under the influence of such a major spell I'd insisted that you wouldn't die, Zorrin. That was his major mistake, underestimating the power of the bond between brother and sister. For when he went to kill you and I moved to stop him, he stated that the agreement was broken. Hence the enchantment combusted.'

'Thank Xenos for the love of a sister.' Zorrin threw a ball of bread at Flick. Just before she caught it, it morphed into a single white rose. 'Why did Karlan have you release the goblin band? He and Tevo have been enemies in the past. Theirs seems an unlikely link.'

'Karlan needed allies. Deep in the dungeons, he made a pact with Tevo. He would get me to release all of them and hand over the Sword of Alwyn. In return they had to accompany us and fight for him. The goblins were more than happy to agree, as they love a battle. Furthermore, Tevo would have agreed to almost anything to get the Sword of Alwyn back.'

'Which unfortunately they have achieved. That will be a problem for another day,' sighed Zorrin.

A grunt escaped Smuddy Binks, lying sleeping on a chair.

Alex glanced over towards him. 'Why did the badger help? Risked his life for us. Seems odd, when we only met him today.'

Flick told them all about Smuddy Binks's visit to her room and how he'd subsequently lied for her. 'I wasn't sure of him at that point, which is why it seemed safer to imprison him with the others, but he's certainly proved his loyalty to us.'

Zorrin pushed back his chair and stood up. 'I'm going to the forward deck to fish for a while.'

With an uncomfortably overfull stomach, Alex followed Zorrin, Skoodle in his pocket. The moonlight seemed suspiciously bright. Alex suspected that Zorrin had somehow turned the brilliance up a few notches. The sea lapped at the gently rocking boat as a few clouds drifted across the heavens.

Zorrin was sitting on an air cushion, a drink and a bowl of nuts on a table beside him, the fishing line aiming straight upwards towards the moon. Figstaff slept nearby, his breathing so shallow that he resembled a statue of Buddha. Zorrin threw a Brazil nut at him. One of the frog's eyes opened, his mouth yawned wide and the nut vanished down his throat. His heavy lids closed and he started snoring.

'Asleep again in less than three seconds,' said Zorrin. 'Not a record, but close.'

Skoodle yawned. 'This boat is awesome. Better than the caves. On an enjoyment scale of nought to ten this is ten – the encounter with Hypnos being about minus forty-two point three.'

'So precise?' asked Zorrin.

'I don't want to exaggerate.'

'What are you hoping to catch?' Alex asked, gazing up into the dark heavens in which the stars stood out as tiny bright holes in the velvet canopy.

'Sky fish.'

There was a tug on Zorrin's line. He reeled it in to find a pale blue octopus-shaped cloud. Zorrin unhooked the undulating mass. He glanced up at Alex. 'I've got a reasonable chance of tracing your parents, as we know where the time tears that blew them away came from.'

'I've just clicked. Is that why you kept Rectoria talking?' asked Alex. 'I thought you were stalling for time.'

'No, fishing for information. If I can find more time tears at the same place, they should transport me to the same era as your parents. Then I can bring them back to the present.'

Zorrin turned the luminous shape over, viewing it from all sides. 'Only a dream.' He allowed the cloud to float away then let the line play out, as it glinted silver in the moonlight.

'We may have sent Karlan and Virida to the same time zone as your parents. However, I feel that Virginia and Mark should be a reasonable match for two displaced wizards.'

Alex picked up a Brazil nut. About to shove it in his mouth, he realised that he couldn't stuff anything else in. He lobbed it to Figstaff. There was a pop as his mouth opened and the nut vanished. The frog closed his eyes, instantly asleep again.

'Three seconds,' said Alex. 'Equalling you on my first attempt.'

'Luck. Your final task on Eridor will be helping me return the sapphire to the heart of Makusha.' He gave a wry smile as Alex shuddered. 'The journey will not be bad at all this time. As the stone is in my possession, we'll find a sunny tropical morning when we arrive.'

Zorrin gave his line an impatient shake. There was a strange stiffness in his body and his speech sounded odd. It's like he's being really formal, thought Alex. Then another thought crossed his mind. Or brave. Suddenly, he understood.

Zorrin's line straightened a little, swaying in the weak current, the hook drifting in the air. 'Once you've replaced the sapphire you can return to your own country.'

'Yes,' shouted Skoodle, punching the air. 'What do you think, Uncle Toomba? Leaving this place with poisonous snakes, evil wizards and exploding aqualates to return to safe old England… what?… yes, I know we haven't found… but surely… oh, fine… thanks a whole heap.'

'What did he say?' asked Alex.

'He didn't answer.'

Alex scratched Skoodle behind the ears. 'Toomba's right. Since I know now that my parents are alive somewhere, I have to try to find them. Anyway, Eridor feels more like home than my aunt's house ever did.' Alex picked up a second rod and let his own line float towards the stars. 'So you're stuck with us for a while.'

As Alex's hook drifted up to join his own, Zorrin grinned. 'Ice.'